Urban America, 2nd ed. New York: Aldine.

Schneider, M. (1980) *Suburban Growth.* Brunswick, Ohio: King's Court Communications.

Schumpeter, J.A. (1950)   *Capitalism, Socialism and Democracy.*   New York: Harper and Row.

Schwab, W.A. (1981)   Urban neighborhood revitalization: Theoretical and empirical issues, *Urban Affairs Papers, 3*(3).

Schwirian, K.P. (1983) Models of neighborhood change, *Annual Review of Sociology, 9*: 83-102.

Sclar, E.D. (1981) Social cost minimization: A national policy approach to grassroots action.   In J.C. Raines, L.E. Berson, and D.M. Gracie (Eds.), *Community and Capital in Conflict.*   Philadelphia: Temple University Press.

Senate Committee on Banking, Housing and Urban Affairs, Subcommittee on Housing and Urban Affairs (1973) *The Central City Problem and Urban Renewal Policy*, prepared by the Congressional Research Service, Library of Congress.   Washington, DC: Government Printing Office.

Smith, Michael Peter (1984) Urban structure, social theory, and political power.   In M.P. Smith (Ed.), *Cities in Transformation.*   Beverly Hills: Sage.

Smith, Michael Peter (1988) *City, State and Market: The Political Economy of Urban Society.*   Oxford and New York: Basil Blackwell.

Smith, Michael Peter. and Dennis R. Judd (1984) American cities: The production of ideology.   In M.P. Smith (Ed.), *Cities in Transformation* Beverly Hills: Sage.

Smith, Neil (1979) Toward a theory of gentrification: A back to the city movement of capital, not people, *Journal of the American Planning Association* (October):   538-548.

Smith, Neil (1986) Gentrification, the frontier, and the restructuring of urban space.   In N. Smith and P. Williams (Eds.), *Gentrification of the City.* Boston: Allen and Unwin.

Smith, Neil (1987) Of yuppies and housing: Gentrification, social restructuring, and the urban dream, *Society and Space, 5*(2).

Smith, Neil and M. LeFaivre. (1984) A class analysis of gentrificaton.   In J.J. Palen and B. London (Eds.), *Gentrification, Displacement, and Neighborhood Revitalization.* Albany, NY: SUNY Press.

Solomon, A.P. and K.D. Vandell (1982) Alternative perspectives on neighborhood decline, *Journal of the American Planning Association* (Winter):   81-98.

Stanback, T.M., et al. (1981) *Services: The New Economy.* Totowa, NJ: Allanheld, Osmun.

Sternlieb, G. and J.W. Hughes. (1983) The uncertain future of the central city, *Urban Affairs Quarterly, 18*: 455-472.

Stone, Clarence N. (1976) *Economic Growth and Neighborhood Discontent.* Chapel Hill, NC: University of North Carolina Press.

Stone, Clarence N. and H. Sanders (Eds.) (1987) *The Politics of Urban Development.* Lawrence, KS: University Press of Kansas.

Sumka, H.J. (1979) Neighborhood revitalization and displacement: A review of the evidence, *Journal of the American Planning Association, 45* (October): 480-487.

Sumka, H.J. (1980) Federal antidisplacement policy in a context of urban decline. In S.B. Laska and D. Spain (Eds.), *Back to the City.* New York: Pergamon Press.

Swanstrom, Todd F. (1985) *The Crisis of Growth Politics: Cleveland, Kucinich, and the Challenge of Urban Populism.* Philadelphia: Temple University Press.

Swanstrom, Todd F. (forthcoming) No room at the inn: Housing policy and the homeless, *Journal of Urban and Contemporary Law.*

Tabb, William K. (1984) Urban development and regional restructuring: An overview. In L. Sawers and W.K. Tabb (Eds.), *Sunbelt Snowbelt.* New York: Oxford University Press.

Thurow, Lester C. (1980) *The Zero-Sum Society.* New York: Penguin.

U.S. Dept. of Housing and Urban Development (1979) *Displacement Report.* Washington, DC: Author.

U.S. Dept. of Housing and Urban Development (1982) *The President's National Urban Policy Report.* Washington, DC: Government Printing Office.

Vaughan, R.J. (1977) *The Urban Impact of Federal Policies*, Vol. 2, Economic Development. Santa Monica, CA: Rand.

Watkins, A.J. (1980) *The Practice of Urban Economics.* Beverly Hills: Sage.

Whitt, J.A. (1982) *Urban Elites and Mass Transportation: The Dialectics of Power.* Princeton, NJ: Princeton University Press.

Whyte, W.F. (1985) New approaches to industrial development and community development. In W. Woodworth, C. Meek, and W.F. Whyte (Eds.), *Industrial Democracy: Strategies for Community Revitalizatin.* Beverly Hills, CA: Sage.

Wills, G. (1977) Carter and the end of liberalism, *New York Review of Books, 24*(8) (May 12).

Wolfe, A. (1981) *America's Impasse: The Rise and Fall of the Politics of Growth.* New York: Pantheon.

Zukin, Sharon (1987) Gentrification: Culture and capital in the urban core, *Annual Review of Sociology, 1*: 129-147.

Biographical Statements

Jeffrey Broadbent received his B.A. from University of California, Berkeley, his M.A. in Regional Studies East Asia from Harvard University and his Ph.D. in Sociology from Harvard University in 1982. His doctoral research in Japan was supported by a Fulbright Fellowship and the Harvard Japan Institute (1978-81). Subsequently, he was a Fellow of the Michigan Society of Fellows. He is currently Assistant Professor in the Department of Sociology at the University of Minnesota and is conducting new research in Japan supported by the Fulbright/Japan-U.S. Educational Commission fellowship.

Mike Douglass received his Ph.D. in urban planning from University of California, Los Angeles and has been active in urban and regional planning, research and education in several Pacific Rim countries, including Japan, Indonesia, Korea and Thailand, for many years. He is currently an Associate Professor in the Department of Urban and Regional Planning at the University of Hawaii. His most recent research has focused on the transnationalization of capital and urbanization in Japan, land use and the environment in Indonesia, and national urban development strategies in China.

Kuniko Fujita is an affiliated faculty member in the Department of Sociology at Michigan State University. Her recent publications include "Women workers, state policy and the International Division of Labor: The case of Silicon Island in Japan," *Bulletin of Concerned Asian Scholars* (1988) and "The Technopolis: High technology and regional development in Japan," *International Journal of Urban and Regional Research* (1988). Her current research interests include "Global Toyotaism" and "Japanese Cities in the World Economy."

Jeffrey Henderson is currently Senior Lecturer in Sociology and Urban Studies at the University of Hong Kong. He formerly taught urban and Regional Studies at the University of Birmingham and has held visiting appointments at the Universities of Lodz, Warwick, California (at Berkeley and Santa Cruz), Glasgow, Melbourne, and New England. His publications include *Urban Political Economy and Social Theory* (Gower, 1982), *Race, Class and State Housing* (Gower, 1987), *Global Restructuring and Territorial Development* (Sage, 1987), and *The Globalisation of High Technology Production* (Routledge, 1989). His current research interests include the comparative analysis of the dynamics and consequences of industrial restructuring, and the determinants of state economic policy in East Asia.

Richard Child Hill is a Professor of Sociology and Urban Affairs at

Michigan State University. His recent publications include a co-authored book, *Detroit: Race and Uneven Development* (Temple University Press, 1988) and "Comparing transnational production systems: The case of the automobile industry in the United States and Japan," *International Journal of Urban and Regional Research* (1989). He is currently engaged in comparative research on the social impact and political response to industrial restructuring in the U.S. and Japan.

Robert Kerstein is a Professor of Political Science and Urban Studies at the University of Tampa. He has published articles on urban policy and on election reform. He is currently completing research on stage models of neighborhood change and is also examining the political-economy of growth in Tampa.

Peter J. Rimmer is a Senior Fellow in the Department of Human Geography, Research School of Pacific Studies, The Australian National University. He was educated at Manchester, Cambridge and Canterbury Universities. As a researcher he has been working in Southeast and Northeast Asia for 20 years. As mirrored in *Rikisha to Rapid Transit: Urban Public Transport Systems and Policy in Southeast Asia*, his main interest has been in transport systems. This has now broadened to encompass urban and regional development as a whole as reflected in a series of papers on domestic developments in Japan and their international repercussions.

Todd Swanstrom is an Assistant Professor in the Rockefeller College of Public Affairs and Policy at the State University of New York at Albany. Previously he was Staff Director of the Albany Strategic Planning Project and a planner for the city of Cleveland. He holds a Ph.D. in Political Science from Princeton University and is author of *The Crisis of Growth Politics: Cleveland, Kucinich, and the Challenge of Urban Populism* (Temple University Press, 1985). He is currently doing research on homelessness and the history of the relationship between business and cities. He is also co-editor (with John Logan) of a series by Temple University Press called "Conflicts in Urban and Regional Development."

David C. Thorns is Reader and Head of the Sociology Department at the University of Canterbury, Christchurch, New Zealand. He is author or joint author of six recent books including *Suburbia, Quest for Community*, and *Social Theory and the Australian City* (1984), as well as numerous articles. Currently he is engaged in research designed to explore the effects of economic restructuring on urban regions, labor markets, local life styles and the development of local consciousness and social movements.

—-

Cover photo by Michelle Monique Photography |
www.michellemoniquephoto.com
Cover model: Nicole Whittaker
—-

AISN: B00DH5FT4M
ISBN-13: 978-1490436524
ISBN-10: 1490436529

J.A. Redmerski | KILLING SARAI | 2nd Edition
Fiction – Crime – Suspense – Assassinations

KILLING SARAI

#1 - IN THE COMPANY OF KILLERS

J.A. REDMERSKI

KILLING SARAI

PRAISE FOR KILLING SARAI

"5 Holy Mother of WTF Stars."
- *The Book Enthusiast*

"Say goodbye to your nails."
- *Amazon reviewer*

"Wow. Killing Sarai was amazing. It was brutal, heartbreaking, gripping and raw."
- *Goodreads reviewer*

"Be still my heart…left me damn near speechless…Just W-O-W."
- *Amazon reviewer*

"This book was A-FUCK-MAZING."
- *Goodreads reviewer*

"I was hooked from page one, and my heart was pounding all the way to the end."
- *Amazon reviewer*

"Killing Sarai is lovely suspense, beautiful executed."
-*Goodreads reviewer*

ABOUT KILLING SARAI

Sarai was only fourteen when her mother uprooted her to live in Mexico with a notorious drug lord. Over time she forgot what it was like to live a normal life, but she never let go of her hope to escape the compound where she has been held for the past nine years.

Victor is a cold-blooded assassin who, like Sarai, has known only death and violence since he was a young boy. When Victor arrives at the compound to collect details and payment for a hit, Sarai sees him as her only opportunity for escape. But things don't go as planned and instead of finding transport back to Tucson, she finds herself free from one dangerous man and caught in the clutches of another.

While on the run, Victor strays from his primal nature as he succumbs to his conscience and resolves to help Sarai. As they grow closer, he finds himself willing to risk everything to keep her alive; even his relationship with his devoted brother and liaison, Niklas, who now like everyone else wants Sarai dead.

As Victor and Sarai slowly build a trust, the differences between them seem to lessen, and an unlikely attraction intensifies. But Victor's brutal skills and experience may not be enough in the end to save her, as the power she unknowingly holds over him may ultimately be what gets her killed.

TABLE OF CONTENTS

ONE

SARAI

Somewhere in Mexico

It's been nine years since I saw the last American here. *Nine* years. I was beginning to think Javier killed them all.

"Who is he?" my only friend, Lydia, asks as she pushes herself further into view. "How do you know he's American?"

I press my index finger against my lips and Lydia lowers her whisper, knowing as well as I do that Javier, or that God-awful sister of his will hear us and punish us for eavesdropping. Always paranoid. Always assuming the worst. Always approaching everything with caution and weapons, and rightfully so. Such is the way of life filled with drugs and murder and slavery.

I peer through the sliver in the door, letting my vision focus on the tall, lean white man who looks as though he was born with the inability to smile.

"I don't know," I whisper softly. "I can just tell."

Lydia squints her eyes as though it might help her to hear better. I can feel the heat from her breath warming the skin on my throat as she presses harder against me. We watch the man from the shadow of the tiny room that we have shared since they brought her here a year ago. One door. One window. One bed. Four dingy walls and a bookshelf with a few books in the English language which I have read more times than I can count. But we aren't locked in and have never been. Javier knows that if we ever try to escape that we won't get far. I don't even know where in Mexico I am. But I know that wherever it is, it wouldn't be easy for a young woman like me to find her way back into the United States alone. The second I walk out that door and make my way down that dark, dusty road alone is the second I choose suicide as my path.

The American, wearing a long black trench coat over black clothes sits on the wooden chair in the living room, his back straight, and his gaze expertly filtering every motion within the room. But no one seems to notice this but me. Something tells me that even though Lydia and I are completely hidden inside our room down a dark hallway which barely allows us to see the living room, that this man *knows* we're watching. He knows everything that is going on around him: one of Javier's men standing in the shadow of the opposite hall with his gun hidden at the ready; the six men standing in wait outside on the porch, the two men directly behind him with assault rifles cemented to their hands. These two haven't taken their eyes off the American's back, but I think the American, although not facing them, sees more of them than they do of him. And then there are the more obvious people in the room: Javier, a dangerous Mexican drug lord who sits directly in front of the American. Smiling and confident and completely unafraid. And then there is Javier's sister, wearing her usual whorish dress so short that she doesn't need to bend over for everyone in the room to see that she doesn't wear panties. She wants the American. She wants anyone who she can sexually abuse, but this man…there's something more obsessive in her eyes when it comes to him. And the American knows this, too.

"I only agreed to meet with you," the American says in fluent Spanish, "because I was assured that you would not waste my time." He glances at Javier's sister briefly. She licks her lips. He is unfazed. "I do business only with you. Get rid of the whore or we have nothing to discuss." His unmoving expression never falters.

Javier's sister, Izel, looks like someone just slapped her across the face. She starts to speak, but Javier hushes her with only a look and then jerks his head back slightly to demand she leave the room. She does as she's told, but as usual not without a string of curses that follow her out the front door.

Javier smirks at the American and raises a mug of coffee to his lips. After taking a sip he says, "My offer is three million American dollars." He sets the mug on the table that separates the two of them and then leans casually back against the chair, one leg crossed over the other. "I understand that your price was *two* million?" Javier turns his chin at an angle, looking to the American for recognition of his generous offer.

The American doesn't give him any.

"I still don't know how you can understand what they're saying so easily," Lydia whispers quietly.

I want to hush her so that I can hear everything between Javier and the American, but I don't.

"Live among only Spanish-speaking people for years and you learn to understand it," I say, but I never take my eyes off Javier and the American. "In time, you'll be as fluent as I am."

I sense Lydia's body tense. She wants to go home as much as I did when I was brought here at fourteen. But she knows as well as I did that she might be here forever and the heavy weight of that reality is what ultimately makes her quiet again.

"The only reason a man such as yourself," the American begins, "would offer *over* the going rate would be to secure some kind of hold over me." He lets out a small, aggravated breath and leans his back against the chair, letting his hands slide away from his knees. "Either that, or you're desperate, which leads me to believe that my mark, the one you want me to kill, would be willing to pay me more to kill *you*."

Javier's confident grin disappears from his face. He swallows hard and straightens his back awkwardly, but tries to retain some confidence over the situation. For all he knows, that might be exactly why the American is here.

"My reasons are not important," Javier says.

He takes another sip from the mug to hide his discomfort.

"You're right," the American says so calmly. "The only important thing here is that you tell Guillermo back there to lower the gun from behind me and that if he doesn't within three seconds he will be dead."

Javier and one of the men standing behind the American lock eyes. But three seconds goes by too quickly and I hear a near-silent shot resound and a *pop!* as a splatter of blood sprays the other man standing beside him. 'Guillermo' hits the floor, dead. No one, not even me, seems to know how the American pulled that shot off. He hasn't even moved. The man standing next to the dead man freezes in his spot, his black eyes wide beneath his oily black hair. Javier purses his lips and swallows again, having a harder time hiding that discomfort of his every unnerving second that passes. His men outnumber the American, but it's obvious that Javier doesn't want him dead. Not right now. He raises a hand palm forward to order the others to lower their weapons.

The American pulls his hand from inside his trench coat and places his gun on his leg for all to see. His finger remains on the trigger. Javier glances down nervously at the gun once.

Lydia is digging her fingernails into my ribs. I reach down carefully and move her hands away, feeling her body relax now that she realizes what she's doing. Her breathing is rapid. I drape my arm around her shoulder and pull her into my chest. She's not used to seeing people die. Not yet. But one day she will be. Cupping one side of her head within my hand, I press my lips against her hair to calm her.

Javier gestures with the dismissing wave of two fingers and says, "Clean this mess up," to the other gunman standing behind the American. The gunman seems more than happy to oblige, not wanting to end up like his comrade. Every eye in the room is on the American. Not that they weren't before, but now they are more obvious, much more observant.

"You've made your point," Javier says.

"I wasn't trying to make one," the American corrects him.

Javier nods in acknowledgment.

"Three million American dollars," Javier says. "Do you accept the offer?"

It's obvious that the American has done more than take Javier down a few notches. He may not be running away in fear or cowering in the corner, but it's clear that he's been put in his place. And this is not easy to do. It worries me what Javier might do in retaliation when he feels he has the opportunity. It worries me only because I need that American to get me out of here.

"What are they saying?" Lydia asks, frustrated that she has a long way to go before she will be able to decipher anything said around this place.

I don't answer, but I squeeze her shoulder once to indicate that I need her to stop talking.

"Three and a half is my price," the American says.

Javier's face falls and I think his nostrils just flared. He's not used to being second best.

"But you said—"

"The price went up," the American says, leaning his back against the chair again and tapping the barrel of his gun softly against his black pants. He offers no more explanation and doesn't need to. Javier already seems accepting.

Javier nods. "Sí. Sí. Three and a half million. Can you have it done in one week?"

The American stands up, his long black coat falling about his body. He is tall and intimidating with short brown hair buzzed around the back and slightly longer and spiky on top.

I pull Lydia away from the door and shut it softly.

"What are you doing?" she asks as I rush over to the rickety chest of drawers that holds all of the clothes that she and I share when I'm allowed to stay here with her.

"We're leaving," I say as I shove whatever I can down inside a pillowcase. "Get your shoes on."

"*What?*"

"Lydia, we don't have time for this. Just get your shoes. We can make it out of here with the American."

I stuff the pillowcase half full and move to help her since she's slow to understand what exactly is going on. I grab her by the arm and push her against the bed.

"I'll help you," I say as I kneel in front of her and go to slip her bare feet into her shoes.

But she stops me.

"No...Sarai, I-I can't leave."

I let out a heavy breath. We don't have time for this but I need to make time long enough to convince her that she *needs* to leave with me. I look up into her eyes. "We will be safe. We can get out of here—Lydia, he is the first American I've seen in years. He's our only chance."

"He's a killer."

"You're *surrounded* by killers. Now come on!"

"No! I'm afraid!"

I shoot up from my kneeling position and thrust my hand over her mouth. "Shhh! Lydia, please listen to me—"

She places her fingers over mine and peels my hand from her lips.

Tears stream from her eyes and she shakes her head rapidly. "I won't go. We'll get caught and Javier will beat us. Or worse, Izel will torture and kill us. I'm staying here."

I know that I can't change her mind. She has that look in her eyes. The one that says she's been broken and she will probably always be broken. I put my hands on her shoulders and look at her.

"Get under the covers and pretend that you've been asleep," I say. "Stay like that until someone comes in and finds you. If they know you knew about me leaving and didn't tell anyone, they will kill you."

Lydia nods in a nervous jerking motion.

"I will come back for you." I shake her by the shoulders, hoping she'll believe me. "I promise. The first thing I'll do when I get over the border is go to the police."

"But how will you find me?"

Tears choke her voice.

"I don't know," I admit. "But the American will know. He will help me."

That look in her eyes, it's hopelessness. She doesn't believe for a second that this insane plan of mine is going to work. And I probably wouldn't have either nine years ago, but desperation makes a person do crazy things. Lydia's face hardens and she reaches up to wipe the tears from her cheeks. It's as if she knows this is the last time she will ever see me.

I kiss her hard on the forehead.

"I *will* come back for you."

She nods slowly and I push my way through the tiny room with the pillowcase slung over my back.

"Get under the covers," I hiss at her as I push open the window.

As Lydia hides under the blanket, I climb my way out the window and into the mild October heat. I crouch low behind the house and make my way around the side and through the hole in the fence surrounding the south side of the compound. Javier has gunmen everywhere, but I've always found them rather dense and lacking in the guard-the-compound-from-escapees area because rarely does anyone try to escape. Mostly the guards all stand around talking and smoking cigarettes and making vulgar gestures to the other girls who are enslaved here. The one standing at the entrance to the armory is the one who tried to rape me six weeks ago. The only reason Javier didn't kill him is because that one is his brother.

But brother or not, he is now a eunuch.

Weaving my way in between small buildings, I make it to the tree line and stop in the shadows cast by the nearby house. I stand up straight and press my back against the stucco and make my way carefully around to the front where the twelve-foot barbwire fence starts at the front gate. Outsiders are always made to park their vehicles just beyond it where they are escorted into the compound on foot.

The American would not have been allowed in any differently. I'm sure of it. I hope.

A large swath of light from the post covers the space between me and the area of the gate that I need to get to. There is one guard posted there, but he's younger and I think I can take him. I've had plenty of time to work these things out. All of my teenage life. I stole a handgun from Izel's room last year and have kept it hidden under a floorboard in mine and Lydia's room ever since. The second I saw the American enter the house I had pulled back the floorboard to retrieve it and shoved it in the back of my shorts. I knew I'd need it tonight.

I inhale a deep breath and dash across the light in the wide open and just hope that no one spots me. I run hard and fast with the pillowcase beating against my back and the gun gripped in my hand so tight it hurts the bones in my fingers. I make it to the fence and breathe a sigh of relief when I find another shadow to hide within. Shadows move at a distance, coming from the house I just left. I feel sick to my stomach and could actually vomit if I didn't know I had more important things to do and fast. My heart is hammering against my ribcage.

I spot the guard out ahead standing near the front gate and leaning against a tree. The hot ember of a cigarette glows around his copper-colored face and then fades as he pulls his lips away from the filter. The silhouette of his assault rifle gives the impression that he has the gun strap tossed over one shoulder. Thankfully he isn't holding it at the ready. I walk quickly along the edge of the fence, trying to stay hidden in the shadow cast by the trees on the other side of it. My worn out flip-flops move over the soft sand making no sound at all. The guard is so close that I can smell the funk of his body odor and see the oil glistening in his unwashed air.

I creep up closer, hoping my movement doesn't attract him. I'm right behind him now and I'm about to pee myself. My legs are shaking and my throat has closed up almost to the point that I can hardly breathe. Carefully, and as quietly as possible, I pull my gun back and hit him over the head with the butt as hard as I can. A loud *whack!* and a *crunch!* turns my stomach. He falls over unconscious and the burning cigarette hits the sand beside his knees. I grab his gun, practically having to tear it off his arm because of the heavy weight of his body, and then I take off running through the cracked gate and outside the compound.

Just as I had hoped, there is only one vehicle parked out front: a slick black car that is probably the most out-of-place object in this area for miles. Nothing here but slums and filth. This is an expensive city car with shiny rims and an attitude.

One more hurdle. But upon seeing the car my confidence in the American having left the doors unlocked are diminishing. Surely he wouldn't in these parts. I place my hand on the back passenger's side door and I hold my breath. The door pops open. I don't have time to be relieved when I hear voices coming through the front gate and I catch a glimpse of a moving shadow from the corner of my eye. I crawl in the back floorboard and shut the door quickly before those approaching are close enough to hear it shut.

Oh no…the overhead light.

I grit my teeth watching the light fade above me so slowly that it's torturous, until finally it blinks out and leaves me in darkness. After shoving the pillowcase underneath the driver's seat I try to hide the stolen rifle just behind the seat between the leather and the door. It leaves me with enough time to squeeze my little body as far into the floorboard as I can. I wrap my arms tight around my knees which are pressed against my chest and I arc my back over and hold the awkward position.

The voices fade and all that is left is the sound of one pair of legs approaching the car. The trunk pops open and seconds later it closes again.

I hold my breath when the front driver's side door opens and the overhead light pops on again. The American shuts the door behind him and I feel the car move as he positions himself in the front seat. One. Two. Three. Four. Five. Six. Finally the light fades. I hear the key being slid into the ignition and then the engine purrs to life.

Why aren't we moving? Why are we just sitting here? Maybe he's reading something.

And then he says aloud in Spanish, "Cocoa butter lotion. Warm breath. Sweat."

It takes a moment for my brain to register the meaning behind his strange words and to realize that he's actually talking to me.

I rise up quickly from behind the seat and cock the handgun, pressing the barrel against the back of his head.

"Just drive," I say in English, my hands shaking holding the gun in place. I've never killed anyone before and I don't want to, but I'm not going back into that compound.

The American slowly raises his hands. The glint of his thick silver watch catches my eye but I don't let it distract me. Without another word he places one hand on the steering wheel and the other on the gear shift, putting the car into Drive.

"You're American," he says calmly, but I detect only the tiniest ounce of interest in his voice.

"Yes, I'm American, now please just drive."

Keeping the gun pointed at his head, I maneuver myself into the backseat and I pull the gun away from his reach. I catch him glimpse me in the rearview mirror, but it's so dark inside the car with just the low lights from the dashboard that all I can see are his eyes for a brief moment as they sweep over me.

Finally the car goes into forward motion and he puts both hands on the steering wheel. He's being calm and cautious, but I get the feeling he isn't the slightest bit worried about me or what I might be capable of doing. This scares me. I think I'd rather him be begging for his life, stuttering over words of plea, promising me the world. But he looks as dangerous and as uninterested as he did back inside the house even when he put a bullet in that gunman's head he so casually named 'Guillermo'.

TWO

SARAI

We've been driving for twenty-eight minutes. I've been watching the clock in the dashboard, the glowing blue numbers already starting to burn through to my subconscious. The American hasn't said a word. Not one word. I know it has nothing to do with being afraid. I'm the one with the gun but I'm the only one of us who is afraid. And I don't understand why he hasn't spoken. Maybe if he would just turn the radio on...*something*...because the silence is killing me. I've been trying to keep my eyes on him while at the same time trying to get some kind of idea of my whereabouts. But so far the only landmarks that I've seen are trees and the occasional stucco house or dilapidated building—it all looks the same as the compound.

Thirty-two minutes in and I realize I've already lowered the gun at some point. My finger is still on the trigger and I'm ready to use it if I have to, but I was stupid to think I could hold it up pointed directly at him for longer than a few minutes.

I don't know what I'm going to do when I get tired. Thankfully the adrenaline is keeping me wide awake for now.

"What's your name?" I ask him, hoping to stir the silence.

I need to get him to trust me, to *want* to help me.

"My name is inconsequential."

"Why?"

He doesn't respond.

I swallow a lump in my throat, but another one just forms in its place.

"My name is Sarai."

Still no response.

It kind of feels like torture, the way he ignores me. I'm beginning to think that is exactly what he's doing: torturing me with silence.

"I need you to help me," I say. "I've been a prisoner of Javier's since I was fourteen-years-old."

"And you assume I'm going to help you because I am also American," he says simply.

I hesitate before I answer, "I-I…well, why *wouldn't* you?"

"It is not my business to interfere."

"Then what *is* your business?" I ask with a trace of distaste. "To murder people in cold blood?"

"Yes."

A shiver moves through my back.

Not knowing what to say to something like that, or even if I should, I decide it's best to change the subject.

"Can you just get me across the border?" I ask, becoming more desperate. "I'll—" I lower my eyes in shame. "I'll do whatever you want. But please, *please* just help me get over the border." I feel tears trying to force their way to the surface, but I don't want him to see me cry. I don't know why, but I just can't let him. And I know he understands what it means to do whatever he wants. I hate myself for offering my body to him, but like I said before about desperation.

"If you are referring to the United States border," he says and for some reason his voice surprises me, "then you must know the distance is longer than I care to have you in my car."

I raise my back from the seat just a little.

"W-Well how long would you allow me?"

I catch his dark eyes in the rearview mirror again. They lock on mine and this too sends a shiver through my back.

He doesn't answer.

"Why won't you *help* me?" I ask, finally accepting the fact that no matter what I say to him, it's futile. And when he still doesn't answer I say with exasperation, "Then pull over and let me out. I'll walk the rest of the way myself."

I think his eyes just faintly smiled at me through the mirror. Yes, I'm positive that's what I saw. He knows as well as I do that I'm better off getting dragged back to the compound than being let out of the car and on my own.

"You will need more than the six bullets you have in that handgun."

"So then give me more bullets," I say, getting angrier. "And this isn't the only gun I have."

That seems to have piqued his interest, although small.

"I took the rifle off the guard I hit over the head when I got past the fence."

He nods once, so subtly that if I would've blinked in that moment I never would've seen it.

"It is a good start," he says and then puts his eyes back on the dirt road for a moment and turns left at the end. "But what will you do when you run out? Because you will."

I hate him.

"Then I'll run."

"And they will catch you."

"Then I'll stab them."

Suddenly the American veers slowly off the road and stops the car.

No, no, no! This isn't how it was supposed to happen. I expected him to keep driving because he knew if he left me out here all alone like this that whatever happened to me would be on his conscience. But I guess he doesn't have much of one.

His dark eyes gaze evenly at me through the mirror, not a trace of compassion or concern in them. I want to shoot him in the back of the head on principle. He just stares at me with that small what-are-you-waiting-for? look and I don't budge. I glance carefully at the door and then back at him and then down at my gun and back at him again.

"You can use me as leverage," I say because it's all I have left.

His eyebrows barely move, but it's enough that I've gotten his attention.

"I'm Javier's favorite," I go on. "I'm…different…from the other girls."

"What makes you think I need leverage?" he asks.

"Well, did Javier pay you the whole three and a half million?"

"That is not how it works," he says.

"No, but I know how Javier works and if he didn't give you the full amount before you left then he never will."

"Are you going to get out?"

I sigh heavily and glance out the window again and then I raise the gun back up and say, "You're going to drive me to the border."

The American licks the dryness from his lips and then the car starts moving again. I'm playing everything by ear now. All of the planned parts of my escape ended when I got inside this car.

When the American spoke of the United States border, it came off to me as if I am closer to the borders of other countries than the U.S. and this terrifies me. If I'm closer to Guatemala or Belize than the United States then I very much doubt that I will make it out of this alive. I have looked at maps. I have sat within that room many times and ran the tip of my finger over the little roads between Zamora and San Luis Potosí and between Los Mochis and Ciudad Juárez. But I always blocked the possibility of being farther south completely from my mind because I never wanted to accept that I could be that far away from home.

Home. That really is such a placeholder word. I don't have a home in the United States at all. I don't think I ever really did. But just the same, it was where I was born and where I was raised, though little did my mother do to raise me, really. But I want to go home because it will always be better than where I've spent the last nine years of my life.

I position my back partially against the door and partially against the seat so that I can keep my eyes straight on the American. How long I can keep this going is still up in the air. And he knows it.

Maybe I should just shoot him and take the car. But then again, little good it will do when I'm driving around aimlessly in this foreign country that I have seen nothing from other than violence and rape and murder and everything else unimaginable. And Javier is a very powerful man. Very rich. The compound is filthy and misleading. He could be like the drug lords I saw when I used to have the luxury of American television, the ones with rich, immaculate homes with swimming pools and ten bathrooms, but Javier seems to prefer the façade. I don't know what he spends his fortune on, but it's not on real estate as far as I know.

It's been over an hour. I'm getting tired. I can feel the burning behind my eyes, spreading thinly around the edges of my eyelids. I don't know who it is I think I'm kidding. I have to sleep sometime and the second that I doze off is when I'll wake up either back at the compound tied to the chair in Javier's room, or when I don't wake up at all.

I need to keep talking to help me stay awake.

"Can't you just tell me your name?" I try once more. "Look, I know I'm not getting out of this country alive. Or your car for that matter. I know that my attempt to escape was wasted the second I stepped out of that gate. So the least you can do is talk to me. Think of it as my last meal."

"I am not good at being the shoulder to cry on, I am afraid."

"Then what are you good at?" I ask. "Besides killing people, of course."

I notice his jaw move slightly, but he hasn't looked at me in the rearview mirror in a while.

"Driving," he answers.

OK, this is going nowhere.

I want to cry out of frustration.

Fifteen more minutes of silence passes and I notice that my surroundings are beginning to feel all too familiar. We're going in circles and have been all this time. For a split second I start to say something about it, but I decide it's probably better that I don't let him know I'm onto him.

I lean up a little from the seat and point the gun at him and say, "Turn left up here." And I do this for the next twenty minutes, forcing him to go my way even though I have no idea where I'm taking us. And he plays along, never breaking a sweat, never giving me the slightest impression that he's worried or afraid of having a gun at his back. The longer we do this the more I begin to realize that even though I'm the one with the gun, he has this whole situation under more control than I thought I did.

What did I get myself into?

More long minutes pass and I've lost track of time. I'm so tired. My lids are getting heavier. I snap my head away from the seat behind me and press my finger against the window button to lower the glass. The warm night air rushes inside the car, tossing my auburn hair about my face. I force my eyes open wide and position myself in a more uncomfortable way to help keep me awake, but it doesn't take long to notice that nothing is working.

The American watches every move I make from the mirror. I notice him every once in a while.

"What makes you his favorite?" he asks and it stuns me.

I was sure he'd been waiting all this time for me to doze off; if he would've waited a few more minutes that's probably what would've happened. Now he's *talking* to me? I'm thoroughly confused, but I'll take it.

"I wasn't bought," I answer.

Finally he asks me a direct question which could lead to conversation and maybe his help, but ironically the topic makes it difficult to take advantage of the opportunity. It's hard to talk about even though I'm the one who initially brought it up.

I wait for a long moment before I go on.

"I was brought here a long time ago…by my mother. Javier saw something in me he didn't see in the other girls. I call it a sickening obsession, he calls it love."

"I see," he says and although his words are few, I can tell they hold more weight than they appear.

"I'm from Tucson," I say. "All I want is to get back there. I'll pay you. If you don't want…me…I'll find a way to pay you cash. I'm good for my word. I wouldn't try to hide from you. I would eventually pay my debt."

"If a drug lord believes he is in love with you," he says casually, "it would not be me you had to hide from."

"Then you know that I'm in a lot of danger," I say.

"Yes, but that still does not make you my problem."

"Are you *human*?" I hate him more every time he speaks. "What kind of man would not want to help a defenseless young woman out of a life of bondage and violence, especially when she has escaped her captors and is directly pleading for your help?"

He doesn't answer. Why doesn't that surprise me?

I sigh heavily and press my back against the seat again. My trigger finger is cramped from being in the same curled position for so long against the metal. Lowering the gun farther behind the seat so that he can't see, I switch hands long enough to wriggle my fingers around for a moment, and then I place my thumb over the top of each finger individually and press down to ease the stiffness. You don't realize how heavy a gun is until you hold it nonstop for long periods of time.

"I'm not lying to you," I say. "About Javier and your money."

I catch his eyes looking at me in the mirror again.

"I've had plenty of time to see how he does business," I go on as I grip the gun in my right hand again, to the argument of my aching fingers. "He would rather kill you than pay you."

His eyes are greenish blue. I can see them more clearly now that we're riding through a small town with street lights. And small is an understatement because in under a minute we're engulfed by the darkness of the desolate highway again with nothing in sight except the starlit desert-like landscape.

And then I just start talking, my last ditch attempt to keep myself awake. I don't care anymore if he adds to the one-sided conversation, I just need to stay conscious.

"I guess if you had a daughter or a sister you might care a little more. I had somewhat of a life before my mother brought me here. It wasn't much of one, but it was one, nonetheless. We lived in a tiny trailer with cockroaches and walls so thin it felt like sleeping right on the desert floor in the winter. My mother was a slave to heroin. Crack. Meth. You name it she loved it. But not me. I wanted to finish school and get a scholarship to whatever college would have me, and make a life for myself. But then I was brought here and all that changed. Javier was sleeping with my mother for a while, but he always had his eyes on me."

I think I just dozed off for a second.

I snap my eyes open and take a deep breath, pressing my face near the open window to let the air hit me.

Then I feel a white-hot pain to the side of my head and everything goes black.

THREE

SARAI

The sound of trickling water wakes me. My eyes creep open, flinching at the light pouring in through some nearby window. I can tell that I'm in a room somewhere. My vision is blurred and my head feels like it was banged against a brick wall the night before. The left side of my face feels swollen.

I try to lift up but something is tied around my wrists and my ankles. When my eyes gradually blur into focus I see that I'm lying on a bed in a dingy room with tan tapestry wallpaper and dusty mismatched furniture. The television looks just like the one at the compound: ancient and probably only picks up one channel which I'm sure is the one that runs the dramatic Spanish soap operas. In my direct line of vision I see the thick green curtains on the window and pushed against them is a tiny square table with a single wooden chair. A long black trench coat hangs over the back of it.

Realizing what must've happened and my instincts finally catching up to me, I force my body onto my back so that I can see the rest of the room. So I can find the American who I know brought me here, wherever here is.

He tied me up. Oh no...he tied me up.

When I notice him sitting in a chair on the other side of the bed, it startles me and I yelp and fall off the bed and onto the floor, my hands and legs bound tight so I can't do anything to brace for the impact. I hit the floor hard and pain shoots up from my hip and through my back. "*Oww!*" I moan loudly. In no time I'm trying to twist the fabric loose from my wrists as I squirm around on the floor.

The American stands over me like a ghost come from out of nowhere.

"Why did you tie me up?" I'm shaking so bad I hope he doesn't notice. I don't want him to know the true level of my fear.

He leans over and picks me up from the floor and lays me back on the bed. I try to kick and hit him until I realize how stupid that is because the only thing it might do is cause me to fall and hit the floor again. Without answering, he goes back around to the other side where he was sitting and puts his hand in a bowl of water on the nightstand. He wrings the water from a rag and brings it toward my face, but I try to pull away. It doesn't faze him. Nothing ever seems to, really. I know I'm not going anywhere right now so I just lie here very still, staring directly into his eyes even though he's not looking back into mine.

I want him to see me, to see the anger in my face, but he doesn't care to look.

"You *punched* me?" I can't believe it, but then again I can.

"Yes." He dabs the cold wet cloth over my left eye and around the bone.

"So you're a murderer *and* a woman beater."

His dark eyes finally look directly into mine and his hand stops moving as if my accusation struck him the wrong way.

He looks away and goes back to dabbing my face.

"I don't hit women," he says, "unless they have a gun pointed at my head."

I don't respond to that. He makes a notable argument, if it can be called an argument.

"Do I have a black eye?"

"No," he says, pulling the wet rag away. "I did not hit you that hard. Just a little swollen."

I look at him like he's crazy. "No? Yet you hit me hard enough to knock me unconscious the whole night?"

He stands up from the bed, his tall height looming over me, and walks over to his coat hanging over the back of the chair. He reaches inside one of the pockets and pulls out a bottle of pills.

"You woke up shortly after I knocked you out," he says as he twists the cap off the bottle. "I had to drug you."

I blink back the stun.

He shuffles a little white pill into the palm of his hand and holds it out to me. I'm still looking at him like he's crazy, maybe now even more-so.

"You *drugged* me? What *is* that?"

I want to slap him. If my hands weren't bound I would.

"Sleeping pill," he says, putting the pill to my lips. "Harmless. I take it myself. You, on the other hand, only need half of one, I know that now."

I spit the pill onto the yellowed sheet beneath me.

"I think I've slept enough."

"Suit yourself." He slides the bottle back inside his coat and moves toward the door.

"Where are you going?"

He stops at the window instead and pulls the curtain closed the rest of the way but remains at it watching out through a crack in the thick fabric. With his back to me, I try quietly to work my wrists free.

"Nowhere at the moment," he says and then turns around again and I stop struggling with my bonds in an instant so that he doesn't notice.

"OK…well then what are we doing here and why am I tied up?"
He looks right at me. "Waiting on the men Javier sent to get you."

I just swallowed my throat. Tears spring instantly from the corners of my eyes. I start to thrash around, trying my hardest to get my hands and legs free, but to no avail. He tied me better than they tied the pigs back at the compound.

"Please! You can't let them take me! I'm *begging* you!"

"It is out of my hands," he says looking back out the window. "It is why I offered the pill. I thought you'd prefer to be unconscious when they arrive."

I feel like I'm going to be sick. My heart is beating too fast, my insides are stiffening and I feel like I can't breathe. I force my body to sit upright and I throw my legs over the side of the bed and try to stand.

"Sit down," he says turning to look at me again.

Tears barrel from my eyes and I raise my bound hands out toward him. "*Please…*" I choke on my tears, my chest shuddering and jerking with fast, uneven breaths. "Don't let them take me back there!"

"I will ask you one more time," he says turning to face me fully. "Do you want to be awake for what is about to happen?"

"I don't *want* it to happen!" I scream.

I pull my arms up and try working the fabric loose from my wrists with my teeth. The American ignores me and moves over to a long black flat suitcase of sorts sitting on the floor propped against the far wall. Carrying it by the handle he places it on the end of the bed near me and flips the latches to raise the lid, blocking my view from what's hidden inside.

A sharp glint of reflective sunlight beams against the back of the curtain and the sound of squeaky brakes outside twists my stomach into knots further. I freeze on the edge of the bed, my teeth still clenched around the fabric, my eyes wide and locked with fear. I look to and from the door and the American who stands at the foot of the bed twisting a long metal thing on the end of a slick black handgun. And then so fast, yet as casual as an early morning walk, he closes the suitcase and slides it underneath the bed and out of sight.

He comes toward me.

I try to kick him again but my bound ankles keep me from doing anything but nearly causing me to fall off the bed.

"No! Leave me alone! Please don't do this!"

With his free hand he grabs me by the elbow and pulls me harshly to my feet, the gun pointed at the floor in his other hand and then he walks me awkwardly across the small room and toward a tiny restroom.

There is a knock at the door but the American pays no attention to it. He drags me into the restroom and practically pushes me into the disgusting tub. I think my head is going to hit the side but he holds me by the fabric on my wrists and lowers me in the rest of the way safely.

"Stay down low. Don't raise your head and don't move."

"What?" I blink back the confusion. I'm so scared I feel like I'm going to lose control of my bladder any second now.

"Do you understand?" he asks, looming over me. The seriousness in his eyes is palpable.

I hesitate because, no, I *don't* understand, but then I just nod in fast, jerking motions.

He reaches around to the back of his pants and slides a knife out from somewhere. My eyes grow wider as the sharp silver moves toward me. Just when I think he's going to cut me, even though I don't know why he'd go through all of this just to kill me, he cuts the bonds from my ankles.

"Stay down," he demands one last time.

And just like that he leaves the restroom and shuts the door behind him.

Frozen in shock, it takes me a moment to get my head together. I gaze down at my unbound feet and I wonder why he did it. Why keep my hands bound but allow me the use of my legs again so that I can run away? It doesn't matter. I need to free my hands, too. I bite down on the tight knots again, working at them furiously but only getting frustrated. I barely lift my head from the tub to get a better view of the restroom, looking for anything that might work as a knife or scissors so I can try cutting it away instead. Nothing. Just a bone-dry deep plastic industrial-type sink with paint, oil and dirt stains and a disgusting toilet with no lid.

The door opens to the motel room and I hear voices inside.

"Where is she?"

Oh no…that's Izel's voice!

My heart speeds up so fast I feel lightheaded as the blood rushes quickly to my head. I bite down on the fabric even harder, twisting the impossible knots with my teeth until it hurts.

"Javier wonders why you didn't just bring her back yourself," Izel adds with her trademark sultry, sarcastic tone.

There are more voices, male, speaking Spanish amongst themselves while Izel talks only to the American. Their voices are muffled. I can't make out what they're saying.

"Have a seat," the American says calmly.

"We didn't come here to visit," Izel refuses. "Give me Sarai…"—I can picture her walking toward the American like the slithering snake she is—"or, you and I can be alone together for a while first. I would like that."

Her voice stops abruptly and her seductive tone disappears in an instant. "Fine! Fine! Fucking *puto*. You'd rather shoot me than fuck me?"

"Yes. I would rather," the American answers.

"Bring her out here," Izel demands, her voice laced with contempt.

"Sit first," the American says.

Suddenly I hear guns cocking and instinctively I lower my body back into the tub as flat as I can make myself. I'm beginning to understand why he forced me in here like this.

"There are five of us and one of you," Izel points out venomously.

Then a shot rings out and I stiffen against the hard plastic beneath me. More shots. Bullets pepper the walls; two move straight through the wall into the restroom where I lay huddled. I hear glass shatter and what sounds like bodies stampeding through the room beyond me. More shots ring out and Izel screams curses over the chaos. The walls shake all around me, knocking thick layers of dust from the exposed light bulb hanging from the water damaged ceiling above. I hear a loud *crunch* and then the sound of the large window in the room shattering as if someone or something was just pushed through it.

Then everything goes silent. All that I can hear now is my heart beating so fast and violently. I'm so scared I can't even manage tears anymore and my body has stopped shaking. I'm paralyzed with fear.

The acrid smell of gun smoke lingers in the air.

Is the American dead? It's all I can think about. Maybe they're all dead and I can get out of here alive.

I go to climb my way out of the tub but then I hear Izel:

"Fuck you. I won't tell you shit!"

There is a brief bout of silence and then I hear the American say calmly, "You've already told me most of what I need to know."

"How is that?"

"If Javier wanted me alive to kill Guzmán your men never would have drawn on me."

"He *did* want you to kill him."

"So then your men are simply stupid."

Izel says nothing in response, but I can picture the expression she wears: sour mixed with evil.

Quietly, I crawl out of the tub, careful not to make any abrupt movements and I reach out for the door handle. It comes open the second my fingers touch it as though it hadn't been shut all the way before, though I know that it had. It must've been jarred loose when I heard someone bash against it during the fight.

I push it open barely a crack. The mirror over the sink just outside the door is in view. All that's left of it now are three large uneven shards of broken glass barely hanging onto the wall.

I can see the American's back through the reflection.

"I should tell you," he says. "There will be a new deal now."

"You're not the one to be making deals," Izel spits out the words.

"I believe that I am," he replies. "First, you will tell me what Javier's plans were in bringing me to the compound."

"I'll tell you shit!"

A muffled shot makes a quick *fuddup* sound and then Izel screams out in pain. "You fucking *shot* me!"

The American moves over and out of sight of the mirror, leaving me to glimpse Izel sitting on the chair next to the wall. Her face glistens with sweat and blood drains from the gunshot wound on her thigh, her hands pressed over it trying to stop the flow. Her bronzed face is contorted in agony and anger. She spits at the floor defiantly.

"Merely a flesh wound," the American says.

I push myself farther against the door. A pair of hands lay open near Izel's feet: one of the men the American just killed. I swallow hard and try to calm my breathing. The door moves as my hip brushes against it and I suck in sharply that breath I just took. Izel's head darts sideways to face the mirror. She knows I'm hiding in here. I try to step away from the door and move back into the darkness of the restroom, but she sees me. A grin spreads across her face.

"Come out, Sarai," she says harmoniously. "Javier misses you."

I don't move. Maybe if I remain still, what she sees in the reflection of the mirror she'll start to believe is just the light playing tricks on her eyes.

She turns her gaze away from me as if the American has done something to regain her attention.

"Javier wants Guzmán dead," Izel says. "He wouldn't have hired you and let you leave with that money if he didn't." She sneers and shakes her head at the American and adds, "You're a fool."

I hear the bed creak as if he just sat on the end of it, facing her. While she's distracted, I position myself farther back from the edge of the door, but in a way that I can get a better view of the room through the reflection in the mirror. I glimpse another body lying haphazardly against the wall on the other side of her.

"And if I kill Guzmán," the American says, "I will have no trouble getting the other half of my money." It was a statement, but at the same time, a question.

Izel grins. "Of course." She tilts her head to one side. "She's gotten to you already."

No answer. I know Izel is referring to me.

"The girl wasn't bought or sold, just so you know," she adds.

"I didn't ask."

"You didn't need to."

Izel looks toward the mirror again, without moving her head.

"Going to be the hero?" she says, sarcasm lacing her voice.

"Hardly," the American says. "I'm going to use her as leverage."

I swallow hard.

Should've kept my mouth shut.

"That won't sit well with Javier. She wasn't part of the deal. You keep the girl and Javier will not be happy." A strand of black hair falls into her face. She reaches up as if to move the rest of her hair away, but her hand stops halfway and she places it back down beside her. Anger helps to hide the fear in her expression somewhat. She knows that he'll blow her brains out the back of her head.

"The girl stays with me until I kill Guzmán and then we will make the trade: her for the rest of my money."

"And what if Javier doesn't give a shit?"

"You wouldn't be here now if he didn't."

FOUR

SARAI

Izel rounds her chin defiantly, the skin around her dark eyes peppered with tiny flecks of blood splatter.

"You're making a mistake," she spats, defeat in her voice. "If you want a girl, Javier will give you one. Just not *that* one. You'll only make him your enemy by doing this."

I know that worry in her voice all too well. When Javier is unhappy, he tends to blame it on Izel. If she doesn't return to the compound with me, he'll beat her senseless. As much as I hate her for the things she's done to me, I can't help but pity her sometimes, too.

"Your offer offends my intelligence," the American says. "She is the one I want *because* she is the one he treasures the most. If Javier has no ill intentions then he should have nothing to worry about." Izel glances toward the bathroom door quickly while he speaks. "I keep the girl until I kill Guzmán. Javier pays me the remainder of my money. I give the girl back. We all leave with what we want."

I want to dash out of the bathroom and try for one of the cars outside, but I know I won't make it. My palms are sweating and stinging. I cut my left hand somewhere at some point. I can't remember when it happened.

Izel curses him in Spanish and presses the palms of her hands on the seat beneath her and begins to rise into a stand.

The American very casually raises his gun and she freezes, anger and resistance twisting her face.

"Fold your hands together behind the chair," the American says.

"Go fuck yourself."

Thwap! Izel's body jerks sideways, almost knocking the chair over with her in it. "Mother*fucker!*" she cries out, holding her hand over a fresh bullet wound on the opposite thigh to match the other one.

The American never moves, his expression and posture always casual and controlled.

"Fold your hands together behind the chair," he says once more with the same amount of calm as before.

This time, Izel is compliant. Reluctant and defiant as always, but compliant.

"Come out of the bathroom," I hear the American say.

I don't want to. I quietly push my back against the wall, thrusting my bound hands over my chest and lock my fingers together nervously in front of me. I sniffle back the tears, the taste of salt draining down the back of my throat. What should I do? If I just stand here like this it'll only prolong the inevitable. There's no way out of this bathroom except through *that* door.

Finally I do as he says.

Trying to push the door open the rest of the way, I have to shoulder it hard because of the body lying on the floor on the other side. I try not to look when I step around the man's left arm, contorted unnaturally behind him, but I glimpse enough that it makes my stomach churn. Especially when I see his eyes. It's always the eyes, lifeless and empty and glazed over, that makes me sick to my stomach. I take a deep breath and step over him. Izel smiles across at me, not as affected by two gunshot wounds as I imagine anyone else might be. Her breathing is labored and she strains to keep her composure for the sake of taunting me.

"Come here," the American says and I do.

He pulls the knife from his pocket again and his eyes avert to my wrists briefly. Assuming—and hoping—it's what he wants, I hold my shaking hands out to him. He slides the blade behind the fabric and cuts me loose.

"Did you tell him that you're a whore?" Izel asks.

I swallow what saliva is left in my mouth. I'm no whore, but she has always had a way with somehow making me feel ashamed by her accusations. I pretend to be more fixated on my wrists, now that they are no longer tied together.

Izel turns to the American, her hands still folded loosely behind her back. She says with a spiteful smile, "If you're feeling sorry for her, don't. That little puta is treated better than anyone, even better than me and I am his sister. Javier has her anytime he wants her. And he doesn't have to take it."

I feel my fingers digging into my palms down at my sides now, but shame eclipses my anger. What she says is only halfway true, but right now isn't the time to defend myself. Nothing that I say will matter. Not to the American and certainly not to her. I only care what the American thinks because I need him to help me. If he thinks of me as a whore, he'll surely be less inclined later on. If I can ever convince him to help, that is, which is doubtful.

Showing absolutely no interest in Izel's obvious attempt to mar my character, the American points to his bag on the table by the window and says to me, "Left zipper, inside pocket you'll find a rope."

I walk across the room carefully, my heart pounding violently against my ribs when I go between the two, the hairs on my arms and the back of my neck stand on end as I pass them. I halfway expected Izel to use the opportunity to reach out and grab me, but am relieved when she doesn't dare move. Making my way through more bodies and debris scattered about the small area, this time

I'm too afraid of the two still alive in the room to let myself notice the dead eyes staring up at me from the floor. I smell the blood. At least, I'm pretty sure that faint metallic stench is blood. There's so much of it all around me. The curtain on the broken window blows inward as a small gust of warm wind pushes through. I reach inside the American's black bag and shuffle around looking for the rope. I'm too nervous to look inside the bag. There's no telling what he carries in this thing.

With the wad of rope in my hand, I briefly wonder why he didn't use this tougher stuff on me instead of strips of fabric from the bed sheet. I turn around and look only at the American waiting for whatever he might tell me to do next, trying to make as little eye contact with Izel as possible. It never takes her much to intimidate me.

The American nods toward Izel.

"Tie her hands behind the chair at her wrists," he instructs.

My heart leaps. Still trying my best to keep from looking at her, the attempt is thrown out the window with his words and look at her is exactly what I do. She'll surely grab me if I'm standing that close.

The conflict in my eyes tells the American everything that the words I can't get out, can't.

He moves the gun in his hand subtly at Izel, his wrist still propped on his leg. "She will not touch you," he says, looking only at me. "If she so much as flinches in a manner that I feel is threatening, I'll kill her and she knows it."

From the corner of my eye, I see Izel's nostrils flare and her mouth twist in anger.

The American nods toward her again to indicate that I should proceed.

Fumbling the rope in my fingers, I step over the bodies again and slowly make my way toward Izel, finding it impossible not to look at her the closer I get. Her smile spreads. My hands are shaking so conspicuously she takes notice; her brown eyes skirt them briefly without moving her head.

"You really did it this time," she taunts. "How did you get out of the fence? Did Lydia help you?"

I'm almost behind her when she says Lydia's name and I stop dead in my tracks. Izel notices my reaction exactly for what it is: worry. And she runs with it.

An even more sadistic grin tugs the corners of her lips. "Ah, I see," she says. "So she *did* help you." She clicks her tongue. "Unfortunate for poor Lydia, she will be punished. But you already knew that, didn't you, Sarai?"

"Lydia had *nothing* to do with it!" I yell in Spanish, as if I'm still back at the compound.

I know she's trying to get to me, but I also know that what she's saying about Lydia being punished is true and already I'm regretting my reaction. Because it's exactly what she wanted to see. This entire situation just changed in the worst way. It's not just about me anymore. I should've known this before I crawled out that window. Javier and Izel knew how close Lydia and I became in her short time there.

A large part of me wants to give up and go back, but now with the American controlling the situation, that's no longer in the cards.

"Stop talking and tie her hands behind her," the American says from behind.

"Fine. Go ahead. Do what you want with her," I say to Izel as I walk around behind her chair. "I got out. She didn't. It's sad, but there's nothing I can do about it. I'm not going back to that place, not even for her." I hope she believes me, that I don't care what happens to Lydia, so maybe they won't use her against me.

"I said stop talking."

The unnatural frustration in the American's tone, though restrained, is enough to get our attention. Izel and I look over at him at the same time.

I do exactly as he says, fearing he might just shoot me in the leg next, and I crouch behind Izel and start tying her wrists together.

The American watches Izel seemingly without blinking, waiting for her to slip up and give him more reason to shoot her. I bind her wrists good, wrapping the semi-stretchy rope three times, tying it into a knot each round. Once the rope pinches her skin, Izel tosses her head to the side in an attempt to see me, her teeth gritting in anger. "Watch it," she snaps and her long black hair falls to one side around her face. I tie the last knot even tighter, just because I can. If looks could kill, I'd be dead ten times over.

"Now step away from her," the American instructs.

He stands from the bed and slides his elongated suitcase out from underneath it.

I step away and with the backward tilt of his head I continue to follow his instructions and make my way over next to him. He takes my wrist in one hand and his suitcase in the other and walks me toward the door. He only lets go of my wrist long enough to pick his bag up from the table and shoulder it.

He leaves his long black coat. Surely he sees it, but I get the feeling he's leaving it draped over the back of the chair on purpose.

"I'll kill you if you leave me here like this," Izel growls through gritted teeth, but her threat comes out thickly with desperation. She begins to struggle in the chair, trying to work her hands free. "Don't leave me like this! How can I tell Javier what you want if I'm stuck in this room?"

Sunlight fills the room when the American opens the door with two fingers from the hand holding the suitcase.

"You'll get yourself free in time," he says and steps out the door with me at his side. "Inform Javier that I will be in touch and not to lose or discard the cell phone number that I last called him on." He pulls the door shut with the same two fingers and I hear Izel's livid voice screaming curses at us from inside as we leave her there.

He guides me around to the front passenger's seat and closes the door behind me once I'm inside. The trunk pops open and he hides his suitcase and black duffle bag away inside of it.

I hear four muffled shots outside the car as he takes out two tires on each of the trucks parked out front.

He shuts the driver's side door and looks over at me.

"Put on your seatbelt," he says and looks away from my eyes, turning the key in the ignition.

The car hums to life as I click my seatbelt in place quickly.

"You shoot women," I say quietly.

He backs out of the dirt-covered space in front of the odd road-side motel, which really looks more like a five-room shack.

The American presses his foot on the brake and looks over at me again. "Flesh wounds," he says and shifts the car into Drive. "She'll live. And that one was hardly a woman." He pulls away, the sleek black car stirring up a cloud of dirt behind us.

He's right in that aspect—Izel is a woman, but she doesn't deserve to be treated like one and it's her own fault.

As we're speeding down the dusty highway and away from the motel, the American reaches into the console between us and retrieves a small black cell phone. Running his finger over the screen, the speakerphone comes on and suddenly Izel's voice fills the car. I'm confused by it at first but soon understand that, if I'm right, there was a reason he left his long coat in the room, after all.

I listen to Izel's voice stream through the tiny speaker:

"He's gone! Get up and untie me! Hurry!"

A rustling sound muffles her voice and then other strange, uniden-tifiable noises.

"Get me out of these ropes!"

One of the men was left alive?

I glance over at the American whose eyes remain fixed on the road out ahead, but his ears are fully open to the voices in his hand. He knew. He knew all along that one of them lay there pretending to be dead. I shudder to think I walked over his body, or around it, so close he could've grabbed me by the ankle and took me down with him.

More shuffling and cracking noises funnel through the speaker-phone. I hear Izel tell the man to give her a phone and seconds later she's speaking to Javier:

"Sí, Javier. He took her. He killed them. No."

She becomes quiet as Javier, I know without having to hear him, threatens her on the other end of the phone.

"Sí," she says gravelly *as if forcing herself to agree though it takes everything in her to do so.*

Then I hear a loud shot and shortly after a *thump!* and I can only assume that she just killed the man who helped her, likely out of anger for whatever Javier said.

Everything becomes quiet now. Maybe Izel left the room. Several seconds pass and still nothing, only the low static hum of the speakerphone itself. The American, although not famous for facial expressions, seems disappointed. He hangs the phone up, rolls the window down beside him and tosses it onto the highway. Then he makes a sharp U-turn and drives in the opposite direction.

"I take it you didn't hear what you wanted to?" I ask carefully.

His right hand drops from the steering wheel and rests along the top of his leg.

"No," he answers.

"You still doubt what I told you," I say.

In my peripheral vision, I see him turn his head slightly to look at me. I'm not comfortable enough with him to meet his eyes when he instigates it. I never will be.

But he doesn't answer.

A minute later, I say, "I'm not a whore. She was only trying to get to you in case you have any pity for me."

Maybe I'm insulting his intelligence, just like Izel had at one point, but this is my way of defending myself from her accusation. I want him to know. And I don't want him to think that way of me.

I go on, finally looking at him now that his eyes are back on the road again.

"But you never had any pity for me to begin with."

Again, my attempt to engage him in conversation seems to go unnoticed and I give up and lay my head against the car window.

"I know you're not a whore," he says.

FIVE

SARAI

It's been on rare occasion that I saw much of any other part of Mexico during the day, other than the compound. Javier wasn't big on sightseeing, or an early Sunday morning drive. I spent much of my life cooped up behind those fences, only leaving when Lydia and I were relocated with the other girls before other dangerous drug lords came to meet with Javier. It was Javier's way of keeping us 'safe' in case a deal went bad. But we always traveled at night, so despite the predicament I'm in now, I find myself in mild awe as I look out the car window while the bright Mexican landscape flies by.

We've been driving for two hours.

"I'm hungry," I say.

A few quiet seconds pass before he answers.

"I have nothing to eat in this car."

"Well, can't we stop somewhere?"

"No."

If I could at least get him to stop answering my questions like that, I'd almost be satisfied.

"If you're worried about me trying to run off," I say, turning sideways to better see him, "then go to a drive-thru. I haven't had anything to eat since early morning yesterday. Please…"

"There are no drive-thrus here."

"Where is *here*, anyway?" Suddenly my hunger has taken the backseat. "At least tell me where I've spent the last nine years of my life."

I saw one road sign several minutes back, but I didn't recognize the name from anything I've seen on the maps I've poured over time and time again, mostly the maps in an American high school textbook from 1997.

"We are now five miles south of Nacozari de García."

I sigh, frustrated with myself for not having any idea where that is, either.

"You're less than two hours from the United States border," he says and stuns me.

I whip around, turning fully on the seat, my back pressing against the car door.

"But you said I was—you made it sound like I was *days* from the border."

"No. I simply stated the distance was farther than I wanted you as my company."

I cross my arms angrily over my chest. I've no idea where I even get off being angry at all with someone like him and even remotely showing it. Reminding myself quickly of where I am and who I'm with, I put on my timid face again.

"Is that where we're going?" I ask. "Is this man you're supposed to kill for Javier in the United States?"

"Yes."

Silence.

I burst into tears. They come out of nowhere, burning behind my eyes and through my sinuses. But I'm not crying because I'm so close to home, I'm crying because his strange, stoic personality and one-word answers are enough to make me want to figuratively shoot myself. I sob into the palms of my hands, letting my fear and frustration of the American out, along with everything else buried inside: relief that I've finally gotten away, fear of being sent back there again, worried about how badly Izel will beat Lydia, the mere fact that I'm in a situation far from anything easy to solve, the hunger in my stomach, the dryness of my throat, not having had a bath in two days now, the fact that I could die at any moment. The only good thing I can account for is that I am, in fact, still alive and not as far away from home as I thought I was.

I feel the car veer off to the right as he pulls onto another highway.

I look over at him, sniffling back the rest of my tears. I reach up and wipe my cheeks with my palms. He never says anything, he doesn't try to console me or ask questions. He doesn't seem to care and I don't care anymore that he doesn't. I never expected him to.

Another thirty minutes or so and we're pulling up to the front of an old roadside convenience store. Only one truck is parked out front, a white Ford with rust along the doors.

"If you want food," the American says, turning off the engine, "come inside and eat."

I'm surprised that we've stopped at all, much less to feed me. He walks around to my side of the car and opens the door, likely just to make sure he stays by my side at all times rather than to be gentlemanly. He stands there waiting patiently for me to get out. Finally I do, just after slipping my bare feet down into my flip-flops in the floorboard.

This place can't be called a roadside diner or convenience store; I think it would need a few more tables for that, but there is a place to sit and eat, off in a dark corner near a single black door. I have a microwaved chicken sandwich from the freezer; the American, nothing but black coffee. The two of us look out-of-place here. Both of us obviously with no Spanish genes, in a place that is clearly not a tourist town, him dressed in expensive black slacks and shoes, which were probably shiny at one time but are now covered in a fine layer of dust. I know I must smell pretty bad. I don't remember the last time I wore deodorant.

I scarf down half of the chicken sandwich and gulp the bottled water until it's nearly empty. I learned a long time ago never to drink the water in these parts, that if it isn't from an unopened bottle, it'll probably make me sick.

The American sips his coffee gradually, reading the contents of a local newspaper of sorts. If I didn't know better, we could almost pass for an unconventional married couple having breakfast in any typical American town. Unconventional because I'm only twenty-three, and the American, he's older than me. Middle to late thirties, maybe. If I didn't know what he was and I just saw him sitting here one day, like he is now with both feet on the floor and his dress-shirt-covered elbows on the table, I'd find him attractive for an older man. He's clean cut, though with stubble in a pattern along his face. He has sharp cheekbones and piercing greenish blue eyes that seem to contain everything but reveal nothing. And he's very tall, lean and frightening. I find it notable how he scares me more than Javier ever did, yet without having to say a word. At the same time, I feel like I'm better off with the American than I ever was with the likes of Javier.

At least, for now. That'll change, I'm sure, when he tries to hand me back over to him.

But I'll die before I let that happen.

"Are you ever going to tell me your name?" I ask.

He raises his eyes from the newspaper without moving his head.

I can sense immediately that he doesn't care to tell me, to get that personal with his 'hostage', but finally he throws me a bone.

"Victor."

I'm so stunned he even told me that it takes me a second to think of what to say next.

I sip my water.

"Where are you from?" I ask.

It's worth a try.

"Why don't you finish your food," he suggests and peers back down into the paper.

"You know my name. You know where I'm from. Why don't you humor me, *Victor*?" The bitterness in my tone wasn't an accident.

I figure that if he was going to kill me, I'd be dead already, so I'm not really as afraid of him as my conscience is telling me I should be.

He sighs with annoyance and shakes his head subtly.

"I was born in Boston," he says. "I have a sister. A year younger than me. My mother is somewhere in Budapest. My father, he's dead. He was my first kill."

That small ounce of bravery I summoned evaporates right out of my pores. I look carefully to both sides of me, looking for the man behind the counter who sold us the food. He's on the opposite side of the store, sweeping the floor and not paying a lick of attention to us.

I look back at Victor, nervously swallowing what's left of the saliva in my mouth.

"You killed your father?" I have to believe it was for some obvious reason: his father beat his mother, something along those lines.

He nods.

"Why? How old were you?"

"I think you know enough about me," he says and takes a sip of his coffee, his long manicured fingers curled gently around the tiny white Styrofoam cup. "You asked to know more about me and I told you. It was a favor. Not an invitation to ask more questions."

I wonder why he told me something like that to begin with. Maybe he was just trying to scare me into submission so I'd stop talking altogether.

I stand up from the tiny table. He raises his eyes from the newspaper again.

"I need to use the restroom," I say.

Setting the newspaper on the table beside his coffee, he stands up to join me. He takes my wrist gently into his hand and I pull it away, shaking my head no. "I can go by myself," I insist.

"Yes, but I'm going to go with you."

I cross my arms over my chest and blink with surprise. "You can't be serious. I'm not using it with you standing there."

"Then you're not going to use it."

My mouth falls open with a spat of air. I look back and forth between him and the door behind him that I'm hoping is a restroom—there are no obvious signs indicating anything. I can detect his annoyance with me, faintly in his face; it makes me feel like I just interrupted his nightly love affair with a glass of wine and classical music.

It doesn't take me long to understand, really.

"I doubt it'll be like it is in the movies," I say. "I try to climb out the window after you make the rookie decision to let me go in alone." I'm not trying to be mouthy, I'm only stating the obvious. I hope he gets that.

"Take it or leave it," he says. "If you don't go now, you might be holding it a while."

I bite down on the inside of my cheek. "Fine," I give in and step around and in front of him.

He walks behind me into the restroom. There is one toilet that looks as though it has never once been cleaned in the decades it has been here. Four dirty walls with peeling paint and a burn mark near the tiny window that I doubt I would've been able to squeeze through if I had been given the chance to try. The room is so small I can reach out and touch Victor as he stands facing the door with his back to me, his hands folded down in front of him. Feeling only a little embarrassed—unfortunately, peeing in front of a madman isn't new to me, either—I pull my shorts and panties down and take a seat. When I'm done, I have to drip dry. Toilet paper really is a luxury that Americans take for granted.

As I'm pulling up my clothes, I notice Victor's shoulders from behind tense up. And then I hear voices as though someone just came inside the store.

Victor reaches around to the back of his pants and slips his hand underneath his shirt, pulling a gun into view, his strong index finger already wrapped around the trigger.

"What is it?" I ask, fearful; already my hands are shaking.

Victor cracks open the door and peers outside, putting up his free hand behind him as if to tell me to be quiet.

Then he turns his head to me briefly and whispers, "Stay here," and before I can question him, or protest, he disappears out the door and I'm left hiding inside yet another restroom. Only, this one doesn't have a bathtub to help shield me from flying bullets and I find no comfort in that.

Despite my fears, I can't stop myself from trying to get a glimpse of what's going on, so I step up to the door and crack it just like Victor had and press my body against it, looking out. My hot, unsteady breath fills the confined space between the door and my face. I can barely make out the counter where the store owner stands off to the side with the broom still clutched in his old, chubby hands. But I can't see his face. And I can't see Victor. Several long anxiety-filled seconds go by and still no gunshots. I take that as a good sign. I notice a figure pass my line of vision, but it's not Victor. And then another man walks by.

I hear voices in Spanish, though not entirely clear to me from my position behind the door. Something about a car part and a few seconds later the store owner says he has one, but he'll have to go around back to get it. I still see no sign of Victor. Did he leave me here? That thought strangely makes me even more afraid and I crack the door open just a little more, trying to get a better visual. At first my misplaced panic of being left alone here makes me second guess my sanity, but then I realize all over again that despite Victor being an assassin and the fact that I'm being used as leverage in a dangerous game of pay-up-or-die, I'm still a girl all alone in the most dangerous parts of a country that I'm not a native of.

Like it or not, Victor is my only protection until I can get over that border, and I'm going to stick with him for as long as I can, regardless of my desperate need to get away from *him*, too.

SIX

SARAI

Finally I glimpse the faces of both men, relieved that they don't look at all familiar. I start to believe they are just passing through. Getting a little claustrophobic, I take it upon myself to open the door the rest of the way. I inhale a deep breath to compose myself and then step out of the restroom as casually as any other customer who just got done using the toilet.

Victor is sitting back at our table reading the paper like he was before, when I make it around the corner.

He barely glances at me, enough to let only me know that he is not pleased.

"Are you ready?" I ask in English. "*I* certainly am. That restroom is *disgusting*," I add, feigning displeasure of the facilities with the attitude of a snotty American girl.

I hope I'm convincing enough.

Victor stands up and takes me by the hand rather than the wrist this time, his fingers interlocking with mine. The gesture at first surprises me. But I soon realize he's only playing along.

The two customers and the store owner look right at me and somehow I get the feeling that my little tourist act is drawing more attention than deterring it. And maybe it's because tourists never come to these parts.

Victor squeezes my hand with disapproval.

Seconds later in a motion seemingly too fast for me to track, the two customers each take a single shot to the head and drop dead in front of me on the floor. I stumble backward into Victor's chest, covering my ears in a delayed reaction to the suppressed sound of the shots. Victor releases my hand and grabs me around the waist, catching me with one arm, his gun clasped in his other hand.

I hear a door slam on the side of the store and I look up still pressed against Victor, using his body for support, to see the store owner through the glassless window running away to no telling where. Victor pushes me to the side and aims his gun at the man through the window. A single shot takes him down before he gets out of range, his body hitting the ground and dust flying up all around him before being carried off by the wind.

I push my way through the store, over the two bodies and toward Victor, my heart pounding erratically.

"What was *that* for?!"

He grabs my wrist again and drags me with him back to the bodies. I try pulling away, but his grip is too tight.

"They were harmless," I say exasperatedly, feeling the tears burning the back of my throat again. "And the owner—what—why did you kill him?!"

We stop next to one of the bodies and Victor lets go of my wrist so that he can kneel down beside it. Reaching into the man's back pocket on his jeans, he pulls out a wad of Mexican money. Sifting through the bills and finding nothing of note, he tosses the money on the dead man's back and rummages the rest of his pockets, finding a gun hidden behind his belt. But there's nothing out of the ordinary about that. He does the same to the other man, still not finding anything noteworthy except a set of keys that he decides to pocket.

"What are you looking for?"

"You should've stayed in the restroom like I told you."

I'm surprised at the accusation in his voice; it's so unlike him to show that much emotion, although it's still not much.

"They weren't Javier's men," I protest. "I was there long enough to remember every single one of them."

Victor rises into a stand, seeming even taller than before, but I know it's just my fear of him playing tricks on my eyes.

"You remember the ones you've *seen*," he says. "But you're a foolish girl if you think they are his only men."

I sigh. "But they were only asking about car parts. Maybe they were having car troubles. I heard them talking."

"You heard code," he corrects me. "He asked the owner for a part that doesn't belong on that truck." He looks toward the front window of the store where another truck is parked out front. "When the store owner said that yes he had the part, he was telling them that you were here."

Feeling foolish, I continue pretending, trying to come back from my moment of stupidity. "Then why didn't they do anything?"

He shakes his head lightly at me.

"They were keeping tabs on us," he says. "Or, they were going to try and stall us, long enough to get more men here. Now come on. We have to leave."

When I don't follow fast enough, he takes my hand and leads me out of the store and we head straight for the newer truck parked out front, still nothing but a hunk of old metal, but newer than that old rusty Ford that had to have belonged to the owner.

He opens the door on the passenger's side.

"Get in," he demands.

Confused, I just look at him, but the next thing I know, he's lifting me from the ground and forcing me into the cab. Not daring to fight him on this, or waste anymore of what little time I know we have left, I wait until he gets his guns and bags from his car and shoves it all between us on the seat. He slams the heavy metal door once he gets in on the other side.

"What are we doing exactly?"

He finds the right key to start the engine on the first try and the truck rumbles and spits to life. He reaches up to the gear shift next to the steering wheel and slams the truck into gear, narrowly missing the rickety wooden awning covering the front of the store as he makes a close, wide turn and speeds away.

"The car is too much of a giveaway," he says. "I needed to get rid of it sooner, but running across a vehicle around here that won't break down in twenty miles is a hit or miss."

"I wondered why you drove something as nice as that here to begin with," I say.

"I wasn't a target then."

"But now you are because of me."

I look into the side mirror, watching the dirt swirl chaotically in the truck's wake. We ride fast over the barren landscape, the truck lurching and bouncing over holes until we make it back onto a paved highway.

"Victor?" I ask, and he glances over at me as if me calling him by his name has hit some enigmatic nerve.

I decide not to say what I intended because I've already said it before and it made no difference then.

I look away and I feel his eyes leave me, too.

"Never mind," I say.

Stick to the new plan, Sarai, I think to myself and feel ridiculous when for a split second I worry if he can hear my thoughts, too.

I'll wait until we get over the border and then I'll do whatever it takes to get away from him, even if it means I have to kill him.

———

Two hours later, we make it over the border and into Arizona without any trouble from border patrol. Victor spoke to a Border Patrol Inspector, who clearly saw that we had a suspicious-looking suitcase and two duffle bags sitting between us on the seat. They had words in Spanish, though they were few and didn't make much sense to me, which led me to believe that, like the men back at the convenience store, it was all some kind of code.

Neither the suitcase, nor the bag or even the truck was checked. I don't care to know why. It doesn't make any difference to me if Victor has connections of some kind with border patrol which allows him easy access into and out of the United States. That remains obvious to me. But I don't care. All I care about is my next move.

It takes everything in me to hide my relief and anxiety, knowing that after nine years I'm finally on U.S. soil again. I want to open the door on this truck right now driving fifty-miles per hour down the highway and jump out, rolling bruised and bloody across the desert-like landscape and to my freedom. But I can't. I have to wait just a little longer, at least until we stop somewhere where there are places I can hide. A city, perhaps. A little lone gas station out in the middle of nowhere won't do. If I was lucky enough to manage to get away, the only place I could go is out into the wide open, which encompasses every space in every direction as far as I can see.

I don't want to end up like the store owner, face down in the dirt with a bullet in my back.

Finally I see a small cluster of lights and buildings on the horizon, dwarfed by a cascade of mountains in the background. We soon come to a stop in a parking lot behind a five-story hotel in Douglas, Arizona.

I get out of the truck and shut the door while Victor grabs his bags from the front seat. Scanning the area, looking for the best way to run which might provide me a place to hide when he comes after me, I see the only way to go is across the street where more buildings are situated.

I glance covertly over at Victor and use that second he's shouldering his duffle bags to take off running toward the street. Dashing through the light traffic and easily missing the cars, I make it to the other side, running full-throttle past a small building with arched windows. My flip-flops snap underneath my heels as I run. I nearly trip when my feet come down hard on the pavement and the worn-out rubber gets twisted underfoot. But I catch my balance in time and push harder, glancing back only once to see if Victor is coming after me. I see him, running through a small crowd of people and my legs go into overdrive, trying to get as far away from him as I can. Already nearly out of breath, I force my body forward, running past a row of parked cars and behind another series of buildings. I see a woman carrying a purse on one shoulder, walking out ahead of me.

"Lady! Please help me!"

She looks up as I get closer, her blond hair falling about her shoulders.

"Please, you have to help me! Call the—"

Victor emerges from my right, having gone around to the other side of the nearest building instead of staying directly behind me. He remains next to the building letting it hide his whereabouts. Only I can see him. I glimpse the gun in his hand held down at his side, pressed against the side of his leg.

"What happened? Are you OK?" the woman asks, fixing her purse firmly underneath her arm, probably in case I might try to take it from her.

My eyes stray between the two of them, back and forth, and at one point the woman turns to her left to see what I'm looking at, but Victor stays hidden in the shadows.

I know why he's not moving. I know why his gun is in his hand rather than hidden away in the back of his slacks—whether this woman lives or dies is entirely up to me.

"Miss?" she asks again, appearing concerned, but wary of me just the same. "Do I need to call the police?"

I try to catch my breath, pressing my hand to my chest, but I realize that it's no longer the running that's stealing it away. The thought of Victor shooting this woman because of me—

She reaches inside her purse and pulls out a cell phone.

Victor raises the gun just a little.

"No!" I shout and the woman stops cold with the phone clutched in her ring-decorated hand.

I gesture wildly at her. "I'm sorry. I thought you were someone else."

She doesn't look convinced. She narrows her eyes at me.

I fake a small laugh. "Really, I am so sorry. My friends and I were...never mind. I've got to go." I turn and start to jog lightly back in the direction I came, leaving her standing there dumbfounded.

Minutes later, I stand against the side of the truck, my arms crossed as I wait. Two more people walk by, one even nods and smiles at me, but I can't ask them for help, either. I don't want to risk it.

Victor walks up as casually as if he had just come back from an early morning stroll. He opens the driver's side door again and shoulders his duffle bags. With my back turned to him, I feel his eyes on me from the other side of the truck.

"You're a murderous bastard," I say calmly, nervously pressing my fingertips around my biceps.

"Let's get inside," he says, but then adds as an afterthought, "And if you try to run again or pull anything else, I'll make sure word gets back about how that friend of yours—Lydia was it?—*did* help you escape."

The truck door shuts with a bang while I stand here paralyzed.

I willingly follow him into the hotel.

The lobby is a vast space decorated by skylights and beautiful paintings. A stained glass mural stretches many feet across the mezzanine at the top of the marble staircase. The massive ceilings are held up by tall marble columns. On the inside, this building seems unfitting of the small dusty town that surrounds it. Victor leads me up the stairs after checking in and my interest in the surroundings diminishes with his voice.

"You can shower if you'd like."

He drops one duffle bag on the floor between the beds, the other on the table near the window overlooking the town. His shiny suitcase with what I'm assuming are his guns inside, he sets on the foot of the queen-sized bed closest to the door.

He reaches up with both arms and opens the curtains wide on the window. It's getting darker out. I see the faint glow from the few streetlights outside.

"Victor," I say, but he stops me.

"I'd prefer it if you didn't call me by my name."

"Why not? It's your name. What else am I supposed to call you?" I surprise myself every time I defy him in the slightest way. Because on the inside, I'm utterly terrified of what he might do to me.

"It doesn't matter," he says, sitting down at the table and unzipping his bag. "Just get your shower."

"Look," I say, walking around the beds toward him, "I'm scared. You scare the hell out of me. I'm not going to pretend otherwise. I'm terrified of what's happening to me—"

"You have a strange way of showing it," he says, not even offering me the luxury of his eyes. He pulls out a digital device of sorts, smaller than a laptop. "I would say you've been too numbed by trauma to let it affect you the way that it should." He sets the device on the tabletop and then the duffle bag on the floor beside his feet. I think the device is one of those digital tablets.

I swallow, rounding my chin. "Maybe I have. Somewhat. But what does that have to do with me calling you by your name?" What he accuses me of is spot on, but what I've been through is none of his business. Not unless he intends to help me, which we've already established as being nothing more than wishful thinking. "And why do you care?"

"I never said I did."

"Then don't probe," I snap.

The mere fact that he won't even look at me half the time when he's speaking to me, makes me angry. And the more he does it, acts as if I'm not worth looking in the eye, the more it infuriates me. And when I get mad, I always cry. It's how I've been for as long as I can remember. And I hate it. I never shout or curse or hit things or people. I cry. Every damn time.

As the tears start to well up in my eyes, I turn my back to him and march quickly toward the restroom. But I stop and turn around to face him once more, my fingernails digging into the palms of my hands down at my sides. "Go to hell!" is all I can say, my poor attempt at lashing out with words instead of tears.

SEVEN

SARAI

It seems like forever since I've had a hot shower like this. I had showers on occasion at the compound—I was the only girl given that luxury—but never one like this. They were always lukewarm at best, but never so hot the water could burn the skin off my back. I don't even turn the cold on at first, allowing myself to bask in the heat until it becomes too much and I'm forced to. I want to stay in here forever and not think about what is waiting for me on the other side of that door, but the reality of it all wins out and it's *all* I think about. I sit down on the floor of the tub and draw my knees toward my chest, wrapping my arms loosely around them and let the water stream down on me from above.

I think a lot about Lydia, wondering if she's OK or if Izel beat her for a much longer time than usual, all because of me. I know she did. And although there was nothing I could do to stop it, I made a promise to Lydia that I fully intend to fulfill. I won't let it go on forever.

But if they find out that she knew I was leaving…

After what seems like an hour, the hot water starts to run cold and I get out, wrapping my hair in a towel folded neatly on the back of the toilet. I wish I had a clean set of clothes, panties at least—lost my pillowcase of clothes in Victor's car when we left it behind. I slip my filthy running shorts on over my panties and then pull the light blue tank top down over my breasts. Javier forbade me ever to wear a bra.

When I step out of the restroom, Victor is still sitting in the same spot he was in before. But the suitcase is no longer on the foot of the bed.

As I walk toward the bed where the suitcase had been and start to sit down, Victor looks up and catches my eyes. He doesn't say a word, but I can sense that something is different about him. For a moment, I'm unsettled by his unusual demeanor, but that quiet look in his eyes which I somehow doubt he knows I can see right away, completely catches my interest. It feels almost…tragic.

"Tell me about your mother," he says.

He turns on the chair to face me, giving me his full attention, resting his arms over the length of the chair arms and letting his fingers dangle casually over the ends. His white dress sleeves have been pushed up just below his elbows.

Completely taken aback by his question, I just stare across the room at him blankly.

"Why?" I ask simply, unsure of his intentions with the information. I go ahead and sit down on the foot of the bed, working the towel in my hair with both hands to dry it. But it's all just for show; every fiber of my consciousness is focused on Victor and every move he makes.

He doesn't elaborate. And in case he decides to change his mind and go back to not giving a damn, I speak up before it's too late:

"What do you want to know?"

I squeeze one last section of hair with the towel and then drop it on the floor.

Victor tilts his head gently to one side and then interlocks his hands in front of him, his elbows still resting on the chair arms.

"How did she meet Javier?"

I think back on it for a moment. "I don't know," I say. "I mean, I know it had to do with drugs and sex. The same way she met every man she brought into our home. My mother and I didn't talk much."

He tilts his head to the other side reflectively. What's he waiting for? I study him for a moment, trying to get some idea of what brought his interest in my mother on and finally I choose to tell him whatever I can. Maybe because I've needed someone to listen for the longest time. Lydia and the other girls were too traumatized by their own abductions and experiences within the compound for me to confide in them. And their lives were much more chaotic than mine, much more…unfair. I could never bring myself to talk to the other girls about *my* insignificant problems while *they* were being beaten and raped and mentally and emotionally tortured.

I was in paradise compared to them.

I shake off the imagery and look back over at Victor.

"The first time I saw Javier, I knew he was different from the other men my mother brought home. More powerful somehow. He walked with this proud air about him. Unafraid. Confident. The other men—and there were a lot—were scumbags. They couldn't wait to get through our tiny living room and past me before feeling my mother up. They were disgusting, pathetic."

"And Javier wasn't?" he asks.

I shake my head, gazing off toward the wall now. "He was disgusting because of what he was and how he used my mother, yes, but he was too professional to be pathetic."

"Professional?" He looks at me with slight curiosity.

"Yes," I say with another nod. "Like I said, he was powerful. Though I wasn't aware of it at the time, about what he was, I knew he was different. I stopped worrying about my mother and the things she got herself into when I was twelve-years-old. I was used to it all by then. She always managed to make it home. Despite being strung-out and sometimes beaten, she never called the police or seemed scared of anything so I guess I started believing in her safety as much as she did." I look at the wall again, my hands pressed against the edge of the bed on either side of me, my body slouching down in between my shoulders. "But when I saw Javier, I was scared for her again. I was scared for *me*."

I lock eyes with Victor and say, "The moment he saw me, I knew my life was over. I didn't know how or why at that time, but I just knew. The way he looked at me. I knew…"

My gaze drops to the carpeted floor.

"Why are you asking me this stuff, anyway?" I turn to him again. "Why the interest all of a sudden?"

I catch him glance over at the digital tablet lying on the table next to him. I look at the tablet for a split second, too, wondering about all of the secrets it holds. Victor stands up from the table and my eyes follow him as he walks toward me.

"Turn around," he says, standing over me.

I tilt my head back enough to see his face; he's too close, crowding my space and it's frightening. "What?" I ask, confused and getting the worst feeling.

He leans over and reaches inside the duffle bag in between the beds and retrieves another rope just like the one I used to tie Izel to the chair with.

"Turn around," he says again.

I shake my head frantically. "No," I say and start to back my way across the bed.

He grabs me by the waist and flips me over onto my stomach.

"I have to get some sleep," he says, pressing his knee, although carefully, into the center of my back. "You'll have to make do. I'm sorry."

"Don't tie me up! Please!" I try to wiggle myself free, but he grabs one of my wrists with his free hand and fastens it against my back. I struggle and kick and thrash about, but he's too strong and I feel like a fawn under the paw of a lion. "You're sorry?! Then don't do it! Please, Victor!"

His grip around my wrists, now with both restrained behind me, tightens harshly and I can't help but believe it has everything to do with me calling him by his name, rather than my struggling against him. With one side of my face pressed into the mattress, I feel the rope wind around my wrists and then he ties it into several firm knots. After he's satisfied that I'm unable to get my hands free, he stands up from the bed and grabs my ankles next. I pull one foot back and manage to kick him square in the stomach, but it doesn't faze him. He just looks at me, catches my leg in midair on the second attempt and binds my ankles together with one hand.

Tears barrel from my eyes. But I stop fighting.

He carefully rolls me over onto my side, facing me toward the wall with my back to the bed where I know he'll be sleeping. The thought of him being behind me like that all night and unable to see him unnerves me to no end.

The lamp between the bed switches off, leaving the room bathed in partial darkness. It's still early, just after sundown, but I'm exhausted enough that it feels like it's two o'clock in the morning.

I cry softly into my pillow for a little while. Thinking about my mom and all of the things Victor forced me to remember. And I think about Lydia and Mrs. Gregory who lived two trailers over from me; they are really the only family I've ever had. And when the uncomfortable position my arms have been put into becomes painful, I roll my body awkwardly onto the opposite side. I peer through the darkness to see Victor on the other bed lying on his side with his back facing me. He's still fully clothed. I notice that he did at least take his shoes off, but his feet are covered by thin black dress socks. I wonder if he's still awake.

"Victor?"

"Go to sleep," he says without moving a muscle.

"When you take me back to Javier, will you at least give me a gun?"

Silence filters through the space between us.

"Will you?" I ask again, stirring that silence. "It will give me a fighting chance. I'll either kill Javier myself, or I'll die knowing that I tried."

Victor's shoulder rises and falls slowly as if he'd just taken a deep breath.

"I'll think about it. Now go to sleep."

EIGHT

VICTOR

I'm awoken at 3:42 A.M. staring down the barrel of my 9MM.

"What's the password?" the girl demands.

She's keeping a respectable distance. Impressive.

"The password," she repeats sternly, motioning her head toward the table where my iPad sits.

I don't move. She may have guts, but she's still fidgety and it would be unfortunate if she shot me by accident.

"Uppercase F, six, eight, lowercase 'k', three, zero, zero, five, uppercase L, uppercase P, lowercase 'w', six." I could easily take the gun from her before she got a shot off, the angle she's standing, but I'm not ready to. Not yet.

She tries to recall each character precisely the way I said them. Without her having to ask, I repeat it for her and even that gesture seems to confuse her.

Carefully, I lift my back from the bed and she grips the gun tighter. If she happened to pull the trigger, she'd only hit my cheekbone. The bullet might pass through my jaw. I'd be disfigured, but I'd live.

"You don't want to see what's on that computer," I say.

"You admit it, then," she says nervously. "Something happened. You found out while I was in the shower."

I'm standing up now. She still hasn't shot me. She's not going to unless I try to go after her. Though I'm not so impressed anymore. If I was her, I would have put a bullet in my skull by now.

I nod my answer. I'm only mildly surprised that she figured that much out. I should never have asked about her mother. She's a smart girl, this one, though still far too sympathetic and human to get out of this by herself alive.

Leaving the gun in her right hand and keeping her eyes on me, she takes three and a half steps backward and reaches for the iPad, glancing between it and me, one second each, long enough to type in the password. After one full minute of frustration, unable to find anything, the girl points the gun at the iPad and steps away from the table closer to the wall.

"*You* pull it up," she demands. "Whatever it is."

Her hands, both gripping the gun handle now, are shaking.

"I will tell you one last time, you don't want to see it."

"Just *show* me!"

She's crying now. Tears roll down her cheeks. I notice her lip quiver on the right side. She's probably sick to her stomach, her nerves frayed to nothing. I glimpse the ropes I tied her up with lying on the floor. They haven't been cut. She has small hands, small wrists. Quite the escape artist to have worked herself free from those knots. I glimpse the clock between the beds. But it took her far too long to pull it off, I see.

"*Hurry!*"

Her eyes are red and glistening with moisture.

I turn the iPad around on the table to face me. Using my finger, I open my private email account and then the folder where I filed away the attachment message I received last night from my liaison:

"What have you done?" Fleischer inquired the night before through the live video feed. "The girl was not part of the deal." His German accent always bleeding heavily through his English.

"Guzmán's daughter was there," I said. "I saw her on the compound before I entered the house." I looked once toward the restroom where the girl was still showering after fifteen minutes. "Javier Ruiz has an impressive operation."

"Are you certain you saw the same girl?"

I was offended by Fleischer's lack of confidence in me, that after years of working together and never being wrong in my assessments that he would still second guess my findings.

"It was the same girl," I confirmed evenly. "I took half of the money Javier agreed to and left, as I was ordered to do."

"And then how did you end up with the other girl?"

"She escaped the compound and hid in my car."

"And you did not know she was there?" He appeared surprised.

"Yes, I knew," I confirmed.

"Then explain why—"

"Remember, Fleischer, that you are not my employer. It would be wise not to speak to me as if you were."

Fleischer swallowed his pride and raised his chin to appear more confident in his moment beneath me.

"What did Javier offer to have Guzmán killed?"

"Not a fraction of what Guzmán offered to kill Javier and Izel and for the safe return of his daughter."

I added, "I could have fulfilled the contract while I was there."

"Yes," Fleischer said. "But that was not part of the plan, the same as keeping the runaway with you."

"The girl will be useful."

"So far, she has proven anything but," Fleischer said, regaining the confidence I stripped from him before. "Everything has changed. The plan. The contract. Your orders."

"What are my new orders?" I asked.

"Vonnegut has given no new orders yet," he said. "He awaits my contact. Your new orders will depend on the information I get from you now."

Fleischer and I locked eyes in this moment, both of us sharing the same thoughts: You are my brother and I will do nothing to betray you, no matter our profession or the orders that either of us are ever given.

No one but the two of us know that we share the same father. But over the years since our recruit by The Order when we were young boys, we have grown apart. It is often easy to forget that we share the same blood, especially by Fleischer, first name Niklas, who has lived in my shadow in The Order for so many years.

I simply nodded, knowing that Niklas would relay to our employer, Vonnegut, whatever I needed him to.

To retain the relationship between my brother and me, I offered him information he never asked for:

"The girl will be useful, Niklas," I repeated, calling him by his first name to offer a truce. "It seems that she is more to Javier than Javier would like us to know."

Niklas nodded in response, understanding my intent.

"You mean to use the girl to trade for Guzmán's daughter," he stated.

"If it comes down to that, yes," I said. "Tell Vonnegut that I have it under control, but that I will await whatever orders he chooses."

"I will tell him," Niklas agreed.

I clicked on the 'play' button then to watch the video Javier sent to Vonnegut, in which Fleischer, as my liaison, was then ordered to pass along to me.

It's just as I thought: Javier has the girl's friend, Lydia, in a compromising position. He wants the girl to see it, to know that if she doesn't give herself up or convince me to take her back to him, Lydia will die. I knew then as I watched the scene unfold on the video before me that this Mexican drug lord was far more brutal than The Order knew.

I heard the shower shut off and I ran my finger over the screen to turn off the video, shutting the iPad down afterwards.

The girl will be devastated. If she finds out about this, it will make her unstable.

But I can use this also to my advantage.

With the recorded video now playing on the screen, I twist the iPad around on the table to face the girl's direction. She glances down at it for only seconds, the gun shaking in her grasp, and then back at me again, fearful that I might make a move. But when she sees her friend, Lydia, she turns her attention solely on the video, abandoning her upper-hand. I don't take advantage of it. I slide my hands into my pants pockets and stand here watching the girl's eyes widen with trepidation as the video plays.

Javier circles Lydia who sits bound to a chair, a red bandanna is stuffed in her mouth. Tears and sweat soak her face. Her left eye is swollen and bruised. A trickle of blood beads from one nostril.

"For you, Sarai," Javier says into the camera as Izel stands next to Lydia, her hair wrenched in Izel's fist. "I want you back here in thirty-six hours." The girl clasps her free hand over her trembling lips; the gun hasn't been pointed directly at me for the past several long seconds. "Or she'll die and it'll be your fault."

Izel pulls back her fist and buries it in Lydia's already bruised and beaten face. Lydia's bound body lurches backward and more tears spring from her eyes. Blood erupts from her bottom lip.

The girl drops the gun on the floor and reaches for the iPad, shoving it clean off the table and then she falls to the floor onto her knees, sobbing into her hands.

I sit down on the end of the bed, leaving the gun on the floor and the girl alone in her moment of despair.

NINE

SARAI

I can't see straight. Through the burning tears, through the blur in front of my eyes, through the anger and hatred and hurt shorting out my nervous system. My body has somehow found its way onto the floor. I lay with my face pressed against the carpet.

Not Lydia...anyone but her. She's innocent and frail. She'll never be able to endure it. Not like me...

It takes me far too long to come to the realization that I'm no longer the one holding the gun, that I'm no longer the one in control. One moment of weakness, traumatized by the suffering of my friend, has stripped that privilege from me. And I deserve it. I deserve whatever punishment fate deems fit to serve because I got away and Lydia didn't. I should have used the phone not five feet from me on the nightstand between the beds, to call the police. I should have called them before I forced him awake, but I was too insistent on knowing what information Victor knew that I didn't. I had still hoped that maybe he would help me, at least by telling me the location of the compound so I'd have something to tell the authorities.

I should have shot him when I had the chance.

From the corner of my eye, I see Victor's black dress socks planted unmoving on the floor. Tilting my head back just a little, my eyes trail from the bottom of his pants up to his waist. His forearms are resting along the length of the tops of his legs, the palms of his hands gently cupping his knees. He sits with his back fairly straight, his gaze fixated out ahead.

Finally his head moves as he averts his eyes to me.

"I am sorry," he says with absolutely no emotion in his words, yet somehow I detect the faintest hint of emotion hidden behind his eyes.

"You have to take me back," I say, rising into a stand. "You can't let her die." My voice trembles.

Victor takes a seat at the table again and begins to sift through his duffle bag. I don't care to know what he's doing or what he plans to do from here on out. Mostly what I think about is Lydia and what I saw on that video; that image will be seared into my mind forever. A part of me wants to blame Victor for all of this, simply because he is what he is and that he could've become human just long enough to help me get her out of there. But I'm back to blaming myself because, in truth, I never once asked Victor to help me free her. He refused to help *me* even ,so I knew he wouldn't go back there for *her*.

It's all my fault. I could have done things differently, planned my escape differently. I could have forced Lydia out that window with me that night.

Seems there are a lot of things I could have and should have done. I never imagined I'd be the dumb girl in the horror movie running into the scary house or tripping over my own feet as I stumbled through the dark woods. I guess by default we're all the ones shaking our heads at the stupidity of others until we're forced into traumatic experiences ourselves.

The early morning sunlight slowly begins to flood the room. The only movement I made all night was to turn onto my other side on the floor to keep Victor in my sights. I'm not afraid of him. Not anymore. But I couldn't help but know where he was, nonetheless.

My back hurts and my face itches from the imprint the scruffy carpet left on my skin.

Victor sits in the chair next to the table now with his shoes on as if he's been quietly waiting for the day to come.

I lift my aching body from the floor and push myself into a stand.

"I don't care anymore what you do with me," I say. "Just please take me back to Javier. I don't have much time."

Victor's face reveals curiosity. "You'll not be going back to the compound."

I blink back the stun of his words. "What? No..." I shake my head in protest. "No—you *have* to take me back! You saw the video! They will kill her!"

He stands from the chair and straightens the sleeves of his white dress shirt now tucked neatly into his pants and buttoned back around his strong wrists.

"The plan has changed," he says calmly.

I practically throw myself toward him, stopping just inches from his body, my eyes wide and feral and unbelieving. "No, Victor!" He flinches. "I have to go back! Don't you understand?! We—*I* have to help her! I want Izel dead! I want *Javier* dead for what he's done!"

"He will be," Victor says.

He turns to the side and zips the duffle bag closed.

I push myself the last few inches through the space between us and then shove him with both hands. "I'm going back with or without you!" He catches me by the wrists, securing them firmly within his grasp. "*Please...*" The word comes out with every ounce of desperation in me.

He scans my face, so close I can feel the warm breath emitting from his nostrils. "Just be patient," he says, stunning me into stillness.

He lets go of my wrists when he senses me beginning to step backward and away from him.

"Patient?" I can't believe what he's saying to me. "There's no time to be patient! How can you say that?"

He bends over and fixes his hands underneath the mattress of the bed nearest the window and lifts it onto its side revealing a hollow space underneath surrounded by the wood frame that holds the bed up. He grabs the duffle bags, hiding them inside and then the suitcase, setting the mattress back down afterwards.

"I'm awaiting word," he says.

"Word from who?"

He sighs, annoyed with my questions. "From Javier."

"Why?"

I don't know what to say, or what to believe, all I do know is that my mind is spinning with everything going on and I can't keep up.

Victor walks to the door and looks back at me.

"Come on," he says, nodding with the backward tilt of his head for me to follow.

"What, you're not going to tie my hands together, or drag me down the hallway by my wrist? What if I run away?"

"You won't."

"You don't think so?" I counter.

He shakes his head once. "No you won't because I'm the only one of us who knows the way back to Javier."

I just stand here.

Victor places his hand on the silver lever and opens the door. "Are you coming, or are you staying here?"

I stare across the room at him blankly.

Maybe he's going to help me after all. Maybe after seeing what Izel and Javier are doing to Lydia, Victor has remembered how it feels to be remorseful, if he's ever known what that feels like at all.

"Where are we going?" I ask, knowing that it can't be far if he's leaving his bags here.

"To breakfast."

TEN

VICTOR

More than two hours have passed and there has been no word. Nothing from Niklas or Vonnegut. Nothing from Javier or Guzmán. The girl is beyond the point of restless. I bought her breakfast in the hotel, but she hardly ate a bite, just picked at her omelet with her fork. It may be a result of her concern for her friend, but I find her sudden inability to ask continuous questions or try to converse with me, refreshing.

I do wonder why she has yet to try contacting family members. I find it difficult to believe that, despite the grave situation with her dear friend, she would not also show interest in calling a sister, grandmother or an aunt. That she did not use the one opportunity she had last night while I was sleeping.

This leaves me with two theories: she cares more about the life of her friend, or she has no family left. Perhaps it's both. I'm fairly certain that it is.

I feel my cell phone vibrating against my leg and I stand up from the table in the lobby and reach inside to retrieve it.

The girl is instantly attentive to me.

My brother's code name reads on the screen.

"Who is it?" the girl asks, standing up with me.

I run my finger over the answer bar, but hold the phone, face down against my chest. Gesturing for the girl to sit back down, I say, "I want you to stay here. I'm going right outside to take this call. I trust that you'll be here when I get back." I know she's not going anywhere.

Clearly wanting nothing more than to follow me out and hang on my every word, she takes a deep, heavy breath, crosses her arms and takes her seat again.

"OK." She grits her teeth behind her softly pressed lips.

I walk out the front doors and put the phone to my ear.

"I am going to put Javier on this call," Niklas says. "Are you prepared?"

"Yes," I answer and wait while Niklas makes the transfer.

Javier's voice seethes with barely controlled anger when he is patched through:

"You'll die for what you've done," he says in English. "Sarai should've been brought back to me the second you found her!"

"What's done is done," I say. "Get to the reason for your contact."

I hear him breathe heavily on the three-way call. Niklas sits listening quietly.

Finally Javier contains himself.

"I still want the hit on Guzmán carried out for the price we agreed on, but I will give you another one million American to also kill Sarai."

Kill her? I did not expect my communication with Javier would cause me surprise. This is very interesting, indeed.

"Why would you want her dead?" I ask.

"That doesn't matter," he says. "The reasons never matter in this business. You should know that."

I do know that, and this is the first time I've ever asked why a client wanted a mark killed.

"I have a better offer for you," I announce. "You bring the girl's friend, Lydia, and one other girl at your compound—a photo will be sent to you immediately following this call—to Green Valley, Arizona in twenty-four hours. I trade you *this* girl for those two and then afterwards I will kill Guzmán and then give you the girls back once I have been paid in full."

I don't have to hear Niklas comment to know that he is in complete disagreement with this, but he remains quiet.

"You mean Guzmán's daughter," Javier probes, knowing. "Am I right?"

"Yes," I say. "If it isn't already obvious, Guzmán paid to have her returned to him."

Javier laughs. "And all this time I thought he was trying to have *me* killed!" He pulls himself from his humorous revelation. "You *are* good," he says. "I give you that. Knock out two contracts at once—show Guzmán his daughter, take the money for bringing her to him, then turn around and kill him and take the money I paid to have him killed." He laughs again.

I remain calm and unemotional.

"Is it a deal, or not?"

"So then you're passing on the contract to kill Sarai?" he asks.

"Right now," I begin, "she is my only leverage. Once I do what you paid me to do and I give her back to you, do what you want with her. It is not of my concern."

Niklas ends the call after we have come to another agreement. He calls me back once he knows that Javier's line has been disconnected.

"Victor, you cannot do this," Niklas argues. "You are making deals without—"

"What are Vonnegut's new orders?" I ask.

I glance through the window to see the girl still sitting anxiously in the hotel lobby.

"He has not given them yet," Niklas says. "You're not permitted to agree to such deals, only to enforce them."

"Then tell Vonnegut I was only attempting to maintain the upper-hand," I explain. "The moment that Javier realizes that I have no authority to offer and agree to such terms is the moment he believes he can get away with demanding more. I mean no disrespect, but Vonnegut must trust me on this. He has always trusted my decisions before. He has been given no reason to stop now."

Niklas remains quiet. I believe he holds this fact against me, that The Order trusts me, yet they have never given him the same luxury.

"Very well," Niklas agrees. "I will tell Vonnegut. But Victor, you're becoming ungoverned." He pauses as if to decide whether or not he should go on. "Since the mission in Budapest last year. I've noticed the difference in you. The Order I believe hasn't, but it's only a matter of time."

"Niklas," I say to him carefully as my brother and not my liaison, "I thank you for your discretion. Now, will you do something for me?"

"When have I ever refused?"

I leave Niklas, tucking the phone back in my pocket and I head inside to find the girl.

She had been pacing the floor and when she notices me, she stops and her arms come uncrossed and fall to her sides, a look of question heavy on her face.

"Come with me," I say, taking her by the elbow.

"Where are we going?" She follows alongside me without argument.

"To Green Valley."

"But why, Victor? What's going on?"

I glance over at her momentarily and tug on her arm as we round the corner at the top of the stairs.

"I will tell you soon," I say, "but first, there are some things that *you* need to tell *me*."

We make our way down the hallway and stand in front of the door at our room as I fish around inside my pocket for the card key.

The girl looks bewildered.

"You need to tell me why Javier Ruiz would want you dead."

Her expression falls under a veil of shock.

ELEVEN

SARAI

Victor walks quickly, but casually over to get the mattress and box springs lifted. With one arm holding them up, he reaches in and grabs each bag, one by one and sets them aside.

"I don't understand," I say, crossing my arms and rubbing them with the opposite hands, up and down as if there's a chill in the air. "Did he say he was going to *kill* me?"

Victor unzips the duffle bag on the tabletop and sifts through the contents.

"No, he offered me one million to kill you *for* him."

I blink back the stun and just stand here in disbelief, more goose bumps breaking out all over my body.

Victor comes up in front of me and places both hands on my shoulders. He pushes me gently down on the edge of the bed where I sit willingly. Then he takes a seat in one of the chairs underneath the table, turning it around fully so that he can face me.

"Why would Javier want you dead enough to pay that much to have you killed?"

Absently, I raise my eyes to look up at him, still a bit lost in my thoughts.

"I-I don't know," I stutter.

"Yes you do," he insists. "Perhaps not directly, but something tells me that deep down a part of you has some idea—think."

I look away from his eyes, trying to recall my time at the compound, searching for what could be the answer. When many long seconds pass and I've found nothing, Victor lifts his bottom from the chair long enough to scoot closer to me. That gets my attention again.

"I need you to tell me everything," Victor says with gentle intent. "Tell me about your relationship with Javier. You said he believes he is in love with you."

I nod in a slow, rapid motion. "Yes. He told me once that he was in love with me, but I know better. He's crazy. Possessive. But he protected me from the things the other girls had to go through. Usually..."

I don't like to think about these things, much less talk openly about them. I am ashamed and I hate myself for what they endured. And what I endured.

"He protected you?" Victor asks, needing more information.

"Yes. I was off-limits to Javier's men. And Izel, well, Javier nearly killed her when she hit me in the face once. After that, she wasn't allowed to touch me. And I was allowed luxuries the other girls weren't, too. Hot showers and good food and I got to see places outside of the compound. I even flew on a small plane with him several times. Javier would rarely let me out of his sight. Izel hated me for it, accused Javier of 'going soft', falling for a 'stupid American girl.'"

A spark of intrigue passes over Victor's features.

"What kind of places were you taken?"

I shrug softly and let my hands fall in between my thighs, my fingers curling nervously around one another.

"Sometimes," I begin, "he'd take me with him to other rich men's houses, with sparkling blue pools shaped like horseshoes and other strange things. Javier said it was just to mingle but I knew we were there for drug deals. And girls. Sometimes we came back with a new one. He would dress up in a nice suit and shiny black shoes just like yours." I glance down at Victor's shoes briefly. "He didn't look like the scumbag you saw the other day, living in filth. He is rich, despite what you saw."

"I gathered that much."

I go on:

"And of course he'd make *me* dress up, too."

I lower my eyes shamefully, mostly because sometimes I enjoyed it, dressing up and being treated like a princess. That was how I always thought of it: a princess, as disturbing as the circumstances were.

"I felt like an arm trophy."

"That is exactly what you were," he says and I look back up at him again, quietly stung by his words. "Do you remember anything about the men whose homes you were taken to?"

"Yes," I say with a nod. "But I think they were vacation homes, or something."

"Why?"

"Because they mentioned things about how they were only in Mexico for a few weeks, or how they were heading back to California, or Nevada or Florida, places like that."

"They were Americans?"

"Some of them were, I'm pretty sure they were," I say. "They didn't have accents, foreign anyway. They definitely weren't Mexican, that's for sure."

They may have been American, but I knew they wouldn't help me like I hoped Victor would. They were just as evil as Javier. Two of them even tried to buy me from him. No, none of them would ever have helped me escape so this is why I consider Victor the first American I've seen in nine years. Those men lost that privilege by association.

"Do you remember any of their names?"

Victor looks more eager now than I have ever seen him, yet he still manages to maintain an almost flawless unemotional façade.

I think back, trying to recall and coming up short.

"No," I say, frustrated with myself, "not right now, but I did hear their names on occasion when one would introduce one to another." I pause and say with more emotion, "Victor, what is it?"

His dangerous eyes lock on mine.

"At the compound, or anywhere Javier could keep tabs on you and control you, you weren't a threat to him. But now that you've escaped, you're a bigger threat than anyone because you know too much. It is apparent Izel was right to think him foolish with his feelings for you; he probably never anticipated you leaving. You being alive and free is a threat to his entire operation and anyone involved in it."

I think on it a moment, letting the obvious truth of Victor's words sink into my mind. I may not have ever known where I was kept in Mexico and even right now I wouldn't be able to tell American authorities where Lydia and the other girls are being held against their will, but I do know names, still hidden in the back of my memory, but they're there nonetheless. And I remember faces and conversations, although casual they still held many small bits of information that, I suppose, given to the right people could expose them as drug and sex traffickers.

"Larsaw, or maybe Larsen," I say suddenly as the name appears on the tip of my tongue. "Gerald Larsen. I remember he was the first American I was 'shown off' to when Javier took me to my first house. He had white hair. He was chubby. But I was never directly introduced to anyone. I wasn't allowed to speak. I learned their names by listening to their conversations."

Victor looks deeply in thought and shakes his head suddenly.

"John Gerald *Lansen* is the CEO of Balfour Enterprises and founder of the most reputable charity for ending violence against women in the United States." He looks right at me. "The information you hold, no matter how insignificant you think it all is, could bring down a lot of high profile people. I imagine if word gets out that you have escaped and the right person—a vengeful sister, perhaps," he says, I know referring to Izel, "who decides to tell the right people, more than Guzmán will pay to have Javier killed and Javier knows this."

It hits me like a shock of electricity and I jump from the bed and try to make a run for the door. Victor catches me mid-stride, grabbing me around the waist. I whirl around at him, punching at him blindly. I manage to hit him, but I'm not sure where as my fists move clumsily and in such a chaotic motion that my eyes can't keep up within the scuffle.

My back hits the floor and I look up, my auburn hair whipped savagely around my face, to see Victor pinning me, straddling my waist.

"Let me go! Let me go, goddammit!" I thrash around under his weight, unable to do much with my legs, my hands pinned against the floor above my head, trapped by his own.

"He's going to kill me! Someone help!"

He manages to bind both my wrists with one hand, the other he presses over my mouth to muffle my screams. Tears shoot from my eyes. I beg him over and over again, my voice almost completely shut out by the weight of his hand.

"I'm not going to kill you," he says calmly. "If it was my intention, you'd be dead already."

He waits for my tense body to ease some before I feel his hand loosen ever so slightly.

"Are you going to be quiet?"

I nod because I still can't speak with his hand over my mouth.

Finally after a long moment, Victor moves his hand away slowly.

"Why *wouldn't* you kill me?" I ask, my voice still trembling and choked by tears. "Still using me as leverage?"

"In a way, yes," he answers.

I want to scream again while I have a chance, but his words keep me from it:

"And I don't kill innocent people."

Silence fills the small space between us.

"*No one* is innocent," I snap, surprising myself. "Least of all me. For years I let that disgusting murderer violate me and I never said no. I sat back and watched in silence as he and his men and that bitch sister of his beat and raped and sold the girls I became close to. I did *nothing*. I never screamed or fought back or stood up for any of them. Not a single one." I hear my voice beginning to rise with anger. I clench my fists together on my chest, looking up into his eyes as he remains seated on top of me, pinning me against the floor. "I pretended like nothing bothered me, that Carmen's hands being smashed to bits by that hammer didn't faze me! I didn't flinch when Marisol was forced to have an abortion by a butcher doctor who left her to bleed to death on the table! I didn't shed a single tear when the girl with the red hair and freckles was killed right in front of me because the man who came to purchase her didn't like what he saw!" I bring up my fists and go to slam them down on the tops of his legs out of anger, but he catches my wrists and holds them solidly. "I am *not innocent!*" I roar.

I feel his hands wrench my wrists, but my head is too clouded by emotion to care.

The things I've admitted are things that have haunted me for the longest time. They've been buried in my soul, burning through to the very core of me, rendering me emotionless and turning me into someone entirely different than I was supposed to be.

I let my head fall to the side, feeling the pang of defeat. I can't look at him anymore. Not out of anger or hatred or revenge, but out of shame. I can't look a murder in the eye because not only am I no better than he is, it's possible that I'm *worse*.

"You are very strong," he says and raises his body from mine. "With a strong survival instinct. It is the only thing that separates you from those other girls. Like them, you were still held there against your will. You were still made to do things against your will. You were physically and emotionally abused. You should not blame yourself for their weakness."

He walks back over to the table.

I pick myself up from the floor and just look across at him, trying to make sense of his words. Or, maybe the guilt I've harbored for so long is only trying to force me not to believe them.

He glances over at me and adds, "You did the right thing."

I shake my head. "No. I didn't. I should've done something to help them."

Victor shoulders his duffle bags and takes up the suitcase in the other.

"You did," he says, standing in front of me now. "You kept your cool. You waited for your opportunity. You pretended to the point of acceptance and trust. You're risking your life right now to go back for that girl."

He walks past me and goes toward the door, turning to look back once he gets there.

"You are innocent," he says. "And it's why you're still alive."

Then he opens the door, and hesitantly I follow him out.

TWELVE

SARAI

We arrive in Green Valley nearly three hours later. Both of us sat in silence for most of the drive. I had too much thinking to do, too many unresolved issues to work out, which I didn't come close to doing in such a short time. And it will take me a very long time to lay my guilt to rest, if I ever can. I don't care that the things Victor said made sense, I still feel like the most selfish person in the world for what I did. I'll probably feel this way forever.

And I did ask Victor why we were heading to Green Valley. He had said before that he would tell me what was going on, but when it came down to it, he was vague. He told me that he has an exchange to make near Green Valley, but he wouldn't go into detail. I guess all that talking he did back at the hotel in Douglas went over his conversational word limit. Because he was back to himself again so quickly, the quiet, reserved, intimidating assassin who, for reasons unknown to me, I almost feel completely safe with.

We pull into a parking lot at the end of a road lined by resort homes. I've been here before, once with my best friend when her older sister picked us up from school in her new car. We had gotten lost and she used this place to turn around. It was weeks before my mom forced me to Mexico with her and Javier. This familiar place reminds me that I'm very close to home. I'm so close that I could walk there. It would take several hours, but I could do it.

But where would I go?

Victor shuts the truck's engine off. I look out through the windshield to see a section of trees and brush separating the parking lot from the interstate. A car flies by every few seconds. But the parking lot is empty save one lone car in the distance parked by a dumpster. On the other side of the lot though, over a low concrete wall there are many cars parked outside a shopping center.

I wonder why he chose a public place, although currently quiet and abandoned, to do whatever it is that we came here to do. Because Javier doesn't care about the public or risking an innocent bystander getting caught in his crossfire.

"Stay in the truck," Victor says just before shutting the heavy metal door.

He walks around to the back as a sleek black SUV enters the parking lot from behind the homes. My heart immediately starts pounding. I slink down in the seat, but move around to his side so that I can get a better glimpse out the window. I want to see but I don't want to *be* seen.

Victor meets the SUV halfway, about fifty feet from where I am and it stops in the center of the road. I see a man. A white man it looks like and I'm confused by this. Victor nods and then I see his lips moving. I reach over and roll the window down by the old fashioned crank. It sticks at first, but then the window breaks apart and I manage to open it several inches. But they're too far away for me to hear anything they're saying.

Victor starts walking back toward the truck and the SUV follows. I swallow hard and find myself practically all the way in the floorboard now, the top of my head pressing against the hard steering wheel. The driver's side door opens, exposing me in my awkward position. That other man is standing next to Victor, both of them looking in at me.

The strange man, who I notice looks somewhat like Victor with his tall stature, brown hair, blue eyes and sculpted cheekbones, nods at me as if it's his way of saying hello. Needless to say, I'm too afraid and unsure of him to give him the same courtesy.

The man, though still looking at me as though I'm a peculiar specimen of sorts that deserves study, says something to Victor in another language. It's not Spanish. Victor replies to him in that same language, which I'm starting to think is likely German. The man finally looks at Victor.

"This is Niklas," Victor says to me. "You're going to ride with him and follow me to another location close by."

Instantly, I feel my head shaking back and forth in refusal.

Victor reaches out his hand to me, but I reject it. Instead, I start to climb my way out of the floorboard and go toward the other side of the truck. I feel Victor's hand wrap around part of my thigh.

"He will not harm you," Victor says. "This truck is not safe for you if Javier or his men open fire on us."

I glance through the back window at the SUV, assuming it has some kind of bulletproof windows, maybe. I don't care to ask; I simply don't want to be left alone with this man, safer vehicle or not.

"This one is not very cooperative," the man named Niklas says in English. He definitely has an accent, unlike Victor who seems to speak fluently in whatever language he knows.

"Sarai," Victor says my name and it stuns me immobile; he's never called me by my name before. "I am asking you to cooperate."

I look up into Victor's harsh eyes and hold my gaze for a moment, letting my mind clear out the unexpected reaction that he saying my name has put there. My body relaxes and then soon after Victor's fingers slide away from my thigh. I look back and forth between the two of them slowly, still unsure, but now more willing.

"Will you tell me what's going to happen?" I ask, looking at both of them, but Victor knows the question was meant for him.

Niklas keeps his cold eyes—more blue than green—fixed on me, but it seems more of an observant nature than a possessive one.

"We will meet Javier not far from here in a more secluded area. There, your friend will be handed over to us."

A dark feeling of uncertainty suddenly blooms within the pit of my stomach.

I narrow my gaze on Victor.

"Just like that?" I ask skeptically. "No, Javier won't just give her over. He'll..." I back away again against the passenger's side door, my hand already on the handle in case I need to make a run for it. "... there's no way he'd do that. You're trading her for me, aren't you?" My voice rises. "*Aren't* you!"

"Yes," Victor says.

Niklas remains quiet and calm and ever so observant. It's starting to unnerve me.

But then I come to my senses and look away from them. I stare out the windshield at the landscape and the cars on the other side of the concrete wall, but I really don't see any of it. All I see is Lydia's face in my mind, the way I saw it last on that video: bruised and bloodied and tear-streaked and frightened. I know this is what needs to be done. A trade: me for Lydia. That is something I know Javier would agree to, now more than ever.

But he wants me dead...

My hands clench the tattered leather seat beneath me, my fingers digging into the exposed cushion insulation. My entire body trembles with dread. But then I stubbornly force that fear into the back of my mind. Maybe he won't kill me once he has me back. I could go on pretending like being with him is where I want to be. I could even pretend that Victor kidnapped me. I know I can fool Javier. I know I can! I did it for years! I made him trust me, so much so that he believed he loved me. I can do it again.

Long enough until I get my first chance to kill him.

Yes, that's exactly what I'll do. Because I only care about two things anymore: Lydia's safety and killing Javier. I know that once I do it, I'll sign my own death warrant. Izel or one of Javier's men will hunt me down before I can get a mile from the compound and they'll shoot me dead, just like Victor did that store owner back in Mexico.

But at least Javier will be dead.

And I don't fear death.

I open the truck door to find Niklas standing at it waiting on me. I was so lost in my thoughts that I never even saw him leave and walk around to my side of the truck.

I shut the door and look over the hood of the truck at Victor on the other side. I've never really been able to read his face because his emotions, if he has any, seem impenetrable, but right now I do detect the faintest hint of something unnatural in his eyes. Could it be regret? No, maybe it's indecision or…no, that can't be it.

"I'll do it," I announce, never taking my eyes from Victor's. "If you can get Lydia away safely, I'll do it."

Victor nods. Then he goes to open the truck door and I stop him.

"But Victor, please take her home. I'm begging you. Just take her home. She lives in El Paso, Texas. With her grandparents. Please."

Victor doesn't nod or answer verbally this time, but I know, just by that look in his eyes that he will do it. I'm not sure why I believe that, but I do.

After transferring his bags from the truck to the SUV, he gets inside the truck and the rumble of the engine turning on follows seconds later.

"Come on," Niklas says, taking me by the arm, his fingers wrapped a little more harshly around my bicep than Victor ever did it.

He guides me around to the backseat, opening the door and standing directly behind me as if he's making sure I get in and don't try to run away. Once I'm inside, the smell of new leather and car freshener fills my senses. A metal cage barrier separates the backseat from the front, just like a police officer might have in his patrol car. Already I feel trapped. I hear a clicking sound as Niklas locks all of the doors after he's inside. I glance to my left and right to see that there are no inside lock switches on either of the backseat doors. I *am* truly trapped in here.

We end up on Interstate 19, following close behind Victor in the old beat-up truck.

"You have become quite a wrench in the gears," Niklas says from the driver's seat.

I glance up to meet his eyes in the rearview mirror.

I don't like him much. Not that I should like him at all considering the situation, but at least with Victor, despite being a killer, I felt a sense of safety. Even back at the compound as I watched him through the crack in the door with Lydia, I got the feeling I could trust him, that he would help me. My hunches were completely off, I admit, but he never hurt me. Regardless of what he is or what he's done and what complications I've caused him, he never treated me badly.

Niklas, on the other hand, I get the sense is a little more intolerant.

I try to keep my eyes on the road out ahead, but it's hard not to meet his gaze in the mirror every now and then. Because he's always watching.

I swallow and say, "I didn't mean to cause you and Victor any trouble." His eyes narrow suddenly in the mirror and I catch it immediately. "But I don't understand why it's such a huge *inconvenience* to either one of you, to help me." I tried to mask the bitterness in that, but I didn't do so well.

"*Victor,*" Niklas says icily, which strikes me in the worst way, "since you're now on a first-name basis with him, should have dragged you back to Javier Ruiz the second he found you."

I hate this man.

I grit my teeth and breathe sharply through my nostrils.

"But he didn't," I snap. "And that tells me he's more human than you apparently are."

My acidic words don't faze him like how I had hoped they would. Instead, he does something I least expected. He smiles.

"Oh, I see what you think this is," he says with that evident German accent. "You think you've enchanted him somehow with your innocent girlish wiles. You've done nothing of the sort, just so you know. Victor, everything he does, he does it for the better of our Order. If he believes it better not to set you free or to hand you over, it has nothing to do with your wellbeing."

I don't want to believe him though a small part of me does, but I refuse to give Niklas the satisfaction of knowing he succeeded in getting under my skin.

I round my chin and look away from him, putting my eyes solely on the truck Victor is driving out ahead of us. Soon, we veer off to the right and enter an unpaved dusty road right off the interstate. The road winds through several sections of low-lining bushes and young trees, but mostly there's nothing but dirt and an endless stretch of almost barren land three hundred and sixty-degrees around me. A few houses are perched in the distance on top of dirt hills, but I get the feeling this section of land has not been traveled in a very long time by those who own it, or anyone else for that matter.

The front of the SUV rises higher over the land as we head up a hill. Once we level out at the crest and the dust begins to settle I see four old trucks, much like the one Victor is driving, parked out in the open, waiting for us.

THIRTEEN

SARAI

Eight men stand outside the trucks, shouldering rifles, all of them Javier's men. I grip the leather seat beneath me, finding it harder to penetrate with my fingertips than the worn-out seats in the old truck. We come to a stop about one hundred feet away.

But I don't see Javier. Or Izel.

I begin to panic when at first I don't see Lydia, either, but then I spot her inside the cream-colored Ford. At least, I'm pretty sure that's Lydia. I press my face against the metal cage as closely as I can, trying to see better, but it doesn't help much.

Niklas turns his head to look at me.

"Sit back and stay out of sight," he demands.

I do what he says, not because he ordered it but because it's probably best.

The truck door slams shut. Victor walks out ahead of it toward them. One by one I look at each of the men, wondering which one was sent here to speak for Javier since he's not here himself, but then I see Izel's black hair sliding past the window of the green truck as she gets out.

"This makes twice Javier's been too much of a coward to come himself," I say out loud, not necessarily to Niklas.

"He knows by now that Victor can kill him with little effort," Niklas says, watching out the window. "I'd say it's a smart move on Javier's part."

Izel tries to approach Victor with her usual sultry walk, but she's clearly in pain from the wounds he left on her legs and she stumbles just as she passes the rusted hood. One of the men step over quickly to help her, but she smacks him hard across the face and shouts curses at him, telling him to back off. She hates pity. I think she hates everything, including herself.

Words are exchanged between Izel and Victor. I can't hear what they're saying, but by the body language, I can tell it's the usual: Izel trying to scare him with threats about Javier and how he's made a very dangerous enemy—same opening conversation they had back at the motel that day. And just like before, Victor is unfazed by her and it only adds fuel to the fire in her expression.

I try to hear what they're saying even though I know I can't, but mostly, I try to see Lydia.

Against Niklas' demand, I push up closer to the cage again, trying to glimpse her through the window. I'm positive that's her sitting on the passenger's side. But I think there's someone sitting next to her.

Izel raises her hand to the men by the truck behind her and one of them runs around to open the door. He reaches inside and grabs the one I think is Lydia and drags her out.

"It's her!" I say excitedly, relieved.

Niklas snaps his head around.

"I said *sit back*," he growls through bared teeth. "Don't fuck this up any more than you already have."

I freeze hearing this and I fall backward against the seat again, though only enough that it satisfies him and he turns away.

Lydia looks like hell, but at least she's able to walk. At least she's alive. She's dressed in the same dirty clothes she was wearing when I saw her on that video. The bloodstains left from her mouth and nose are evident on the front of her thin white t-shirt, even from here at a distance. Her hands are bound at the wrists down in front of her. Her light red hair is disheveled and filthy and matted. She's crying, gazing hopelessly toward us in the SUV and I can only imagine she's wondering whether or not I'm in here. I want to run out of here and toward her, to let her know that I'm OK and that she's finally going home, but wishing I could do that I know is all that I *can* do.

The man who pulled her out of the truck jerks on her elbow, pulling her harshly out of the way and over to the side.

Victor says something to Izel and she smiles cunningly. Then she looks back over her bare shoulder and indicates with the wave of two fingers for the other man whom she'd just slapped, to do something. He responds quickly by going around to the open truck door where Lydia was removed and he reaches inside for the other figure I saw had been sitting next to her.

"Oh my God," I say also more to myself. "That's Cordelia. Why did they bring *her*?" I look to Niklas for the answer, but he doesn't offer one.

Cordelia and Lydia are standing side by side now, trembling with tear-streaked faces, unable to stop looking toward the SUV.

Victor waves two fingers toward us.

Niklas turns around. "Are you ready?"

I swallow hard. "Yes."

Niklas opens his door and as he gets out the hidden locks on the SUV click again. He pops the back door open and reaches out his hand to me. Reluctantly I take it.

"Sarai!" I hear Lydia's voice on the air once I step out of the SUV.

I look up as I move around the opened door to see the man holding her by the elbow, push her onto the dirt-covered ground and onto her knees. The other man does the same to Cordelia.

I begin to walk slowly the short distance toward Victor, my legs shaking more with each step. I feel Izel's eyes on me, so cold and predatory, but I won't look at her. I refuse to give her the satisfaction. Instead, I look only at Victor and although he's staring right into my eyes, I know that not an ounce of his vigilant attention has been taken from those around him.

Then he looks away, putting his hand up to me and instinctively I stop.

"Have one of your men bring them," Victor instructs Izel.

Izel sneers, her nostrils flaring, making her look all the more hateful. Then with the backward tilt of her head, she orders the man standing over Lydia to do just that. He swings his rifle hanging from the shoulder strap around toward his back and then reaches out with both hands, grabbing Lydia and Cordelia each in one, lifting them to their feet.

Victor looks at me again. He reaches out his hand and as I walk toward him I feel his seemingly emotionless gaze penetrate my own. There's something in his eyes, something quiet and mysterious and I feel like he's trying to speak to me through them. I place my hand into his and his fingers collapse around it, at first carefully.

Something doesn't feel right, in a way like that furtive look I saw in his eyes seconds ago.

As the man approaches, Victor's hand tightens around mine. I only see Lydia's eyes now, full of fear and hope and relief as she moves closer. And then when they are within Victor's reach, in a quick, unseen motion, I'm shoved onto the ground and I see Victor reach out so fast, grabbing the man by his head and snapping his neck. Lydia and Cordelia fall to their knees, and then Victor has the man's semi-automatic rifle, spraying bullets at Izel and the others.

Lydia and Cordelia try to cling to me as the sound of bullets move vociferously through the air in all directions, but I shove them both onto their stomachs and push theirs faces against the dirt with my hands.

"Stay down!" I scream, dust whipping up into my mouth. "Follow me! Come on!" And I drag my body as fast as I can across the dirt toward the SUV like a soldier crawling through enemy fire.

More shots ring out, two or three hit the sand near us, one pinging off the side of the SUV's open door. And even though the SUV is within fifteen feet, I feel like it's too far away and that we'll never make it. One bullet hits the ground two feet in front of my face, causing me to freeze up and come to a dead stop. I've already lost sight of Victor, but I see Niklas running away from the SUV with a gun gripped in both hands as he fires off several shots in rapid succession.

"Hurry!" I shout over the chaos, twisting my head around so that I can see if Lydia and Cordelia are still following, my arms pressed even harder into the dirt.

Lydia is screaming and I glimpse blood on the sand near her foot. Cordelia, terrified, moves quickly past me, forcing her body through the sand even with her wrists bound. But Lydia is stagnant and I turn back to help her. If I have to drag her across the ground alone and through a hailstorm of bullets, that's what I'll do.

"My foot!" Lydia cries out.

"Don't stop, Lydia! Push through it! You have to keep moving!"

I finally make it back to her and I cover her head with both my arms when another bullet zooms past, narrowly missing us. She buries her face in the crook of my arm now. Sobs rock her body.

The bullets stop, but the eerie silence is almost as frightening as the noise. For what feels like forever, I'm afraid to lift my head and as the dust begins to settle, I only see two upright bodies among the dead.

Viktor and Niklas.

Sobs of utter relief shudder through me, causing my chest to constrict over and over again until I feel like throwing up. I don't even realize that I've managed to sit upright with my bare heels digging into the sand. At some point I lost my flip-flops. Lydia throws herself on me and I wrap my arms around her so tight I feel my fingers digging into her back. She would do the same if her hands weren't restricted by that rope.

"Sarai! Sarai!" Lydia cries into my shoulder. My name is all that she can get out.

"I know, Lydia! I'm so sorry that I left without you. I'm so sorry!" My nose burns from crying so much and so hard.

Lydia pulls away and looks at me, shaking her head. "No, no, you tried," she says as I work furiously on the knots in the rope until I finally get her wrists free. "It was my decision to stay. But look, look Sarai, you kept your word. You promised to come back for me."

I wrap her up in my arms again and we just sit here like this together, on the ground without any care in the world about the dead people laid out not so far away. We only pull away when I see Niklas walking toward us.

Briefly I glance behind me at the SUV and am relieved that Cordelia got away safely, too. She sits huddled in the backseat, her legs drawn up toward her chest as she rocks back and forth in a state of shock.

I turn back to Lydia and cup her bruised and dirty face in my hands, moving her long reddish hair away from her mouth and cheeks with my thumbs. I press my lips against her forehead.

"We're going to take you home," I say and a soft, lip-quivering smile breaks out on my face.

She smiles back at me.

A single shot rings out, ripping through the wide opened space. Lydia's smile fades as I look back into her eyes.

That eerie, foreboding silence is back, bathing us in its infinite cruelty. I feel like time has slowed, that somehow the world around me has flown by and left me behind to suffer this moment. It's just me and Lydia, staring into each other's eyes. Mine in disbelief. Hers glazing over with something that sends chills through me.

It's always the eyes…

I watch those bottomless eyes until the life slips completely out of her and her head falls backward like a broken spring.

One more shot rings out. Even though I watch the bullet pass through the front of Izel's skull, and Victor, as his gun drops again slowly to his side, I feel like I never really took my eyes away from Lydia whose body hangs precariously in my arms.

And then in a whirlwind of color and movement and sound, the world catches up to me again and I scream into whatever part of it is listening, pulling Lydia's lifeless body against my chest, rocking back and forth with her in my arms. Her limp arms fall and sway beneath her. I feel her blood warm and thick as it pools beneath the fabric of her shirt and bleeds through to my hands holding her back.

I cry into her hair until I feel her body being pried away from me.

"No!" I scream out at whoever it is. "Get away from me! Leave her alone!" My voice cracks and strains under the weight of emotion, which I never knew I possessed.

"We must go," Victor's voice says from somewhere above me. "We cannot stay here any longer."

"No!" I lash out, reaching up with one hand and trying to shove him away.

"*Now*, Victor," Niklas says from behind. "There's no fucking time for this."

Victor grabs me around the waist and scoops me up with ease, tossing me belly down over his shoulder. I kick and scream and beat him on the back with my fists as he carries me toward the SUV and away from Lydia's body.

"We can't just *leave* her here!"

"We have to."

He sets me in the backseat with Cordelia.

"Victor! You can't! Please don't leave her here like this!"

There is remorse in his eyes. I see it although hidden behind the ever-present mystery in his face, I see it there as plain as I see anything.

He shuts the door and the locks click in place again.

I ride in absolute silence to wherever it is they're taking us.

FOURTEEN

VICTOR

Niklas has never known when to remain silent. He lacks discipline and because of this our Order has always been fonder of me.

We were together when we were recruited at the ages of seven and nine, but so were two other neighborhood boys who had been good friends of ours. We had been playing ball in the field behind the schoolyard, like we did every Saturday afternoon, when the men came. Niklas and I did not know we were brothers at the time. But we were the best of friends. Inseparable like brothers should be. So perhaps deep down a part of us knew all along.

It wasn't until four years later, after my mother was killed while on a mission that we found out the truth. Niklas' mother told us in secret.

It has been kept a secret ever since.

"What have you done, Victor? What were you thinking? Where is your head?"

Niklas white-knuckles the steering wheel. He turns to look at me every few moments, waiting for me to give him an answer that I cannot give.

Quietly, I bite back the pain searing through my hip.

I look over at Niklas.

"You must tell Vonnegut that they shot first," I say and I see the argument cloud his features instantly. "Tell him that I had no choice."

"Victor." He shakes his head and then hits the steering wheel with the palm of his hand. "What has happened to you?" He grits his teeth, holding back the words he wants to say but knows would be better left unsaid.

He hits the steering wheel again.

"I've always done everything you've ever asked me to do. Not once have I refused you. Rarely do I question you. But I don't because I trust you as I should." He inhales a sharp breath and I notice his eyes stray toward the rearview mirror. And then he looks back at me. "But this is different. You're risking everything: your place in The Order, your relationship with Vonnegut, your life, *my* life." He slashes the air between us with his hand. "All for that girl."

"I am doing nothing of the sort."

"Then what would you call it?" he snaps. "If not for her, then for what? Make me understand, Victor!"

He swerves into the opposite lane of the highway to make it around a slow moving car.

"And why have you told her your name? You've become unstable. They eliminate the unstable ones, Victor, you *know* this."

He forces his eyes back on the road having hit his own nerve. His mother was one of the 'unstable ones'.

"I will not let anything happen to you because of me," I say. "If you feel you must tell Vonnegut the truth, I will understand. I will not hold that against you."

He shakes his head dejectedly. "No. As I've always done, I'll tell him whatever you need me to tell him."

He pauses and grips the steering wheel with both hands, moving the palm of one hand over the ridges of the leather as if to keep his hand from hitting something else.

"I hope one day you'll tell me the truth," he adds, not looking at me, "about what's happening to you. About what really happened in Budapest. And if it has anything to do with what you're doing now."

"There is nothing to tell," I say.

"Dammit! I'm not Vonnegut!"

"No, you are Niklas, the only person in this world whom I trust." I point out ahead. "Drop us off there. I'll need to get a new car."

Despite wanting nothing more than to shout at me all day until I tell him something satisfying, Niklas drops it altogether. Discipline—something he will never have.

We pull through the front gate of a car dealership.

"Around to the side," I say. "Wait for me there."

Without objection, Niklas does as I say and parks on the side of the building next to another vehicle.

Before I get out, I glance back once at the girl, Sarai. She's motionless and lost. Her eyes are open, but whatever it is that she's staring at somehow I know she doesn't really see. I want her to look upon me, just for a moment. But she never does and I walk away.

SARAI

I feel like I should be like Cordelia, sitting next to me wide awake yet unaware of it herself. I know it will take her months of therapy to overcome what she's gone through. I know because I went through the same thing after I watched my mother die.

The only way I'm anything like poor Cordelia is that I can't find the will to speak. I just sit here, letting the time pass and being completely incoherent to it, numb to its efforts to cause me discomfort. Fifteen minutes could be two hours and I truly wouldn't know the difference.

Unlike Cordelia, I'm aware of everything around me. I just don't care.

Sometime later, Victor emerges from the building and opens my door on the SUV. He looks at me for a moment as if waiting for something, I guess for me to get out.

I let my head fall sideways against the seat. "You didn't have to leave her there."

"Yes I did," he says and takes my hand. "She'll be found soon, if she hasn't already. You have my word."

I take Victor's hand, but glance over at Cordelia before I get out. "What about her?"

Victor turns his gaze on Niklas in the driver's seat.

"No long stops in between," he instructs. "Meet Guzmán at the waypoint we discussed. The money for his daughter. Inform him of the turn of events and that we could not control Javier's absence, but the job will be done."

"Whatever you say, Victor," Niklas agrees flatly, his words tinged with bitterness and disappointment.

Victor tugs on my hand and I get out of the SUV.

As we're walking away, Niklas stops us.

"Where will you go?" he asks, hanging partially out the window with his arm resting on the door.

"For now," Victor says, "Tucson. Await my contact for the rest."

Niklas drives away.

As Victor walks alongside me toward a shiny new dark gray car, I fall back behind him for a moment.

"Why are we going to Tucson?"

He stops mid-stride and turns around to face me.

"I'm taking you home."

FIFTEEN

SARAI

When I see 'home' on the horizon many minutes later, it doesn't affect me the way that I always dreamed it would. I don't even lift my head from the passenger's side window to look at it as we roll by. Because I know there's nothing for me here.

Instead of gazing out at the city, I watch the black asphalt move rapidly as we coast over it.

"Where do you live?" Victor asks.

Finally I lift my head and turn to face him.

"Why are you doing this?"

Victor sighs and puts his eyes back on the road.

"Because I think you've seen enough."

He pulls the car into a roadside convenience store parking lot and puts it into Park. It's starting to get dark outside.

"You need to tell me where to take you," he says and I detect the faintest hint of discomfort in his face.

"Your father?" he urges when I don't answer.

Absently, I shake my head. "My father could be one of a hundred men in Tucson. I never knew him."

"A grandmother? An aunt? A distant cousin? Where would you like to go?"

I quite literally have no family. Since I don't know my father, I don't know any of my family on his side. I never had any siblings; my mother got her tubes tied after she had me. My grandparents both died when I was a teenager. My aunt, Jill, lives somewhere in France because she could afford to move there and she disowned my mom when I was thirteen-years-old. And in turn, she disowned me, accused me of being just like my mom even though I was as different from her as night is from day.

Not wanting to give Victor any reason to believe that he owes me anything else, I say the only person that comes to mind so that he can drop me off and leave me to whatever kind of life I can make for myself.

"Mrs. Gregory," I whisper quietly, lost in the memory of the last time I saw her. "She lives about ten minutes from here."

I catch Victor's eyes staring at me from the side and mine meet them for a moment. What is he waiting for? He seems to be studying my face, but I don't know why.

I look away and point in the direction he should go next.

Victor puts the car into Drive and we head for the trailer park where I used to live.

It looks exactly the way it did when I left, with broken toys scattered around in side-yards, old beat-up cars parked in various spots with grass grown up around the flat tires. Window unit air conditioners hum a racket into the early evening air and dogs bark from their short chains wrapped around trees. When we drive by the little blue trailer I lived in for most of my life, I barely look at it. But I do wonder, just for a moment, who lives there now and if they ever managed to get rid of the incessant cockroach infestation that my mom never could.

"Right here," I say quietly, pointing to what I hope is still Mrs. Gregory's home two trailers down.

But seeing the bright red Bronco parked out front, I'm beginning to think that it's not. After nine years I wouldn't expect it to be.

KILLING SARAI

I go to get out, but Victor stops me.

"Take this," he says, reaching into his inside suit jacket pocket.

He pulls out a thick wrapped stack of one hundred dollar bills and hands them out to me. I glance to and from him and the money, hesitant only because it's so unexpected.

"I know it's blood money," he says, putting it into my reach, "but I want you to take it and do whatever you need to with it."

I nod appreciatively and take the stack of bills into my fingers.

"Thank you."

I start to walk away but then I stop and say, "What about Javier? If he's willing to pay that much to have me killed, he'll send someone else to find me if you won't do it."

"He will be dead before that happens."

"Are you going to kill him?" I ask, but then add, "I mean not for me, of course, but for that other man?" I want him to say that, yes, it's for me, but I know that's not the reason.

"You will be safe to live your life now," he says simply.

We share a quiet moment and I get out of the car, shutting the door softly behind me. And then I watch Victor drive away, his brake lights penetrating the partial darkness at the very end of the road. And then he's gone. Just like that.

What just happened?

I doubt I'll ever be able to wrap my mind around the past nine years of my life, and even more-so, the past couple of days. As I stand here at the end of a driveway of a place familiar yet so foreign to me, I realize that I can't feel myself. At least the person I used to be, or the person I was supposed to be but the opportunity was taken from me by Javier. By my mother.

I have lived a life of seclusion and bondage, a prisoner of a Mexican drug lord who although treated me with a strange sort of kindness, abused me in other ways. I have slept with a man I didn't love and who I didn't want to sleep with for most of my young life. And Javier is the only man I've ever been with sexually—willingly.

105

I have seen rape and kidnapping and abuse in every form possible. And I have seen death. So much death. My only friend died in my arms just hours ago. I watched the life leave her body as she looked at me.

After all of this, I feel like, as I sift through those memories casually as though scanning a hand of cards, none of it is affecting me the way that it should, the way it would a normal girl. And I know why. I just hate to admit it to myself—over the years I became used to it. It was how my life was. My mind conformed and adapted the best way that it knew how.

But now here I am back at home in Tucson, free to do whatever I want. I could walk a few blocks to the little store I used to go to everyday after school and buy a soda and a bag of Doritos. If I wanted, I could go to my old elementary school down the road and swing on the swings or lay down in the field that surrounds the building and just look up at the stars until I fall asleep. I could steal that bike in the front yard of lot number twelve and ride to my old friend's house twenty miles away. But the trailer behind me at the end of the cracked concrete driveway is just as good. And it's right there. It's taking me longer than I anticipated to walk up to the door and find out if the only person I knew who could help me now still lives there.

I can do whatever I want, yet I find it eternally difficult to choose where to begin. Or if to begin at all.

I guess now I know what it feels like when a person has spent half of his or her life in prison and is released back out into the world. They don't know what to do with themselves, they don't know how to fit back into society. They constantly look over their shoulder. They can't sleep past five a.m. or believe that they can choose what to eat and when to eat it. Violence and darkness and confinement is so much a part of them that half of them never learn any other way.

I don't want to be like that. But right now, as I stand here staring at the blaring light on the front porch and letting it bring spots in front of my eyes, I feel like it's how I'll be forever whether I want it or not.

A shadow moves across the front window.

I shove the stack of money in the back of my shorts, pulling my tank top down over it and then I take a deep breath.

I walk up the wooden steps and knock lightly on the door.

"Who is it?" a man's voice asks from the other side.

I'm pretty certain now that Mrs. Gregory is long gone from this place.

"It's…Sarai. I used to live over at lot fifteen."

The chain on the door shuffles and then the door breaks apart. A short, chubby man peers out at me.

"How can I help you?"

He's shirtless and his round belly hangs over the elastic of his knee-length gym shorts. The smell of popcorn filters out the door and past me.

"Does Mrs. Gregory live here anymore?" It feels awkward asking because I already know that she doesn't.

The man shakes his head.

"Sorry, but I've lived here for two years now," he says. "And I never knew of a Mrs. Gregory."

"OK, thanks."

I turn my back on him and descend the steps.

"Are you all right?" the man calls out.

I glance up at him momentarily. "Yeah, I'm fine. Thanks for asking."

He nods and closes the door as I leave, the sound of the chain lock being slid back into place is brief.

My bare feet move painlessly over the sand and rock-littered road of the trailer park. The street lights mounted high on the light poles begin to thin out and bathe me in darkness as I make it to the end of the road and leave the property. A car drives by and I'm instantly on edge, thinking it might be Javier here to kill me. But it drives on past and leaves me only with an erratic heartbeat and paranoid thoughts. At least I know that Izel is dead. I picture her last moment lying on her stomach in the sand with that gun in her hand. I didn't flinch or recoil when I saw Victor's bullet pass through her skull and her upper body hit the ground face down like a toddler falling asleep in his birthday cake. No, I felt only the satisfaction of revenge. I was glad to watch her die. Because she had it coming.

I only wish that it had been me who killed her for what she did to Lydia.

Strolling past a line of about a dozen mailboxes, I see the stop sign out ahead where I remember that if I go left it'll lead me to the elementary school. I decide in this moment that that's where I'll go because I have nowhere else to go. And after many long minutes of walking I make it there, glad that nothing about the playground has changed, at least. The same old rusted seesaw I remember sits near the swing set with one seat raised high in the air. Three spring riders: a dolphin, a lion and a walrus, are lined next to each other inside an encased sea of playground pebbles. I make my way through the dry grass and sit down on the same swing I always went straight for during recess. And thankfully it feels the same, too. The way I coil my fingers around the linked chains just above my head, how the conformable plastic seat fits just right against my thighs. But I'm much taller now than I was back then, so my legs are bent awkwardly beneath me. I dig my toes into the cool pebbles and watch a tiny white light from a plane move across the distant sky, making no sound.

And the only face I see in my thoughts is Victor's. He helped me, after all, even when I had accepted that he never would. I think about the conversation that he had with Niklas in the SUV and it only creates for me more questions about Victor. I wonder why he fired first. I wonder why he didn't just go along with the original plan to hand me over, trade me for Lydia and apparently, Cordelia, who I had no idea was any part of this at all. Maybe he knew that Izel would've killed me anyway and afterwards tried to kill Victor and take Lydia and Cordelia back. It's very plausible that Javier ordered Izel to go along with it, make the trade and then the second she had the opportunity, start shooting at us. I don't know; there are many ways that the whole thing could've gone. And there are many reasons why Victor might've done what he did.

All that I'm sure of is that I'm alive because of Victor. I'm home in Tucson because of Victor. I'm free from a life not of my choosing, because of Victor.

Coldblooded murderer-for-hire or not, he saved my life.

I reach around and take the money from the back of my shorts. I run my fingers fast over the edges, letting each bill fall rapidly onto the next, expelling a small blast of air on my face. There has to be at least five thousand dollars here. I start to count the ends of each bill, but stop a quarter of the way and just accept that there's a lot. Enough to rent myself a room for the night so I can get a shower and some rest. I resolve to do just that, relieved that I've come up with a solid first part of a very long plan. But then I realize that I don't even have a driver's license. I don't have a single shred of identification to prove that I'm me, or anyone else. I'll be lucky to find a hotel to rent a room to me without identification, no matter how much money I try to bribe them with. And I need to spend this money wisely, do what I have to do to stretch it out. Because it's all that I've got.

In the back of my mind I know I could simply go to the police and tell them my story and that they would help me. But I feel so overwhelmed by the simplest things that with work, I know, could be remedied that I feel utterly defeated by it all.

I sigh miserably, letting my head fall in between my slouched shoulders and I press my toes into the pebbles some more, moving them around in a circular pattern.

And then for the first time in what feels like forever, I break down in tears of self-pity. Not of anger or anguish or frustration. I cry for myself. Sobs roll through my body. I let the money fall on the ground next to my bare feet and I grip the chains on either side of me and just let it all out.

When I'm done minutes later, I raise my head and wipe the tears from my face.

A set of headlights turns on the street on the opposite side of the school building and I watch the car until it stops on the road about fifty-feet from me.

It's Victor.

SIXTEEN

SARAI

I don't get up right away. I just gaze out over the grass at the car, knowing what I want to do but having a hard time figuring out if it's what I *should* do. But then finally I stand up, giving in to that desire and I pick the money up from the ground and set out for the car.

The window slides down seconds before I get there.

"Who was Mrs. Gregory?" Victor asks with both hands resting casually on the steering wheel.

I open the door and get inside; there's no need for either of us to question or explain why he's here. We both know already. For the most part.

I close the door.

"She was more like a mother to me than my real mother."

A light breeze moves through the opened window and brushes through my hair.

Victor remains quiet looking at me, letting me relive the moments. I keep my eyes trained out ahead, peering into the darkness through the spotless windshield.

"I spent most of my time with her," I go on, seeing only Mrs. Gregory's face in my mind now. "She fed me dinner in the evenings and we'd watch *CSI* together. She loved baking her own seasoned Chex Mix." I glance over, laughing lightly. "She was a mean old woman. Not to me, of course, but she told my mom off a number of times. And once, one of my mom's boyfriends came over to Mrs. Gregory's looking for me"—I glance over—"he was one of the jerks who thought because he was sleeping with my mother that he could tell me what to do. Anyway, he rapped hard on Mrs. Gregory's door, calling out my name. It was so funny." I laugh again, resting my head back on the headrest. "She came to the door with a shotgun in her hand. It wasn't loaded, but it didn't need to be. That guy looked like somebody just kicked him in the nuts. He never came over there looking for me again."

I feel the smile fade from my lips as other memories appear.

"She got real sick once," I say distantly. "Had to have some kind of artery surgery, I don't know, but I remember being so scared she was going to die. But she made it through." My head falls to the side, still resting against the headrest, and I look right into Victor's eyes. "But what I'll always remember her for the most was that she taught me how to play the piano. For five years, from the time I was eight-years-old when I met her, up until I started hanging out with my best friend more, Mrs. Gregory taught me nearly every day it seemed. I'd head over there after school, sometimes forgetting about my homework, and I'd play until my fingers ached." I look downward toward the dashboard, regretful. "I wish I never would've met Bailey. I still feel bad to this day for replacing Mrs. Gregory with my friend."

I can't talk about this anymore. I shake it off and inhale deeply, raising my head from the seat. And then I pass the money over toward him, urging him to take it back.

"Keep it," Victor says, shifting the car into Drive. "You will need it later."

I push it down between my seat and the console.

"You know, you're in danger of becoming a trusted member of society," I jest.

I see his eyes move toward me briefly without moving his head.

"Perhaps," he says, pulling onto the freeway. "Just let it be known that if that's the case, I'll have to tie you up again." He looks over at me and although his lips aren't smiling, I see that his eyes are.

I turn toward the window beside me because unlike Victor, I have absolutely no control over the smile on my face, and I can't risk letting him see it.

———

We stop at a hotel just outside of Tucson and instead of running away this time I help him carry his usual bags up to our room on the third floor. Our room. Two words together that days ago I never would've imagined using so casually. I had asked about having my own, but he insisted that while with him I stay close. I didn't have to ask why. Being on the run with someone like him, I imagine it's better that way, but I do feel that there's something more to it that he's not telling me. I'm sidetracked by those thoughts when I see the blood on the tail of Victor's dress shirt as he pulls the shirt from the top of his slacks.

"Are you *bleeding*?" I walk over to him, trying to get a better look at that side of his body.

"Yes, but I'll be fine."

"But why—were you *shot*?"

He unbuttons his shirt all the way down, exposing his well-defined chest muscles and abs underneath, but all I notice is more blood.

Now I understand why he was in such a hurry to get into the room, why he seemed uncharacteristically uneasy since before we parted ways with Niklas and Cordelia.

"Go down to the front desk and request a bottle of peroxide, gauze and alcohol. They should have a first-aid kit."

I keep looking to and from his eyes and the blood, trying to see the actual wound. He takes his shirt off the rest of the way and drops it on the floor.

Finally I take notice of his physique.

"Sarai?"

I look up at him. "OK, I'll be right back."

I hurry out the door, not running but walking briskly so as not to draw too much attention to myself. God, I feel like a fugitive.

It takes several long minutes for the front desk clerk to find everything that I asked for after having to leave the lobby and look in the housekeeping room. Because she only had a tiny first-aid kit with some Band-Aids and antibiotic ointment, close by behind the desk.

"Sorry, I couldn't find any peroxide, but here's a full bottle of alcohol." The girl hands the bottle and an unopened box of rolled gauze over the counter to me. "What happened? Is everything all right?"

I thank her and take the stuff from the counter.

"Yeah, everything's fine. My uh, boyfriend, cut his hand open on his pocket knife." I shake my head and roll my eyes dramatically. "He was trying to open one of those human-proof plastic packages. I told him I'd come down here and ask for some scissors, but he insisted he 'had it.'" I roll my eyes again for added effect.

The girl laughs lightly. "Sounds like *my* boyfriend."

I laugh with her, thank her again and head back to the elevator feeling like I can't get away from her fast enough.

Victor has his slacks pulled down over one side of his hip by the time I get back. He's standing in front of the mirror, twisting his waist awkwardly so that he can get a better look at the wound, which I see clearly now. There's a small hole in the thicker flesh just behind the top of his hipbone. It doesn't appear to be bleeding much anymore, though there's plenty of blood on this shirt, proof it's already bled its fair share.

I walk over and set the supplies down on the long TV stand in front of the mirror.

"Is the bullet still in there?" I ask, looking at the wound more intently.

"Yes," he says reaching for the rubbing alcohol, "but it's not deep." Twisting the cap off, he pours some over the wound. He grimaces and shuts his eyes momentarily until the burning pain subsides.

"You left it in there all this time?" I ask, finding no reason acceptable. "Why didn't you do this sooner? Or go to a hospital?"

It dawns on me now that he didn't even tend to that wound after he dropped me off—he waited until after he knew I was safe.

"Victor?" I ask upon realizing.

He walks over to his duffle bag on the table by the window and reaches inside.

"Yes?" He barely looks over at me, more occupied with the knife he just fished from the bag.

In the last second I decide not to speak my assumptions aloud. Because I'm probably far off the mark and I don't want to look silly believing something so absurd.

"Never mind," I say. "Do you need help?"

He contemplates the offer. "No, I can do it. I've done it before."

Maybe that lie I told the front desk clerk had some truth to it, after all. I smile faintly thinking about it and then I move across the room toward him with the alcohol and gauze in my hands.

"You can't even *see* it fully," I point out. "I can help. Just tell me what to do. I'm not *completely* useless."

Again, his face appears faintly contemplative and then to my surprise, he takes off his slacks and stands in front of me practically naked, wearing only a pair of tight black boxer briefs that cling to every masculine curve and indentation from his lower waist to the tops of his thighs. It's only natural that I check him out a little, especially since he's so physically fit, but I don't let that distract me. That bullet deserves all of my attention and I make sure to give it.

He burns the blade of his knife with a lighter for a time and hands it out to me. I've never done anything like this before and really feel a bit squeamish just thinking about it, but I try not to let that show on my face. I take the knife by the handle and wait for him to instruct me.

"Like I said, it's not too deep. Just dig it out with the end of the blade."

I wince at the picture his words create in my mind. "But what if I cut you?"

"It can't be worse than what the bullet did. Now hurry," he says, pulling the elastic around his underwear down farther over his hipbone to give me better access.

Covertly I glimpse the rigid curve of his upper pelvic bone muscle and then get to work.

Hesitantly I bring the knife up to his skin and glance up at him, hoping he'll change his mind and do it himself, after all. Because I really don't think I can do this.

"Go on," he urges me. "You're not going to hurt me anymore than it already does."

I kneel down so my eyes are level with the wound and I feel my face flush red hot when I notice the outline of his manhood through the tight fitting boxer briefs. But even still I don't let his obvious good genes distract me from the matter at hand.

Carefully, I insert the tip of the blade into the wound, my face tightening and twisting into something horrible. Nervous at first, it takes me way too long to push it in farther and I don't until he gets tired of waiting.

"It's like pulling a Band-Aid off a sore, Sarai," he says irritably. "Just do it and get it over with. The longer you drag it out the worse it feels."

I bite down on my bottom lip, press the fingers of my free hand around the back of this hard thigh to get a better grip and then I sink the knife in deeper. I feel his muscles constrict beneath my hand, but I'm too nervous to look up and see the pain that I know is on his face.

"Why did you come back for me?" I ask, partly to take my mind off what I'm doing, the rest of me just really wanting to know.

"I never left," he says and I glance up to see his eyes. He looks away and then adds, "I thought you were being followed. I planned to stay back and wait until Javier or whoever he sent for you, showed up where you were."

Taken aback by his admission, I pull the knife out of his flesh and cock my head backward to glare up at him.

"You were using me as *bait*?" I don't know if that pain I suddenly feel is because he risked my life to catch Javier, or if it's because he doesn't care about my wellbeing as much as I had started to believe he might.

Victor sighs faintly, though still irritably, but it seems more-so because of what I said than me taking my time about pulling the damn Band-Aid off.

"No," he says. "Shortly after I pulled onto the main road, I saw another car drive past. A brand new Cadillac. Black with a nice price tag. I thought it didn't quite fit with the neighborhood."

I feel foolish before he even finishes explaining.

"So I turned around and parked on the road and watched it to make sure."

I remember that car now, the only one that drove past me and made me immensely nervous.

I get back to work on finding the bullet, trying to be extra careful.

"I'm sorry," I say.

"For what?"

Finally I see the bullet amid the blood and work it out with the end of the blade.

"For accusing you."

The bullet drops on the floor and a gush of blood pours from the wound.

"Get the gauze," he says casually, pointing at it on the table.

I do as he says while he pours more alcohol on the bloody wound, gritting his teeth even more than before.

I grab the gauze from the table and break it apart from the wrapping, unrolling it all the way, which isn't nearly enough to wrap around his waist twice much less as many times as it will take to help keep the blood from draining.

"Don't I have to sew it up or something?" I ask.

"Not right now," he says. "I don't have anything to sew it up with. You'll have to pack it with the gauze."

"But won't that—"

"It'll be fine," he assures me, nodding toward the gauze dangling from my hand.

"I guess Izel got you back for those flesh wounds you gave her," I say as I kneel back down level with the wound.

"I suppose she did," he says. "Just use your finger to pack it inside. Put a lot of pressure on it."

Not even thinking about my hands getting bloody, I start to pack the hole with the gauze until I can't fit anymore. But I see now that it really isn't that deep, maybe an inch at most, and it really does look worse than it is.

After cutting the excess gauze away, he pulls his underwear back up where it rests just below his hip. "I'm going to shower," he says walking to the bathroom. "Don't open the door for anyone. And stay away from the window. Thank you for your help."

"Sure. Anytime," I say flatly.

I wish he was a little more conversational. I'm going to have to remedy that.

He slips inside the bathroom and seconds later I hear the water running.

I plop down on the end of my bed and turn the television on, searching for the local news. When I find it, I can't do anything but stare at the black-haired reporter as she stands outside the area where 'ten bodies were found shot to death earlier this morning', and the rest of what she says fades into the back of my mind. It hurts to think about Lydia, the horrible way that she died. It hurts knowing that I couldn't help her like I promised and that her grandparents will soon know about her death and that they will be heartbroken.

The only good that I get out of this newscast is knowing that Lydia's body was found, that it wasn't left out there to decay and turn to dust never to be identified.

SEVENTEEN

VICTOR

The girl is asleep when I get out of the shower. I turn off the lights in the room and double-check the door before stopping at the side of her bed. She's curled in the fetal position with one pillow crushed against her chest. She's filthy and could've used a shower herself, but was exhausted by all that has happened.

I study the way her long auburn hair, although disheveled, outlines the contours of her face. She appears peaceful lying there, innocent. Despite exhaustion, after all that she has been through I find it interesting that she can sleep at all.

I'm going to need to get her some new clothes and shoes soon.

Carefully, I pull the bedspread over her body and leave her to her deep sleep, sitting down at the table on the other side of the room.

I'm breaking my own rules keeping her around like this. I know that I should have left her at the trailer park and waited for Javier to come for her—because surely that is one of the first places he'd look—make it easier on myself to eliminate him. But I feel like I owe it to her to keep her alive. At least for now. At least until Javier Ruiz is dead. She has seen too much, experienced too much. She shows all the signs of having lost the ability to react to fear and danger appropriately. She is numb to danger and that in itself is a death sentence.

Once this is over with, I will set her out on her own again. Perhaps she will find her way, though her chances are slim. But it is a risk that I must take. She cannot be with me for much longer; the life I lead will only get her killed.

I make contact with Niklas through a live video feed on my iPad, putting only one ear bud in my ear so that I can control the volume of my voice while speaking with him.

"She's still with you?" Niklas asks, incredulous.

I did not expect anything less of him.

"I will get rid of her once I eliminate Javier Ruiz," I say. "For now, I need her close by. I cannot chase Javier if he's moving from place to place chasing *her*."

"So you're using her as bait?" He appears more accepting of the prospect.

I glance over at Sarai to make sure she isn't awake.

"Yes," I answer looking back, but instantly feel as though I am deceiving my brother, and in-turn, our employer.

Taking matters into my own hands and breaking protocol for the sake of a successful mission, I am known for. Over time my decisions based purely on instinct have been accepted and respected by Vonnegut. Because I have never been wrong. But breaking protocol by outright deceiving The Order is new territory for me.

And I don't yet fully understand why I'm doing it.

"Good," Niklas says. "Onto matters—last known whereabouts of Ruiz was just outside of Nogales. He had trouble crossing the border into Arizona, but was finally granted permission once his insiders planted in border patrol arrived to see him through. We believe he is on his way to Tucson, if he isn't there already."

Niklas adds, "What is your next move? Vonnegut has all but passed off the reins of this mission completely onto you. All that he asks for are updates. And as you can understand I'm sure, he believes it's taking far too long to resolve. Javier should have been killed yesterday and you should be on a plane to your next mission by now."

"I am aware," I point out. "Forty-eight more hours at the most is all that I need."

Niklas accepts, nodding in answer.

"I will take the girl with me to Houston in the morning," I go on. "Inform Safe House Twelve of my arrival."

"Why Twelve?" Niklas looks at me warily. "You always choose Safe House Nine. Twelve is not your...shall I say *type*?"

"I am not going there for that," I tell him.

He believes that, but I can sense that he doesn't particularly agree with it.

Something is different about my brother as my liaison *and* my brother and I intend to find out what.

"Why go to Houston at all?" he asks, seemingly irritated with my decisions entirely. "You could wait for him to come to you and be done with this. Why, Victor, are you dragging this shit out?" Anger and frustration rises up in his voice.

"I'm taking the girl there to keep her safe," I say and there's more than enough question in his face to show that he is beside himself over my reasoning. So for the sake of my relationship with my brother, I add, "Niklas, it is only temporary, I assure you. You must trust me."

"Very well," Niklas agrees with suppressed suspicion. "I'll notify Safe House Twelve of your arrival. She'll be waiting for you."

And then the video feed goes dead.

I run my finger over a series of touch keys, breaking into the system through the backdoor. I choose a long series of commands, wiping the device clean of all evidence of correspondence and then crashing the system afterwards. I walk quietly past Sarai and take the iPad into the bathroom, cleaning my fingerprints from every square inch of it using what's left of the alcohol from before. And then I drop the device into the back of the toilet.

I crawl into the bed by the window and lay on my back, looking up at the ceiling in the darkness.

"He doesn't like me much, does he?"

I'm quietly stunned that she managed to pretend to be sleeping without my knowing.

Was she pretending? Or am I becoming too unfocused because of her?

"No, he does not," I answer without looking at her.

"But *you* do?"

The question stumps me.

She gets up from the bed and my head falls to the side to see her as she approaches. Not knowing what to do, unable to read her because I'm confused by her actions, I don't speak. She lies down beside me. Her knees are drawn up and pressed together, her hands hidden between them, and she looks at me.

"You should get back into your own bed," I say.

"I just want to sleep here. It's not what you think. I'm just afraid."

"You fear nothing," I say, looking back up at the ceiling.

"You're wrong," she counters. "I fear *everything*—what tomorrow will bring and if I'll be alive to see the end of it. I'm afraid of Javier or anyone else coming through that door and killing me in my sleep. I'm afraid of never being able to live a normal life. I don't even know what normal feels like anymore."

"There is a stark difference between fear and uncertainty, Sarai— you fear nothing but are uncertain of everything."

"How can you believe that?" She seems truly confounded by my assessment of her.

I look at her and answer, "Because you didn't go to the police. Because you made no effort to contact anyone else that you knew and you have had dozens of chances to do so. Because you got back in the car. With me. A killer. Because you know that I will kill you without thinking twice about it and I would not be remorseful, yet you're lying next to me. Here in this bed. Alone and willingly."

I reach over and pull the gun from the floor beside the bed and before she knows what's happening, the barrel of it is pressed underneath her chin, forcing her head backward. I push my body against hers, our shoulders touching, the weight of my gun hand held up by her chest. My eyes study hers, the question and surprise within them, although faint. I look at her mouth, her soft and innocent lips pressed together gently.

I lean over and whisper onto the side of her mouth, "Because you're not shaking, Sarai." And then slowly, I pull the gun away, never removing my eyes from hers.

"I am not Javier," I say. "You are mistaken if you believe you can manipulate me as you did him."

She appears offended, though it's very faint in her eyes, I see it. It is exactly the reaction that I wanted. That I *needed*, to know that the accusation is untrue.

Without argument, she looks away from me and rolls over onto her other side. She doesn't get up and move back to her bed.

And I don't force her.

"I wasn't with Javier willingly," she says with her back to me. "I don't have any reason to manipulate you."

A minute of quiet passes; only the shuffling of feet moving down the carpeted hallway outside the door disrupting it.

"I'm glad you came back," she says softly. "And Victor…I should tell you, I've been a liar for the past nine years of my life. Everything I said and did and expressed was a lie. I like to think I've mastered it by now." She pauses and I don't have to wonder long where she's going with this. "I've noticed that every time you talk to that man, Niklas, about me, that you're lying to him." She cranes her head backward to see me behind her. "Thank you for helping me."

And then she turns away again and says nothing to me for the rest of the night.

SARAI

I wake up the next morning tangled in the sheet in the center of Victor's bed.

I wonder if he slept here last night.

"Let's go," he says from somewhere behind me. "We have two hours before our plane leaves and you need some new clothes."

I roll over to see him standing in the room, fully dressed in his suit and bloody white shirt, waiting for me.

I glance at the shirt tucked into his slacks, seeing a bloodstain.

"I'm not the only one that needs new clothes."

I walk over to him and reach out to lift his shirt, but he closes his suit jacket buttoning only one button, to conceal the obvious red against the white of the fabric.

"How are you feeling?" I ask, only a little hurt that he refused me the chance to inspect his wound.

"I'm fine."

"But you need to at least change that gauze."

"I know," he says lightly. "And it will be taken care of when we get to Houston."

We drive to a nearby department store where he parks near the front and gets out. I remain seated, not expecting him to make me go in without shoes and looking the way I do.

Before he shuts the door I say, "I should probably tell you what size I wear."

He closes the door without letting me finish and walks around to my side, opening my door and waiting for me.

"You're a size six," he says, surprising me. "Now get out. You can't stay out here by yourself."

"I can't go inside, either." I point at my bare feet, which are now black on the bottom from walking around without shoes since yesterday. "I'm barefooted. No shirt, no shoes, no service."

Appearing annoyed with me, Victor takes my hand and yanks me out of the car.

I hardly protest.

We're only in the store for fifteen minutes before we make it back outside, me with a new pair of casual gray yoga pants, a plain white t-shirt and a pair of running shoes. He also let me snag a package of low-cut white socks and a six-pack of white cotton panties. The whole time I felt like I was forgetting something, but it's not until we're back inside the car that I remember: I should've bought a bra. It's been so long since I owned one I really did forget their importance.

I had expected to show up at a regular airport and get to fly on a passenger plane, but instead we drive to a place back in Green Valley and board a private jet. It only makes sense since he can't very well get past security in any public airport with a suitcase full of guns, a duffle bag with a mound of cash and another chock full of suspicious items.

While on the tiny plane Victor presents me with my very own fake driver's license, which looks so real it could easily pass for something from the DMV. I wondered where he got it, but never asked, assuming that earlier in the morning just before we left he went down to the front desk in the lobby to pick up a 'package'.

I'm twenty-year-old Izabel Seyfried of San Antonio, Texas, today.

And the photograph, I'm not even sure how he managed to take it, but it's definitely of me and so recent that I'm wearing the same filthy tank top I had been wearing since I escaped the compound. The natural background of the photo has been removed and replaced with the dull blue DMV background, so I don't have any idea where I was when he took the photo, either. I don't know, but I have a driver's license and that's good enough for me.

"The place where we are going," Victor says, "is safe, but the woman there should not know your real name. No one should from here on out. I will refer to you as Izabel and you need to answer to that name as casually as you would your own."

"OK," I agree. "Who is this woman?"

"She is a liaison...of sorts. Though more like a contact."

Confused, I ask, "But if she's one of you, why lie to her?"

He takes a sip of water and sets the glass down on the little table jutting out from the wall of the plane underneath the elliptical shaped window.

"It's just a precaution," he says, leaning his head back against the headrest. "When one person is wanted by many wealthy others, just about anyone can be swayed."

I raise my back from the seat. "Wait a second, what are you saying? Do you think everyone else knows I got away from Javier?"

"I've received no confirmation of that, but it's best to prepare in advance."

As if I wasn't already on edge enough.

EIGHTEEN

SARAI

Our flight lands in Houston just after twelve and there is an ordinary blue car—looks like something my mother used to drive—waiting out front for us. Victor grabs all three bags and conceals them inside the trunk. The woman driving I'm assuming is the contact. But she looks so ordinary, just like her car. I expected more sophistication, like Victor in his black suit and expensive shoes, but really she looks more like me.

"I haven't seen you in years," the woman says after Victor gets settled in the front seat. I sit in the back, just behind him.

"Yes, it has been a while," Victor responds.

When the woman smiles over at him, deep lines form around the corners of her mouth. She has blond hair, her age showing through her hair most of all, judging by the amount of gray mixed in. And she's much older than Victor, by ten years at least. But she's very pretty and clean and I feel embarrassed comparing myself with her in my current state.

We pull away from the building near the private landing strip and head for the freeway.

"I wonder what brought you to my neck of the woods," she adds. Then she glances back at me briefly. "And who did you bring along? Pretty girl. I get the feeling she's not—"

"No, she's not," Victor interrupts.

I'm not what, exactly?

Then he starts speaking to her in French.

Spanish, German, French? How many languages does this man speak? I hate it that I can't understand what they're saying, but I know they're talking about me. The woman glances at me in the mirror a few times, a little knowing smile tugging the corners of her lips. But even in a language that I can't understand, I can tell he's not being completely honest with her. Or, maybe I can't. Maybe it's just because I know deep down that I have nothing to worry about when it comes to Victor.

That fact surprises me more every day.

"It's nice to meet you, Izabel," she says.

I smile slimly at her and decide that since I have no idea what all Victor just told her about me that I'll be better off not speaking much to avoid contradicting his story.

Many minutes later we pull into the driveway of a humble little house situated next to other similar houses. Two boys zoom past along the street on their bicycles when we get out. Directly across the street a man washes his car in the driveway. The woman we're with raises her hand and waves at him and he waves back. It's a very typical neighborhood, the kind that all of my friends from school lived in when I was growing up and was more respected by the popular girls than a trailer park.

The woman pops the trunk from a button inside the car and I join Victor at the back as he grabs his bags. But I don't get a chance to ask him privately about what he might've said when she joins us seconds later.

"You'll have to excuse the mess," she says, fingering her keys; a purse dangles from the other shoulder. "I did clean up, but if I had a few more days to prepare I would've hired the Molly Maids." She waves at us to follow. "Come on in. My poor Pepper is going to tear up my window blinds the longer we stand out here."

I hear the barking of a small dog muffled by a side window as we approach the door underneath the carport. The blind moves erratically behind the curtain. There's another car parked in the drive, under the carport cover, but it's old and looks like it's been sitting up like that for several years. When she opens the door, the smell of food, *delicious* food, instantly causes my stomach to rumble and ache.

"Lunch is ready," the woman says leading us into the kitchen. She sets her purse down on the counter; already her yapping Pomeranian is making its rounds, deciding whose leg to sniff longer, mine or Victor's.

"Have a seat," she says gesturing toward the kitchen table.

Not having to tell me twice, I sit down in the nearest chair where an empty plate awaits me.

Victor takes the chair next to me.

The woman waltzes over with a ceramic bowl filled with whipped potatoes in one hand and a plate full of fried chicken in the other and sets them down in front of us. A smaller bowl of corn and a basket of rolls follow.

Not feeling right about being first, I wait to see if Victor will reach for something before me.

"What would you like to drink?" the woman asks. "I have soda, tea, milk, lemonade."

"Water is fine," Victor says and then he looks at me, casually nods his head toward the food, giving me the OK to start filling my plate. "From the tap," he adds at the last second.

I reach for the chicken first and pick up a piece with the tongs.

"I'll have water, too," I say, looking up at her as I drop a chicken leg on my plate. "Thank you."

She smiles sweetly and walks around the bar toward the refrigerator and begins preparing our drinks, scolding the little dog verbally to send it strutting out of the kitchen and away from us.

By the time she makes it back with our glasses, Victor and I both have put all of the food we want onto our plates.

She sets our drinks in front of us.

I thank her again and feeling better about 'going first' now, I pick up my spoon and start to eat, but Victor stops me, placing two fingers on my wrist and lowering my hand back onto the table. My face flushes and I lower my eyes, hoping the woman doesn't think I have the worst meal etiquette ever. I figure she must be the religious type, that we have to hold hands around the table awkwardly while she talks to Jesus and tells Him how thankful we are for this food and for the troops and all that stuff.

"Oh Victor," she says playfully, "you can't be serious."

He doesn't say anything.

I glance at him, wrinkling my brows. Maybe *he's* the one who feels it necessary to pray.

Surely not...

The woman sighs and rolls her eyes a little bit as she reaches over and slides my plate away from me.

I'm thoroughly confused now. I fold my hands in my lap underneath the table because I'm not sure what else to do with them.

I turn to Victor, momentarily lost in the mysterious depths of his eyes under the bright light from the fixture centered above the table. I swallow nervously and come back to reality when I hear the woman's voice again.

"He doesn't trust anyone," she says to me as she scoops some whipped potatoes from my plate, into her mouth. She points her spoon at me and continues with her mouth full. "Never has. But it's to be expected." She swallows. "And completely understandable, being in his line of work and all."

Her eyes veer to Victor's and suddenly she changes the topic as if he gave her some private look of warning that I missed by the time I turned my head to see him, too.

"Anyway," she goes on, now taking a bite of my chicken, "you two can stay here for as long as you need. Spare room is at the end of the hall." She takes a bite of my corn and then my roll, finally washing the food down with her tea.

Then she slides my plate back to me. I take it hesitantly, fingering the edge of the plate and feeling uncomfortable about eating anything she just double-dipped her spoon in.

Victor slides his plate toward her next and she does the same to his food.

It worries me that in the home of one of his contacts he feels the need to have her eat the food first to prove to him that she didn't poison it. I wonder briefly about our water but realize that must be why he requested it from the tap. He had been watching every move the woman made the whole time while I was metaphorically drooling over my first home cooked meal since I hung out at Mrs. Gregory's house.

Victor nods at me, letting me know that it's OK to eat now. And I don't give the germ exchange another thought and dig right in.

The woman, whose name I learn is 'Samantha', does most of the talking for the next thirty minutes while we eat. Every now and then Victor will add a few comments here and there, but I find that his conversation willingness is even more lacking than it was with me or Niklas. But she doesn't seem to mind. In fact, she's more accepting of it than I would be. If the two of them were on a date right now, it would be obvious to everyone in the restaurant that he is not at all into her and she's completely oblivious to that fact. But this isn't a date and I get the feeling that I'm the only one in this room who is oblivious to what's going on.

My theory is confirmed when after lunch things between the two of them begin to…change.

"Will you two be sharing a bed?" she asks from the doorway of the spare bedroom.

There is only one bed in here. It's a question I've been asking myself since I walked in.

"If not," she goes on, glancing at Victor in a way that perhaps she didn't expect me to notice, "then I can make up a bed for one of you on the couch."

"That will not be necessary," Victor answers and I don't know why, but my heart leaps inside my chest. "I won't be sleeping."

Then my heart goes back to normal. Boring, non-fluttering normal.

Samantha looks pleased.

And for some reason, I'm instantly...jealous.

Trying to familiarize myself with this inane, absurd emotion that just infiltrated my head, I force myself to shake it off. I start looking at random objects within the room: the plain-Jane cream-colored bedspread that covers the full sized bed, the matching dresser and chest of drawers placed against opposite walls, the large oak chest situated at the foot of the bed with a horse carved into the side, the window with equally plain white curtains where a beaded necklace of some sort dangles from one end of the curtain rod.

"All right then," she says standing in the doorway with her hands cradled in front of her. "Make yourselves at home. And Victor..." she glances downward below his waist, "when you're ready to patch that up, you know where to find me."

"I'll be there soon," Victor says and then she smiles politely at us and walks down the hallway, leaving us alone in the room.

"Why are we here exactly?"

Victor opens his gun suitcase on the bed and takes out two sleek black handguns. He puts one underneath the mattress and the other on a small desk in the corner of the room. Then he opens the closet, taking down a new suit after sliding back several others dangling from hangers. Slacks first, then a long-sleeved button-up shirt, lastly, a matching jacket.

"You're going to stay here," he says, "until I kill Javier. I'll be going back to Tucson later tonight, or wherever it is I am told that Javier was last seen and then I'll find him and I'll kill him."

"But why Houston?" I ask, sitting on the edge of the bed. "Wasn't there a...'Safe House' in Arizona somewhere closer? You know, maybe you should've used me as bait, after all. I could help you. I mean, it's likely that whoever is looking for me one of the first places they'll check is where I used to live, around people I used to know." I pause, thinking to myself how glad I am now that Mrs. Gregory no longer lives in that trailer park.

"You're right," he says. "And that's why it's likely I'll be heading right back to Tucson. I've seen where you once lived, where the woman you spent most of your time with, once lived. By taking you there last night, you've already helped me by showing me precisely where Javier might be found. There's no need to risk your life anymore by keeping you there."

"So then you *did* have another agenda by taking me home," I say, feeling very small right now. "You just wanted to see the location."

Victor shakes his head and closes the top drawer on the dresser. He turns to face me and something unfamiliar is evident in his greenish blue eyes.

A long breath emits from his nostrils.

"I took you home because it's what you wanted," he says and goes to the door with all of his clothes draped carefully over one arm.

"Even though you knew they'd go back there looking for me?"

He stops at the door with his back to me, his fingers placed on the knob ready to open it. His head tilts back some and his shoulders fall.

Instantly, I feel like I've offended him.

"I'll use the shower in Samantha's room," he says and it stings. "You should get cleaned up, change into your new clothes."

And then he walks out, leaving me in here all alone.

NINETEEN

SARAI

Instead of a shower, I soak in a long hot bath. My muscles ache something awful and it wasn't long after I slipped into the water that I started feeling the tiny scrapes and cuts all over my body that I hadn't realized were there before. I'm just surprised I don't have a gunshot wound to go with them.

By the time I get out, I'm cleaner than I feel like I've ever been now that I have new clothes to put on and that I've gotten to shave. Victor had told me back at the department store that I could pick whatever I wanted and that it didn't matter how much it cost, just that I needed to be quick about it. I chose the most unfashionable, casual thing I could find. Because I don't care about fashion and honestly can't remember the last time that something like that mattered.

After I'm dressed I pull my wet hair up into a ponytail and then rummage through the things left out on the bathroom sink: deodorant, toothpaste and toothbrush, various bottles of lotion and other random creams of sorts are lined neatly against the mirror. Everything is new and there's no telling how long it's all been sitting here waiting for a guest like me to come along and put it to use. And I definitely put it to use, starting with the deodorant first, a luxury that I rarely had at the compound. Javier, for the most part, made sure that I had necessities and nice things, but he left the shopping up to Izel and since she despised me immensely, she made it a point to go out of her way to buy the cheapest, most useless stuff that she could find. When it came to deodorant, the best I ever got was some strange brand of liquid roll-on that left red, inflamed spots underneath my armpits.

I brush my teeth and even use dental floss for the first time in years and then I find myself standing blankly in front of the mirror. I don't see myself really, but I think about Victor and what he's doing in Samantha's room. Explicit pictures of him fucking her spring up in my mind and it upsets me more than I want to admit to myself.

I can't really be attracted to a man like him, can I? A man who has killed no telling how many people. It doesn't matter that I feel safe with him, or that I trust him; the truth is that he is what he is and I'd be stupid to ever think he wouldn't kill me if he found it in any way necessary.

But I *am* attracted to him. I *do* have strange, unfamiliar feelings for him.

And I *hate* it!

I shake my head angrily at myself, finally taking notice of my own reflection. The area around the outside of my right eye is yellowed by a bruise. My lips are dried and chapped. There's a tiny cut along my left brow bone. I look tired and…used up.

Only the sound of something falling on the floor in another room down the hall snaps me out of my self-loathing.

I crack open the bathroom door first to peer down the hallway. I hear Samantha's voice, but I can't make out what she's saying. Finally leaving the bathroom, I walk quietly down the length of the hall toward her room, tiptoeing across the carpet as carefully as possible. Her door is closed, so I press my ear against the wood and try to listen in, but the moment I touch it, it creaks open a little and my heart falls into my stomach. I shut my eyes tight and hold my breath until I know that I didn't just give myself away.

I shouldn't be doing this, I think to myself, but I just can't help it.

I peer inside the dimly lit room. A television is on, but has been turned down really low or muted, the glow from it providing the room with most of its light. I see Victor's bloody shirt and the rest of his suit hanging over the side of a laundry basket pressed against the wall near the master bathroom. That door is cracked open, too.

Pushing the bedroom door open a little more, just enough for me to squeeze through, I walk inside Samantha's room. And every step I take makes me feel that much more violating and uncouth. But I have to know. Because the thought of him with her is torturing me on the inside. Maybe later I'll try to figure out why. Right now, I just want to know.

I make my way through the room and to the bathroom door, where I wait just outside of it, my heart pounding in my chest, worried they'll catch me eavesdropping. When after a few seconds pass and Samantha is talking again, I feel safe enough to peek inside to get a better look, only hoping that the partial darkness of the room helps to keep me from being seen.

VICTOR

I stand with my hands pressed against the counter, a towel wrapped around my lower body after having just showered. I peer into the mirror over the sink, tilting my chin to one side and then the other, feeling like I should probably shave but decide against it. Samantha sits down on the closed toilet seat with a suture needle and thread in one hand, ready to stitch me up.

"Are you going to drop the towel?" she asks. "I can't very well do this with it in the way. And it's not like I haven't seen it before."

I start to remove the towel just as she says that, but then I notice a sound so faint, like the sound of a sharp breath, that I'm surprised I heard it at all. I glance into the mirror and look behind me at the door seeing nothing but knowing that Sarai is on the other side of it.

"Victor?" Samantha urges me, getting irritated with my slow response.

"No," I finally answer, turning around so that the side where the wound is, is facing her. I reach down and strategically adjust the towel over the back of my hip so that she can access it, afterwards tying it firmly together on the other side to hold it in place.

"If you insist," Samantha says and goes right to work.

I feel the needle slide in once and I grit my teeth for a moment until the pain fades.

"You never did tell me why you stopped coming here," Samantha says.

"It was for the best."

"Bullshit. It was something I did, or said, or maybe it was something I *didn't* do. I just want to know. No hard feelings. No awkwardness. Just answer the question that's been bugging the shit out of me for ten years. I deserve that much."

After the second pass of the needle through my skin, I no longer feel it.

"I respected you," I say. "It didn't feel it right to use you anymore."

"Honey, you know better than that." She smiles up at me briefly. "I didn't mind; hell, I enjoyed it."

"But I *did* mind."

Samantha pushes the needle through again, always carefully. Then she shakes her head. "I wonder how you manage to pull off this job with that conscience of yours. I think you're the only one with a conscience who can."

"Well, it was nothing you did or didn't do," I say, skipping over her comment entirely. "So I hope I've answered the question enough to satisfy you."

"Stop being so technical with me, Victor. You know I hate it."

She stands up from the toilet seat and reaches for the iodine, spilling a small amount onto a wash cloth. She dabs it all over and around the stitched bullet wound.

"I hear you started staying at Safe House Nine over in Dallas when you came through these parts," she goes on and I can predict where she's going with the rest of it. "Is it because that one was younger than me? I mean, it's perfectly fine. I *am* getting up in the years, I admit."

It is exactly what I predicted she'd say.

I sigh and lean against the counter, crossing my arms. She pulls a large square of gauze from a packet to prepare it next.

I look right at her, hoping I can say what I'm about to say without turning her against me. I won't leave Sarai alone with her if she thinks

I chose Safe House Nine over her because of something as absurd as her age. Samantha is a killer. And a woman who feels scorned who is also a killer is a fatal combination.

"I chose Nine because she was a whore and proud of it," I say, laying the truth out the way it needs to be, to make her understand. "I couldn't use you like she let me use her. Because you were and still are my friend. I hope you understand."

She laughs lightly. "You don't have any friends, Victor."

Her gaze skirts me as she places the gauze over the wound and presses two strips of dressing tape along its edges. Then she raises up the rest of the way and looks at me with thoughtful green eyes. I feel the same thing in her eyes that I always felt when I came here, when I slept with her. She might have been someone who could fall in love with me, if I had let it go that far. She started getting too close and I couldn't let that happen. She had always been kind to me. She was different from the others who were more like myself and are only interested in sex. Because anything more is not only reckless and dangerous and foolish, but is completely unacceptable.

"Who do you think you're fooling, Victor?" she asks with a playful, yet inoffensive smile.

I pull the towel the rest of the way back over my hips, tucking it in on itself at the waist.

"What do you mean?" I ask, looking at her curiously.

Samantha starts clearing the countertop of the bandage leftovers and rinsing the blood and iodine down the sink with a burst of water.

"That girl down the hall," she says. "Izabel. Of course we both know that's not her real name, but regardless, what the hell are you doing with her?" She drops a handful of bloody tissues into the wastebasket beside the toilet.

"I told you," I say. "I'm just using her until I eliminate my target. After that, she's on her own."

I never could completely fool Samantha, but what strikes me the most about right now is that she appears to know more about what's going on with me than even I do. And I'm not fond of that idea.

I glance toward the bathroom door several feet away, wondering if Sarai is still hiding there, listening to everything between us. I know she is. I can feel it. But Samantha needs to stop. Right now. Because I can't have her filling Sarai's head with things that might cause her confusion. The girl is confused enough as it is.

"I need to get dressed," I say, hoping to deter her from the topic. I reach for my clean boxer-briefs hanging nearby, but Samantha steps around in front of me.

She crosses her arms and the smile she wore before has been replaced by determination.

"You can't do this. You know that."

I reach around her and grab my boxers anyway, letting the towel drop to the floor and stepping into them.

"Victor," she persists, "you can't be the hero. Not for her or for anyone else. You *know* this. What you're doing, what you're *feeling* is only going to get you killed."

I pull my thumbs from the elastic, letting it snap against my hips, and I shut Samantha up with the hard look in my eyes.

"You're way off the mark, Sam," I say, glaring at her. "You think you see something in me for *her* because it's what you're used to believing you saw in me for *you*." Instantly, I regret my words.

Samantha glares at me coldly, her fingers pressing aggressively into her biceps. "What are you saying? She can't look at me anymore and her eyes stray toward the shower. Because she knows I'm right. I shouldn't have said it, but she can't deny the truth.

Finally she looks at me again, hurt and admission on her features. "You're right," she says. "I have always thought of you in that way. I read into things between us wrong and saw things that weren't there."

I keep silent to let her finish, but it seems that she has.

"I truly am sorry for anything I have done to you," I say and mean it with everything in me.

She shakes her graying blond head. "No, Victor, you did everything right. You saw that I was developing feelings for you before I knew it myself and you did the right thing."

I cup my hands underneath her elbows and she relaxes a little.

"I hope that—"

Uncrossing her arms, my hands fall away.

"Victor," she says, putting up her hands between us, "please don't apologize for not having the same feelings for me that I was having for you. That's not something you can control, I know. And I hope that you'll believe me when I say that you can *always* trust me. You're the one person in The Order that I trust and can truly call… my friend."

"I thought you said I didn't have any friends?" I smile faintly.

Relaxing one arm back against her chest, she pats my shoulder with the other.

"OK, maybe you just have me," she says, smiling back at me. But then she becomes serious again. "And because I'm your only friend, you have to trust me, *listen* to me when I tell you that what you're doing with this girl is going to get you exiled, or killed, or both."

I start buttoning my shirt.

I had hoped she would drop it altogether, especially if Sarai is still listening in from the other room, though I get the strangest feeling that she's not and that relaxes my mind somewhat.

"I'm not doing anything with her other than keeping her safe until this is all over," I insist. "She deserves a shot a normal life after what she's been through and I decided at some point to try and give that to her."

I slip into my black slacks, tucking in my shirt. Samantha pulls my tie from the hanger on the wall and drapes it around the back of my neck.

She sighs. "OK," she says, surrendering. "But tell me, and be honest with *yourself* before you answer…" she hesitates, her fingers paused around the tie. I nod. "Since she's been with you, can you tell yourself that she's going to be any different than you were years after you were taken by The Order?"

Her question quietly shocks me. I had not expected it at all.

"Even I see it, Victor, and I've only spent an afternoon with her so I know you see it, too."

I know now what she's referring to, but I'm still too taken aback by the revelation to comment. Samantha detects this, my need to hear more of what I already know to be true from someone else's lips rather than just my own. Subconsciously needing the validation.

"I know you can't tell me anything about where she came from, who she's running from or how long she was with those she's running from, but judging by what I see in her now I can tell two things." She straightens my finished tie and lets one hand drop to her side, the other briefly holds up two fingers. "One," she drops one finger, "she's already so anesthetized to what is normal that she might never live a normal life. She knew I was testing her food for her because you were making sure it wasn't *poisoned*, but it didn't faze her. She sat at that table with us, scarfing down that lunch like we were a simple family of three sharing an afternoon meal in the suburbs."

She leans against the counter, crossing her arms over her chest.

"And two," she goes on, "for her to be that way I know she had to have been a prisoner, sex slave or no-telling-what for several years, no less than five. And at her young age—what is she twenty-three, twenty-four? (She gestures her hands around in front of her briefly)—that means she had to have been fairly young when she was taken. *Like you.* And we both know that the younger one is, the easier it is to mold them into whoever or whatever you want them to be. Also like you."

Every word that Samantha spoke is true and I know it. I know it better than anyone.

I slip my suit vest on over my shirt and tie and button all four buttons.

"She's in the fifty-fifty zone," I say. "She can go either way with an equal shot at both. And she's strong enough. And intelligent." Lastly, I put on my suit jacket. "I'm just giving her, her one and only shot. Which direction she chooses to take it will be *her* decision. And I won't be there to see it. She'll be on her own then."

Samantha cocks her head to one side. She probably doesn't fully believe me, but she has finally exhausted her warnings.

She comes up to me, the same sweetly seductive smile she always wore minutes before I'd have my way with her in the past. She stops directly in front of me and her fingers dance upward along the fabric of my jacket. She rests her hands on both sides of my neck, brushing lightly against my skin.

"One last kiss," she says looking into my eyes, "for old time's sake. I just want to feel young again, like I always felt when you'd visit me."

I bring my hands up and cradle her face within them, kissing her forehead slowly first. "It was never about you being older than me, Sam. You're still as sexy today as you were to me ten years ago." And then I touch my lips to hers, dragging the tip of my tongue softly across her bottom lip and into her mouth.

TWENTY

SARAI

They've been in the bathroom for a really long time. But it's none of my business what they do. I left the room right before Samantha started stitching Victor up, resolved to come to my senses and let it go. I feel like I should've stayed to hear the things they talked about at least, since I'm pretty sure some of it was about me and I have a right to know, but it was too intrusive. And I admit, I didn't want to see them together.

Despite feeling some jealousy for Victor, which I realize is only natural given the extraordinary situation I've been thrust into with him, I know that he could never be interested in someone like me, or in anyone at all, really.

Except Samantha and others like her, I suppose.

Regardless of their age difference, I know they've been intimate before. I heard her say it right before I left the room and I like to think I'm smart enough to put together the rest of the picture on my own, knowing what little I do know. Whatever their past relationship I feel like even though she's attractive and obviously a kind and smart woman, those probably weren't the things that brought him here. And it wasn't just the sex, either. It was that Samantha knew all along that sex was all it would ever be.

I'm no expert, but it's just what I believe in my heart. Samantha is *like* him, maybe not exactly in what roles they play in their secretive world of crime and danger and death, but she knows he's too disciplined and unemotional to become involved.

Victor could probably never trust himself with anyone on the 'outside'. And when it comes to comparing me with them, I am the epitome of the outside.

I stare off toward the curtain covered window in the spare room where Victor left me earlier. It's pitch black outside even though it's not even nine o'clock yet. I lay on my side on the bed, one arm bent beneath my head underneath my pillow. My feet are cold, but I don't care to get up and break apart a pair of socks from the package Victor bought me, so I press my feet together at the ankles and slide them underneath the blanket.

Victor walks into the room. He leaves the door open to let the light from the hallway filter inside instead of flipping on the switch. I get the feeling he thought at first I might've been asleep.

He's dressed from head to toe in refined sophistication, more-so than I've ever seen him and I can't help but stare across the room at his dangerous beauty. His tall form moves through the path of light at the door and then is bathed in shadow when he approaches the bed where I lay.

"You're leaving, aren't you?"

"Yes," he says and sits down beside me, his back straight, his hands resting along the tops of his legs.

"Are you going to come back?"

It takes him a moment to answer. He keeps his eyes trained on the window out ahead.

"It will probably be best that I didn't," he says.

My heart lurches. I swallow.

"When Javier is dead, either Samantha will take you where you need to go, or I'll send Niklas for you."

The back of my throat is beginning to burn, the top of my nose, just between my eyes is starting to itch.

I force the tears back.

I don't want him to go at all, much less never come back. I want to stay with him, though I don't know why.

"But what if others know?" I remind him, hoping to change his mind without him knowing the real reason why. "What about John Lansen? What about all of the other men I saw? Victor, they might know and maybe Javier won't be the last to come looking for me." I really don't care if they do. That's not what I'm afraid of. I'm afraid of Victor walking out that door and never seeing him again.

Finally I manage to sit up, anger twisting my features at first, until I notice it and let them soften.

I cross my legs Indian-style on the bed and reach out to take his wrist, tugging on the sleeve of his jacket. I halfway expected him to retract it from me, but he doesn't. He rests his hand on the tops of my crossed ankles and just that simple touch, that single gesture, causes my throat to close up with emotion. I look down at his hand, my fingers shaking nervously against the cuff of his dress shirt.

He didn't move his hand away...I keep thinking to myself.

Tears brim my eyelids, but I breathe them back quickly.

"I am sorry, Sarai," he says looking me in the eyes as his churn with conflict and indecision.

I get the feeling that he doesn't want to leave me here. I *feel* it...I *know* it.

Slowly he stands up from the bed. I sit here, frozen in a chasm of self-defeat and anger and fear. *Fear!* How can he accuse me of fearing nothing?! I want to shout at him, tell him how wrong he is as he shoulders his bags and takes up the gun suitcase in one hand.

Instead, I wipe the few tears that did manage to fall from my eyes and I say across the room to him softly:

"Victor, you were wrong."

He turns only his head to look back at me.

"You were wrong when you said I fear nothing. You were *so* wrong…"

He holds his gaze on me for only a second and then turns and walks away, closing the door and letting the darkness of the room consume me again.

———

Samantha left me alone for the next hour and a half. I guess she wanted to give me time to myself because when she did finally come into the room with me minutes ago, I could tell that she felt something for me as I lay curled up on the bed, staring at that window. It makes me wonder what they talked about in her bathroom earlier, makes me regret not staying longer to have found out.

I would hate her for knowing more than me, if she was an easy person to hate.

But I realize I like her too much for that.

"You know, Victor does this stuff all the time, Izabel." She pats me on the hip with the palm of her hand. She's sitting in the same spot next to me where Victor last sat.

"He'll be fine." She smiles. "And I'm sure he knows you're grateful to him for helping you."

"What can you tell me about him?" I ask.

She inhales a deep, concentrated breath and her eyebrows rise with that loaded question sort of look.

"Well, I'm guessing you know what he does for a living already, so you can probably imagine that I'm sworn to a certain amount of secrecy that if I break could get me in a lot of trouble."

True, but she's smiling and really seems kind of itching to talk to me, regardless. It may not turn out to be much, but something is better than nothing, I suppose.

I sit upright, dropping my legs over the side of the bed to sit like her. I rest my hands within my lap.

She smiles over at me in a short glance and reaches out her hand. "Let's talk about it over a cup of coffee."

She stands up and I put my hand in hers and accept.

"I swear it's perfectly poison-free," she jokes as I follow her out the door and into the hall.

"I believe you."

I believe her mostly because if Victor trusted her enough to leave me alone with her then that's enough for me.

I sit down at the kitchen table while she gets the coffee ready at the counter where the coffee pot sits next to an old giant microwave.

"I suppose it's OK to tell you that he's been the way he is pretty much all his life." She scoops a few tablespoons of coffee into the filter and shuts the top of the coffee maker. "But I really only know the things he's told me. Nothing more than that."

"What kinds of things?"

She pours the water in the back of the coffee maker while allowing the different conversations she's had with Victor to materialize.

"Well, I know he loves his coffee black." She smiles. "He loves Thai food and he won't touch tuna fish with someone else's tongue. He prefers a good beer over a fine wine, but only the best beer, preferably German." She sits down at the table with me and props the side of her face in one hand, looking thoughtful. "To tell you the truth, Victor would rather go all the way to Germany for a beer than to drink the beer here." She waves her hand at me once, removing it from her cheek. "He's a very particular man."

"But what about his family?" I ask. "He told me he had a sister and that he killed his father and something about his mother being in...*Budapest*, I think?"

Samantha shakes her head, smiling and maybe even finding what I told her a little amusing. But she's not gloating about it.

"No, doll," she says. "If that's what he told you, it was probably just to get you to stop talking. (Well, she's right about that much, I know.) He would never tell anyone else anything too personal about his life, especially his family. Not even me. I don't even know if he *has* a family."

I stay as far away from the topic of the two of them as I can.

"You need to know, Izabel," she looks at me intently so that I'll meet her gaze, "that Victor is risking a lot…no, he's risking *everything* by helping you. And even though he left tonight and doesn't intend to come back for you, what he's already done where you're concerned, though I have no idea what that might be, it could have already sealed his fate."

My stomach tightens and I get this horrid feeling in the center of my throat.

Her gaze shifts softly and I feel as if she's mourning me, or my feelings in some private way.

She leans her back against the chair. The coffee gurgles and drips into the pot behind her.

"But how do you know that's what he's doing?" I ask. "How do you know he's helping me and that I'm not just part of his mission?"

"Because he would never have brought you here," she says almost sympathetically. "And he wouldn't have asked me not to tell anyone, our employer, *no one*, that he did it."

I raise my gaze from the table to look at her, surprised by the information she just gave.

She nods at me as if to confirm my thoughts even though I never spoke them aloud. "Yes," she says. "Other than Niklas, I am the only one he trusts. Maybe not completely because Victor is incapable of that, but he trusts me. And by hiding you out here and asking me to risk my life by keeping you a secret, *that's* how I know."

She's telling the truth. I can't bring myself to believe otherwise no matter how hard I try. And I *do* try. I think I'm subconsciously attempting to find some reason not to like her or to be suspicious of her because of my jealousy from before.

But I find nothing.

And I can't help but wonder if she holds that against me, if there is any lingering bitterness toward me because Victor asked her to risk her life for me. But I sense that there isn't. It makes me feel ashamed in a way.

She gets up from the table and heads back toward the coffee pot.

But then she stops mid-stride and freezes at the end of the counter as if she came within an inch of walking into a glass wall. Her right hand touches the edge of the counter, her fingers curling into a fist as her head snaps back around to me. Her eyes are wide and alert and the sight of her like that makes me jump in my own skin.

And then I hear something, too, and my heart starts to bang violently against my ribs, reverberating through my bones and into my ears. Shadows move across the kitchen window, and at that moment, Samantha drops low toward the floor, still on her feet, and rushes toward me, pulling me completely from the chair. It happens so fast that I don't get to drop as gracefully as she had. I nearly fall on my butt, but my right foot keeps me grounded where I spin around precariously on it until I catch my balance and then follow her through to the hallway.

"Who is it?" I whisper.

She grabs my arm and pulls me around in front of her. Her dog, Pepper, runs to the back door, barking furiously.

"Stay low and get back to your room!" she hisses. "*Hurry!*"

Crouched as low to the floor as I can possibly be without actually sitting on it, I feel like I'm scuttling across the carpet toward the opened bedroom door. Once I'm inside, Samantha comes in right behind me and dropping the rest of the way to her knees, she thrusts out both arms and presses her hands against the large wooden chest sitting at the foot of the bed. As she's moving the chest, more shadows move across the window and I hear voices whispering outside.

And they're speaking Spanish.

I whirl around to Samantha, tearing my eyes away from the window just in time to see her lifting a small metal door in the floor that had been hidden underneath the chest.

"Get inside! Hurry! Now!"

In that last second, which I don't even think I really have the time to spare, I reach underneath the mattress and grab the gun that Victor left there, shoving it into the back of my pants. Samantha waves her hand at me to hurry and when I'm close enough she grabs my arm and helps me the rest of the way by practically shoving me down into the hole beneath the floor.

The metal door closes over me, shutting out the only light I had which had been shining thinly through the single bedroom window from the streetlight outside. And then I hear the chest being moved back over the metal door and my heart sinks like a stone at the thought of being trapped down here, regardless of what's up there.

Make that one more thing that I fear, Victor: being trapped in a small space.

I hear Samantha's footsteps move across the floor above and then the sound of the bedroom door clicking closed once she makes her way out.

Everything is eerily silent: the heaviness of my breath, the pumping of blood through my ears; I can't hear either of them though I know both should be raucous in the small confined space that conceals me. I can't see a thing, so I reach my hands out in front of me and start feeling my surroundings. I painfully count three walls to my left, right and in front of me, but am relieved that behind me there is no fourth wall to keep me confined. It's a narrow hallway.

I don't have time to investigate it further when I hear the first gunshot, although suppressed like Victor's always sounds, but I know that this time it isn't Victor.

Pepper isn't barking anymore.

I hear a voice. It sounds far off but it echoes from somewhere above me. That's when I feel a small draft on my hairline and I reach up my hand to feel for the ceiling. There's a vent, though far too small of one for me to fit my head through much less the rest of my body, but it's a vent and I know now that's how I heard the echo of the voice.

There's another suppressed shot and this time when I hear the voice that succeeds it, I know that it belongs to Javier.

TWENTY-ONE

SARAI

"I have four bullets left in this gun," Javier says to Samantha some-where in the house. "And I'm going to put one in you every two min-utes that my sweet Sarai is still in hiding."

My hand comes up involuntarily and clutches at my heart.

"Victor is coming back," Samantha says in a weak, strained voice.

It fills me with dread to think of where Javier has already shot her.

"You lie, *puta*! You stink of lies. Now tell me where Sarai is. Because I *know* she's here."

How did he know I was here?

Then in Spanish Javier shouts, "Search the house! Every room. Turn it upside-down and find her!"

Two seconds later the sound of furniture being overturned, glass shattering and feet stomping across the floor echoes through the walls.

"She's *not* here," Samantha says as if pushing the words through her teeth. "Victor was here earlier. With a girl. A little black-haired girl he called Izabel. But he took her with him when he left."

Thwap!

Another shot sounds and Samantha screams out in pain, but then her screams are muffled and I can only imagine that it's by

Javier's hand. Or maybe someone else within the room. Tears stream down my hot cheeks. There's a chill in the air being so close to the cold ground outside, but my blood pressure is so high from the incredible amount of stress on my nerves that it feels like my head is on fire.

"I know she's here," Javier says coldly. "I know she didn't leave with him because I was watching. Now you have six more minutes. The last bullet I'll put in your brain."

Then Javier's voice rises:

"You hear that, Sarai?" he calls out to me. "In six more minutes you'll kill her. Just like you killed Lydia. All I want is to take you home. I could never hurt you, you know that."

My legs are shaking.

After the ransacking noises finally stop, the extra sets of footsteps, two judging by the pattern, move back into the room with Javier.

"Both of you go outside," Javier demands. "Look everywhere, search the neighborhood but don't draw attention. Go!"

I can't leave Samantha up there with him to die.

"I told you there's no one here!" she shouts.

The noise I hear this time I know is Javier's hand across her face and then her body hitting the floor. The floor beams shake above me with the force of her fall.

I turn behind me and start feeling my way through the narrow passage, hoping that it leads me out. Because I won't leave her like this. Javier can take me back. He can kill me if he wants to, but I won't hide under here like a coward and let her die for me.

Thwap!

My breath hitches and my bones lock up, but I keep on moving forward and finally come to the end. There's nothing here, nothing but more walls and the same passage I just walked through. I reach up above me and feel around on the ceiling for another metal door hatch. And sure enough, there is one. And just when I think there's no way I can lift that lid all the way and climb my way out without making enough noise to tell Javier exactly where I am, I stub my toe on a four-step set of moveable stairs shoved into the corner.

I pick the steps up instead of pushing them across the floor to avoid making any unnecessary noise and I set them underneath the hatch. Climbing to the third one, I have to bend over forward to keep from hitting my head on the ceiling. I reach up with both hands, pressing my palms against the hatch and close my eyes as I push, hoping that it's not blocked by anything and that wherever it leads it's not where Javier can see me.

The hatch opens, creaking once which makes me wince and freeze holding it partially open above me. I push again and walk up to the fourth step and my head emerges inside a closet. I see that a foam mattress pad had been folded over and placed on top of the hatch door to conceal it and there is carpet on top of the hatch that matches the carpet on the closet floor; I feel it with my fingertips as I raise the hatch the rest of the way and leave it to lean against the back of the closet wall.

I climb out and quietly push myself through the clothes hanging from the bar above.

Thwap!

"Two more minutes, Sarai!" I hear Javier warn from the living room.

I open the closet door and make my way more quickly now through Samantha's bedroom, down the hall and into the living room where Javier is waiting on me, every bone and muscle in my body trembling.

"Ah, and there she is!" Javier raises both hands out beside him, his gun latched in the right. He smiles and looks genuinely excited to see me. He's crazy.

His hands drop to his sides.

"I've missed you, Sarai." He cocks his head to one side to appear sincere. "If you were unhappy why didn't you just say so? I'd have done anything you wanted, you know that."

I don't care about what he has to say, all I care about is making sure that Samantha is all right. Trying to keep my eyes on Javier, my gaze carefully scans the room out ahead of me, looking for her.

Finally I see her bare feet sticking out from behind the recliner on the other side of the room, her skin stained with blood.

"Samantha, are you OK?"

She doesn't respond so I know she's hurt pretty bad.

I look back at Javier, pleading in my eyes.

"Let's just go. Please. Javier please don't hurt her anymore."

He smiles at me, thoughtful but amused.

He's wearing black from top to bottom: long-sleeved black shirt, black belt, black pants, black shoes. Black heart. He raises his gun at me and motions it for me to go over to him.

He curls his finger at me. "Let me see you."

I walk closer, my bare feet moving over the *Good Housekeeping* magazines scattered about the floor. The grandfather clock standing tall in the corner ticks ominously behind me.

"Javier, she's going to die if we don't call for an ambulance," I urge as I get closer. "Let me call nine-one-one. Then we can leave."

I see her knees now, but it's all that I can see as the rest of her is obscured by the chair and the darkness.

Javier reaches out his hand.

"Did he fuck you?" he asks and pulls me closer to him by my fingers. "Did you let him fuck you, or are you still mine?" He leans inward and inhales the scent of me, a loose strand of hair fallen from my ponytail he plays with in the tips of his fingers.

"No," I say breathily. "I'll always be yours."

He's wearing cologne, the same kind he always wore when he'd come to me in the night. And his hair, somewhat long on top, is clean and groomed, the way he always wore it when he'd dress me up and take me with him to the wealthy houses.

"Don't lie to me," he says quietly and I feel his breath on my neck. "You don't know what you've done to me. You shouldn't have left."

I reach up with my left hand and curl my fingers softly around the back of his neck. I lean into him, the side of my face navigating the opened buttons at the top of his shirt until I feel his chest on my cheek. "I know and I'm sorry." I kiss his skin lightly. "I am so sorry for leaving you like that," I add in Spanish.

I shudder, both from pleasure and from disgust, when he slides his hand down the front of my pants and puts two fingers inside of me. It doesn't matter that he's insane or that he's a murderer or that he might kill me any second, the touch still makes me wet. It's my body betraying me, human nature betraying me, not my mind or my heart. I had conformed years ago to react to him in this way. A twisted survival instinct that they don't teach in self-defense classes. Javier had to believe he was turning me on or he'd know everything else about me was a lie, too, and so my body learned to react in the way that it knew would keep me alive.

He pulls his fingers out and brings them to his lips, inhaling deeply, his eyes closed as if to savor it. Then he puts them in his mouth.

I take a step backward while he's distracted, to put as much distance between us as I can manage although small.

"I'm not sure I want you anymore," he says.

My heart hardens. If he doesn't want me then I know he'll kill me, especially after everything that I've done, all of the trouble that I've caused.

"Javier," I say, trying to hide the nervousness in my voice, "let's go. I'm ready to go back."

His top lip furrows and he shakes his head.

"Izel is dead," he says probingly, probably wondering if I did it. "I know you hated her. I don't blame you. But she was my sister."

I shake my head and start to back up some more.

"I-I didn't kill her," I say. "I didn't know."

Javier laughs.

I take another step back and two to my right, stepping on a sharp piece of plastic from some random object, but it doesn't break the skin. I press my hands against the wall behind me.

And then I see her, Samantha, much clearer from this angle. I abandon my dire need to watch Javier's every move as he approaches me slowly, tauntingly, and all I can see now is Samantha. She's not moving. She sits slumped over with her back against the wall. Her bloody legs are splayed out into the floor. Her arms lie limply on either side of her, her fingers uncurled.

Her eyes. They're open. And they're dead.

Bile churns in my stomach, my hands begin to solidify, hard like metal, down at my sides. I'm shaking all over from anger and hatred and guilt, and goddammit, *fear*.

"You *killed* her," I say, my lips trembling.

"I did," Javier admits proudly. "On the fifth shot."

"But you said…" I look to and from him and Samantha's body, my heart feels like it's closing in on itself. "You said if I didn't—"

Javier raises his gun at me, that last bullet I know now why he didn't use it on her.

I stand frozen, one hand still on the wall behind me, the other somehow made its way to my stomach as if it could keep the vomit down by being there. I stumble on more debris and then press my back against the wall to let it hold me up. Because my body is still betraying me, my legs weak and unstable, threatening to give way beneath me any second.

I stare across the small space separating Javier and I. I stare into his cold, bottomless dark eyes, not the barrel of his gun pointed directly at me, but his eyes. I hear a click, just a click, and we look blankly into each other's faces, confused by what just happened. Then a shot rings out and my head falls against the wall with my back. I feel my body sliding down until I'm sitting on the floor just like Samantha. Limp and spent, just like Samantha. The room spins around in my vision like a thick haze of gray.

And I close my eyes and let the darkness take me.

TWENTY-TWO

VICTOR

I'm forty thousand feet above the Texas landscape when I get the call.

"Victor," Niklas says into the phone, "Javier is not in Tucson. He was reported to have used a known credit card with an old alias, just outside of La Grange, Texas."

I raise my back stiffly from the seat.

"That's less than a two hour drive to Houston," I point out, more to myself. "At what time did the card process?"

"At three-twelve this afternoon."

My body becomes rigid.

Hanging up the phone, I crush it in my fist down at my side as I make my way to the cockpit.

"Turn the plane around," I demand.

Less than an hour later I'm driving through traffic heedlessly, I know drawing unneeded attention. But I speed on through, running a number of stoplights, not knowing how I managed to drive all the way back to Samantha's house without having to lose a cop or two in a high-speed chase on my way there.

There's a car parked out front on the street between Samantha's house and the one next door. I don't remember seeing that one before I left. With my gun in my hand, I stay low as I get out and rush up the driveway, using Samantha's car as a shield just in case. There are no lights on inside the house. It's unusually quiet. Samantha's dog would normally be tangled up in the window blind by now, trying to see out after hearing a vehicle pull up.

I hear another, larger dog, barking in the backyard of the neighbor and I stay crouched low, making my way underneath the carport and next to the car parked there.

One figure emerges from the side of the house just after I move silently across the space and make it to the brick wall underneath the carport. I grab him by the throat too fast for him to react and throw him to the ground. His gun hits the concrete and in that same moment, I put a bullet through his temple before he has a chance to seize it.

Another man calls out a name, looking for the man I just killed. I don't wait for him to come around the side. I step right out in front of him, raise my gun to his face and get my shot off before he sees me fully. His body hits the grass.

I wait only seconds in case there are anymore and then I rush inside the house through the side door underneath the carport.

The house has been destroyed; Samantha's dog, shot to death on the kitchen floor. I smell gun smoke, blood, freshly brewed coffee and unfamiliar cologne.

The first body I see is Samantha's. The second, Javier's.

"Sarai?" I say when I see her sitting against the wall, partially hidden by the darkness. I take off my black gloves and shove them inside my jacket pocket and go over to her. "Sarai?"

She doesn't look up at me, so I crouch in front of her.

The gun I left underneath her mattress lies next to her foot. I slip it into the back of my pants. Her knees are drawn against her chest, her hands lay palm up beside her on the floor.

"He's dead," she says, her words distant as if she's still trying to process the truth. She raises her eyes to me; pain and confusion and disorientation reside within them. "I killed him, Victor."

I reach out and lift her into my arms.

"I'm going to get you out of here."

Holding her close to my chest, I carry her through the death and debris and out of the house. She doesn't speak, but she holds onto me as if she's terrified I'll drop her. Or, perhaps, terrified I'll intentionally let her go.

I set her carefully in the passenger's seat.

Three police cars fly past toward Samantha's house one block over as we leave the scene, doing the speed limit this time around.

Sarai is quiet and motionless, emotionless, all the way back to the private airport where the jet awaits us.

There's only one place to take her now. Home. To *my* home on the New England coast.

My driver picks us up from the airport hours later. Sarai rode all the way to my cliff-side beach house with her head pressed against the backseat window. She never moved. It's the first time since I found her in my car in Mexico that I would welcome her chatty one-sided conversation and annoying questions. But I get nothing from her. And I find myself silently yearning for it.

The first kill is always the hardest, the one you never forget. But the first kill is also what drops the chances of living a normal life by half.

Sarai is no longer in the fifty-fifty zone.

I shouldn't have left her there…

Carrying her across the cobblestone driveway and into the house, I take her inside and lie her down on my sofa. It's been a month since I've been here and it still smells as clean as the day I left and set out on a job to kill a man in Colombia. It is because of jobs like that one that I can afford such luxuries. But it's a shame that because of what has happened with Sarai that I will have to leave here soon, too. I thought perhaps I'd get to stay in one place for at least a year this time, but such is the life I lead, a dark and lonely path lined only with the solitude of death.

Sarai lies on her side, her head propped against a couch pillow.

I remove my suit jacket and drape it over the back of the chair next to me and then start to go into the kitchen to get her some water, but her voice stops me cold.

"The gun jammed."

Standing in the arched kitchen entrance, I turn to look at her across the expanse of marble tile and expensive furniture. I walk toward her again, slowly, breaking apart the button of my shirt cuff.

I wait patiently for her to go on. She still doesn't look at me; she stares out ahead of her seeing only the scene as she relives it.

"I'd be dead if it weren't for that."

I walk closer, still keeping my distance as though some part of me doesn't want to disrupt her thoughts with my presence. I break apart the button on the left cuff and roll up my sleeves.

"I froze," she says, remembering it. "I thought I was dead. I just stood there waiting to die." She moves her head backward just enough to finally see me. "I don't know how I reacted so fast, but when his gun jammed…that look on his face…next thing I know the gun in the back of my pants is in my hand and Javier is on the floor. I didn't hesitate. It was like someone else was inside my head at that moment. *She* was the one who grabbed the gun. *She* was the one who pulled the trigger. Because I didn't realize what had happened until it was over." She looks away again. "I killed him," she adds distantly.

"He deserved it," I say calmly.

Her head snaps back to see me again, making me think that when she looked at me moments ago, she wasn't really seeing me at all. It's as if my voice just woke her.

She raises up from the couch.

I watch her curiously in a vague, sidelong glance. I glimpse her hands shaking and the corners of her mouth trembling. She curls her fingers toward her palms until her hands are balled into fists. And then she lunges at me.

"You left! You bastard! You left!" she cries out, beating her fists against my chest as hard as she can.

I let her. I stand motionless and let her until she can't do it anymore and her body starts to fall exhaustively at my feet. But I catch her before she hits the floor, wrapping my arms around her small frame. She sobs into my chest, choking on her tears, grasping the seams of my suit vest with her trembling fingers. "You left," she repeats over and over again until the words fade into a whisper on her lips. "*You left...*"

I hold her tight. Awkwardly. Because I've never done this before. I've never experienced this type of sorrow and pain and have been the one to be expected to help mend it. My mother was the only one who had ever held me like this when I was a boy and I can't remember the way it felt.

I feel like I want to press my lips against the top of her hair. But I don't. I have the urge to squeeze her a little tighter and take her completely into me. But I can't. I just can't bring myself to do it.

"Sarai," I say, gently pulling her away so that I can see her eyes. "I need you to tell me what happened. Tell me everything. Did Samantha make any phone calls? Did she receive any strange calls that she made mention of?"

Sarai's expression distorts offensively.

"You think *she* had something to do with this?" She pushes herself away from me. "She died *protecting* me! How could you think she had anything to do with it?!"

I sigh deeply. "No, I can't believe that she did. Samantha was trustworthy. But she and Niklas are the only two people besides you and me who knew where you were." I step forward and place my hands on her upper arms in an attempt to make her understand, and when she doesn't push me away I'm relieved. "It had to have been one of them and I'm only trying to get the facts."

"Then it was Niklas," she hisses angrily at the thought of him. Her eyes are wild and narrowed. "He hates me, Victor. He hates it that you've been helping me. He all but said so when I was in the SUV with him. I *know* it was him!"

I step away from her, my hands falling away from her arms and I cross one arm over my stomach, propping the other on it. Rubbing my hand over the short scruff of my face, I contemplate the situation. Sarai is right. Niklas is the obvious answer and although often the obvious turns out not to be the answer at all, this time it must be. Because it's the only thing that makes sense.

My brother betrayed me.

TWENTY-THREE

SARAI

"What are you doing?" I ask as Victor starts for his jacket on the chair.

He reaches inside the pocket and pulls out a cell phone I've never seen him use before and punches in a number.

"I'm going to bring Niklas here."

Stunned, at first I just look at him. But then I start to panic inside. I rush toward him, grabbing him by the elbow.

"No, you can't let him know where we are," I say breathily. "Why bring him *here*? What are you going to do?"

My mind is frantic with scenarios, none of which I can envision ending happily.

I zip my lips when he holds up his hand to hush me as Niklas answers on the other end of the phone.

"Javier Ruiz has been eliminated," Victor says, as calmly and professionally as any other time I've heard him speak to Niklas.

"Yes," he answers a question I can't hear but I still dumbly push my head forward a little as if it'll amplify the volume in some way. "Police arrived at the scene before I made it out of the neighborhood. It was not a clean kill." He listens to Niklas for a moment and goes on, "I believe Samantha led them there. The girl was alive when I arrived just before I took Javier out. He had shot her, but she managed to tell me that she overheard Samantha on the phone with someone just after I left for Tucson. Yes. No, Samantha is dead. Inform Vonnegut that Safe House Twelve has been compromised. A Cleaner should be sent there immediately to confiscate her files. Yes. Yes." He glances at me. "That will not be necessary. The girl died of her wound. I left her there."

My stomach twists into knots. I cross my arms over it.

"Niklas," he says, dropping the professionalism in his tone a degree. "Come to my New England location as soon as you can. We will get the payment squared away and then…I wish to tell you what happened in Budapest."

I tilt my head gently to one side upon hearing those last words. Everything else that Victor told Niklas, I understand it all for what it was: a lie, a ploy to get him here. But the last part felt real, personal. The fact that he said it in front of me strikes me as peculiar. I know it has nothing to do with me, so why would he include it in this particular conversation? It's in this moment that I begin to understand that Niklas is something more to Victor than his liaison, more than someone he works with and that whatever happened in Budapest needs to be said because his conscience needs to be cleared.

That's what people do when they say their goodbyes.

I don't know why, but despite Niklas trying to get me killed, I feel this pain and sadness inside. Because I know what Victor is going to do. I know he's going to kill him. Yet, I feel like it's the last thing that he wants.

He sets his phone on the glass end table next to the chair and breaks apart the buttons of his vest.

"I have nowhere else to go," I tell him from the couch again. "I know I've been a burden and I'm sorry. Samantha told me that you're risking everything, even your life to help me and I don't have anything to give you in return. Other than my gratitude and I know that's not much."

I sigh and add, "And I'm sorry about Samantha."

He tosses his vest and afterwards his tie over the back of the chair with his jacket.

"It was my decision to help you," he says while untucking his dress shirt. "And Samantha was a good woman."

"Did she love you?"

I fold my hands together within my lap.

"No," he says, not looking at me. "She wanted to, but she was incapable."

My brows wrinkle in confusion.

"Incapable of love?" I ask. "No one's incapable of that."

"You can't fall in love with someone who isn't there," he says matter-of-factly. "I left before she had the chance."

"Did you love *her*?" I mentally hold my breath.

"No I did not. Love is an impediment in this business. It'll only get you killed."

Although his answer leaves a bitter taste in my mouth, I can't deny that maybe he's right. Though I think about how Victor, or any-one for that matter, could go through life without loving someone. But then I realize that I've never loved anyone, either. At least, not in the conventional way.

"And I know you have no place to go," he adds, "but when this is over and I know you're safe, you will have to be on your own. I will help set you up, give you a decent start." He stops and looks at me intently, his eyes locking on mine as if to seize my undivided atten-tion. "But this ends soon. You've been with me too long already as it is."

It feels like suddenly he's angry with me, or at least angry with himself for helping me. Maybe it has to do with whatever's going on between him and Niklas, I could never know, but since his phone call with Niklas, Victor is different.

And it fills me with dread.

He turns and walks through a marble archway that leads to another part of this massive house. In a way it reminds me of the places Javier used to take me all dressed up and on his arm, but this house, although massive from what I've seen, is smaller than the others were. And darker, with dark cherry hardwood floors so shiny I can see my reflection, and covered with expensive rugs of the deepest reds and browns and grays. Tall rust-colored curtains dress the expansive windows that cover the entirety of one wall from ceiling to floor and overlooking the turbulent ocean below. Even outside the beach isn't a bright ocean-side paradise with white sands and blue skies. Here it's gray and gloomy and the waves crash angrily against the rocks many feet below, yet it's not even storming.

For the next several hours, Victor stays out of sight. I don't feel like he's intentionally ignoring me, but I know that he wants to be alone.

I think a lot about Samantha. And Lydia. And Izel. And Javier. I've seen so much death. I killed a man tonight, yet, the only thing that picks at my mind more is the fact that I'm already over it. For the most part, that is; I still can't get it off my mind. I still see Javier's dark, almost black eyes staring back at me with that jammed gun in his hand. I still shake—I'm shaking right now—when I think about pulling the trigger, when his eyes followed mine all the way down until his body hit the floor. And I'll never forget what he said to me just before he died:

"I knew you had it in you, Sarai."

And I hate myself for it, but I…well, I feel an out-of-place sense of sadness over Javier. A void. That part of me which grew to accept him as being the only life I had, whether I wanted him to be or not, misses him. I guess because I was used to him after so long.

"Sarai?" Victor's voice snaps me out of the memory.

I look up at him standing over me. I never heard him walking up, or noticed his tall form approaching the couch, I was so absorbed.

"Niklas will be here in about twenty minutes," he says. "You'll need to stay out of sight. You'll go in my room and keep the door closed. Is that understood?"

"Yes."

I hate how cold he feels again, just like he felt when I first met him. All traces of empathy and openness that I felt grow within Victor over the time we've been together are gone.

"What are you going to do?"

"What I have to do."

He walks past me wearing a long-sleeved black pullover shirt and black pants. It's refreshing to see him dressed in something so casual after only ever seeing him in suits. He is attractive in whatever he chooses to wear, I admit to myself.

I follow him to whatever part of the house he's going.

"Victor?" I call out behind him, but he just keeps walking. "I-I could help you." I can't believe I'm saying this. "Have you ever… trained anyone? You know, to be like you?"

Victor stops mid-stride underneath the entrance of some spacious, marble-floored room out ahead.

I see his shoulders rise and fall. Then he turns to me.

"No," he says, "and I never will."

He leaves it at that and walks into the room where I continue to follow, and once I'm inside, the beauty of it takes my breath away. There are four life-sized statues of Greek women wearing flowing gowns, standing tall in all for corners of this round, dome shaped room. To my right another wall-sized window overlooks the turbulent ocean and in front of it, sitting proudly on display is the most beautiful piano I've ever seen.

I try to tear my eyes away from it.

"But why not?" I ask, coming up behind him. "What else am I going to do with my life? I can't go back out there. I have no education, didn't even get to graduate. I have no friends, no family, no work history. Victor, I don't even have a real driver's license or a birth certificate and social security card. I have *no* identity, at least not a legal one."

He leaves the room with the piano, walking through an exit on the other side and I stay close behind him.

Now we're in a smaller side room with a ceiling-to-floor bookshelf situated on the back wall, filled to the brim with books—mostly leather-bound—and an antique-looking black lacquer desk on one wall. A leather recliner sits in the center of the room with a small table and lamp beside it.

"You can get those things back," he says walking toward the table beside the recliner. "It will take some time, but you can get them. As far as an education, you can get a GED, go to a community college." He glances at me and adds, "It will be hard, but it's your only option."

He takes a writing book of sorts from the table and begins flipping through the edge-tattered pages.

"But that's not what I want," I say. "I want to...do what you do. I know it sounds ludicrous but—"

"It *is* ludicrous," he says, snapping the book shut in his hand. "The answer is no. It will always be no, so do not waste your time or mine going on about it anymore."

He walks past me again.

And I follow him out again, through the room with the piano and back into the living room area.

He starts to leave me standing here again, but I stop him.

"I want to stay with you."

With his back to me, he just stands there, quiet and immobile as though my admission stole his movements and voice away. I didn't mean to say that out loud, but I felt it was the only thing I had left with which to throw at him.

For a long moment, I think he's going to respond, even if only just to tell me no again and lecture me about how I don't know what I'm talking about or what I'm asking. But he says nothing. And then finally rounds the corner heading back to his room.

Feeling defeated, I sit down on a barstool in the kitchen and watch the video surveillance television fixed inside the wall; one screen split four ways to show four different areas of the property simultaneously. And each individual square also changes to another camera every few seconds to show yet more areas of the property.

Minutes later, a sleek black car, much like the one Victor had that I hid in when leaving the compound, pulls up to the front gate.

Victor, probably watching the same screen in another room, comes into the kitchen.

"He's here," he announces and gestures for me with one hand. "Remember what I said—stay quiet and don't come out of my room until I tell you."

I nod nervously.

My stomach is swimming again, my heart already beating twice as hard as seconds ago.

I get down from the barstool and walk quickly into Victor's immaculate room where there's, unsurprisingly, another wall sized window. A massive king sized bed is pressed against another wall, dressed by black and gray bedding pulled tight over the mattress so that no wrinkles or imperfections can be found. It seems that's the case in every room I've seen thus far: devoid of imperfections and signs of even the slightest disarray.

Victor shuts the door behind me and I try to mentally prepare for what is about to happen.

TWENTY-FOUR

VICTOR

When Niklas and I were just boys, before we were taken by The Order, he was my best friend. We fought a lot, hand-to-hand, always trying to size the other up, and although we both often came out with bloody noses and once a broken wrist, nothing could make us turn on the other. We would walk off the battlefield, carrying on about what we thought our mother's would have waiting for us for dinner when we got home. And we'd wake up and attend school the next day with matching black eyes.

The ones I gave him were bigger, of course, but then Niklas would say the same about those he gave me.

After we were taken by The Order, things between us began to change. Vonnegut, although rarely ever making a face-to-face appearance—and that hasn't changed even today—said that I showed promise. But he said nothing about Niklas. And the first time I saw Niklas' face when Vonnegut promoted me—younger than any assassin he had ever promoted—to Full Operative when I was just seventeen-years-old, I saw something in Niklas that hardened me against him: a jealous heart.

I knew at that moment that one day I might be forced to kill him.

Niklas is the only family that I have left. And as much as I wish it didn't have to be this way, that I could be wrong about him and go back to the way things were, I know that's not entirely possible. The truth is, I have been watching my back where my brother is concerned since last year.

And our father is to blame for that.

I suppose I should've listened to him.

I meet Niklas at the front door. He walks in, calm and collective as always except when he's angry with me for having my own mind and choosing to do things the way I see fit.

I shut the door behind him.

"This is a much nicer place than the last one," he says, looking up at the scaling ceilings with his hands folded together behind his back.

I find myself privately studying his features, looking for traces of me and our father in him. We have the same eyes, though his are bluer than mine; mine tend to appear more green at times than blue. His face is rounder, mine slimmer. But I think what separates us the most are our accents. Our father and his mother were both German. I was born in France, my mother a French spy for The Order. My father moved us to Germany when I was two-years-old and I did not meet Niklas until I was six. I helped him learn to speak English and French, but he did not have the knack for linguistics that I had and so he never was able to fully lose the accent. But despite the differences we have, I still see only a younger version of me when I look at him. Especially right now as I try to grasp the fact that I'm going to kill him. I don't want to. I want to walk away from this and forget that it ever happened, but that's not an option.

He smiles at me.

We have the same smile, too. I remember our father telling me this.

"Yes," I say about the house, "I thought it was time I slept in something more upscale. I hoped I might get to stay here for a while."

"Has that changed?" he asks curiously, having reason to believe that judging by my tone.

"Unfortunately."

I gesture toward the living room. "Let's sit down," I say and he follows. "We have a lot to discuss."

He takes the chair next to the marble side table.

I remain standing.

I sense that he wonders why I don't sit down as well, but the curiosity disappears from his eyes and is replaced with attention when I begin.

"Niklas," I say, "last year on my mission to Budapest, I wasn't being entirely honest with you."

Niklas laughs lightly, adjusting his back against the chair. He props his left ankle on top of his right knee and interlocks his fingers in front of him, his elbows propped on the chair arms.

"Well, that wouldn't be the first time," he says, still smiling as if this is any other casual conversation between two brothers. "You never were one to tell even me your secrets."

"I went to see our father," I announce.

The smile drops from his face. He turns his chin slightly at an angle, clearly confused by my admission.

"He sent for me," I add.

"What for? Why would he send for you, Victor? After all those years of never seeing him once, why would he send for you and not me?"

I don't answer. I find it more difficult to tell him the truth than I imagined it would be. I always knew it would be hard, but not this hard.

"Victor?" Niklas' eyes are filled with concern and…pain.

He stands up from the chair.

"Just tell me, brother, please."

I swallow hard and take a steady breath.

"Niklas," I finally go on, "your mother was eliminated by The Order because proof was found that she was selling information. You already know this." He nods. "But after that, because she was your mother, The Order could not trust you. Even Vonnegut felt you were unstable, that one day, sooner or later, you would avenge your mother's death and betray The Order."

He continues to listen, his face shadowed more and more by pain and rejection. And it kills me inside to see it.

"I went to Budapest to meet with him," I say and can no longer look at my brother. "He spoke with Vonnegut and they both agreed that you should be eliminated even if only as a precaution, to prevent the inevitable. I was given the order to carry it out."

Niklas' head snaps around.

I meet his eyes.

"Vonnegut, of course," I go on, "did not know that we were brothers and being his Number One, he knew I could carry out the job also because we were so close, you as my liaison. Father wanted me to be the one to kill you because he felt it would be the honorable thing, that if anyone should take your life it should be me because we are family and no other should have that privilege."

Niklas can hardly get his thoughts together. He can barely speak, but finally manages and when he does, it hurts my heart as much as his expression continues to do.

"Father wanted you to *kill* me?"

"Yes," I say gently.

He starts to pace the floor and then brings his hands up to the top of his head, pushing them roughly over his hair. He looks across at me, his eyes brimmed with tears. I have never once in our lives seen my brother cry. Never. Not even when we were children, or when his mother was killed.

I grind my jaw, forcing my own tears back. I grit my teeth so hard that I feel the pressure in my skull. But I keep a straight face, as much of one as I can manage.

"Then why *didn't* you?" he lashes out. "Why am I still alive? Tell me that, Victor." The first of his tears streams down one cheek and he reaches up instinctively to wipe it away, angry at it for betraying him. "You should've killed me!"

"I refused," I say. "You were the one job I could not carry out, Niklas. And so then Father had only one thing left to do: he was going to do it himself."

Niklas' body freezes rigidly, more hurt by this truth than the truth before it. Another tear escapes from his eye, but this time he doesn't have the mind to wipe it away.

"I killed him," I finally say. "Father told me that I would have to because it was the only way he wouldn't finish the job. So I shot him where he stood."

He can't look at me. I feel the conflict within him, his mind and heart trying to choose which emotions to feel and which ones to reject: his hurt for what our father did, or his love for his brother, because both are too much to take on at once.

I go on:

"Being Vonnegut's Number One, I convinced him to spare your life and made him believe that our Father was unhinged, paranoid, and that was why I had to kill him. I told Vonnegut that you were trustworthy and that I wanted a chance to prove that to him and the rest of The Order. I vowed to take full responsibility for you—"

"Full re—," he glares at me, "full *responsibility* for me? What, am I a goddamned child? Everything I have done since I was seven-years old, I've done for The Order. I am the one of us who always did as I was told, who never questioned Vonnegut's orders, who has never given him or anyone else reason to question *me*!" He clenches his hands into fists at his sides. "I have strived to become like you, Victor, to be respected and trusted and showered with the same glory Vonnegut has showered you with since before you were promoted Full Operative! I have done nothing to warrant—"

"You've been lying to Vonnegut for me for years, Niklas. What's not to say that you wouldn't turn against me when the time was right? You've pretended to be Vonnegut's trustworthy soldier, his liaison waiting to be promoted Full Operative, all the while lying to him whenever I asked you to."

"Is that what this is about?!" He points upward and then drops his hand aggressively back at his side. "Have you been testing me all this time?! That's what you've been doing! Isn't it?!"

"No," I say. "I would never use you like that, Niklas. I killed our father to save your life. Why would I then risk your life by setting you up?"

He has no answer. He just stares at me, confused and hurt and angry and not knowing what to do with any of it. He collapses back into the chair, his legs splayed out into the floor, his upper body slouched forward resting his forehead in his hand.

"Why are you telling me this now?" he asks, raising his eyes back to me. "What made you decide that today was going to be the day you turned my life upside-down? Did you just wake up this morning and say to yourself: 'Today I think I'll mindfuck my brother because I have nothing better to do'?"

"I felt I owed it to you," I say. "You should know the truth before you die."

He looks faintly stunned, as if trying to figure out if he heard me right.

His hand drops away from his forehead and he straightens his back against the chair.

"What do you mean?"

"Niklas," I get right to it, "I know you told Javier Ruiz where I hid the girl. Where *I* was with the girl."

His eyes wrinkle with confusion.

"What are you talking about?"

I walk a couple steps, my hands now behind my back to appear to be resting there. My gun is hidden safely in the back of my pants.

"When you called me while I was on my way back to Tucson, you said that the time of Javier's last known whereabouts was at three-twelve in the afternoon." I cock my head to one side. "Why did it take you seven hours to give me this information?"

He still hasn't flinched. I'm beginning to find his ability to act more effective than I gave him credit for.

He thinks about the question for a moment. "I called you as soon as I found out myself. Victor, you know we don't always get that kind of information right when it occurs."

"Maybe so," I say. "But you and Samantha were the only two people who knew where I was and where I planned to leave the girl."

He points at me, his expression twisted with disbelief. "But you told me Samantha was the one. You said the girl told you that Samantha got a call…"

"I lied."

He still hasn't flinched.

Is he telling the truth?

I raise my gun to him.

Niklas' eyes widen and he puts out his hands toward me.

"Victor, I didn't betray you. I swear to you on my life, I told no one *anything!*"

My finger presses carefully on the trigger.

"You are my brother!" he shouts. "I have always done what you asked, kept your secrets, played your game between Vonnegut and the orders he gave you! I would die before I betrayed you!"

When Niklas' eyes avert behind me, I know that Sarai is standing there.

"I told you not to come out." I keep my eyes on Niklas.

He looks back and forth between the two of us, his features riddled by shock and betrayal.

"You said she died."

"I lied about that, too."

I press the trigger a little more.

"So who's lying to who then? Who's been betraying *who*?!"

Back and forth his eyes dart.

"Victor! *It. Wasn't. Me!*" he roars. He's more angry than scared, his face twisted with heartbreak and disbelief, his hands clenched tightly into fists at his sides. "I won't beg for my life. I won't do it, brother. If you must kill me then kill me, be done with it, but know that I did *not* betray you!"

In the last second, I lower my gun and catch the breath I've been holding for the past few minutes.

Then I sit down in the nearby chair and slump against it.

Silence fills the room. I've never been so confused in my life about anything.

"I think he's telling the truth," Sarai says softly behind me. I feel her there, standing with her fingers draped over the back of my chair. For a moment, I almost reach up and touch them.

Finally I raise my eyes to Niklas and say to Sarai, "I believe he is, too."

"How is she alive?" Niklas asks, more concerned with her than the fact that I've decided not to shoot him. He seems to be looking at her more now than me. I can't tell yet what level of discontent he's feeling about this, but maybe once the shock wears off I'll be able to read his face a little easier.

"Samantha didn't tell Javier where we were, either," I say. "I only told you that to get you here because I was certain you were the one. You were the only one *left.*"

"Samantha was killed trying to protect me," Sarai speaks up.

I wish she'd just stop talking and go back into the room.

"Javier killed her," she adds with sadness in her voice.

"And Sarai killed Javier before I got there," I say.

Niklas stares at us for a long time, perhaps still trying to fit all of the pieces together in his mind, and likely still feeling stung by my deceiving him the way I did to get him here.

"Fine," he says, slashing the air in front of him with his hand. "Samantha didn't do it, but neither did I."

Sarai's fingers move from the back of the chair and touch the back of my shoulders, likely involuntarily because she's so nervous. For a moment, I find myself wanting her fingers there, but I get up quickly before my brother gets the wrong idea, if he hasn't already.

"What is all this about?" Niklas asks. "Tell me Victor; what has this girl got to do with you?" He starts pacing again, looking back at me every so often, his mind in overdrive. "You went to Mexico to hear Javier's offer, to see whose offer was worth the contract—his or Guzmán's. And then on the way out, you find a stowaway in your car who clearly belonged to Javier Ruiz—"

"I don't belong to *anyone*," Sarai says acidly. "And my name isn't girl, it's Sarai."

I put my hand up to her and she stops talking, but her harsh gaze grows darker looking across at Niklas. She crosses her arms.

Niklas glares back at her, but he says to me, "I've already reported the lies you told me to get me here to Vonnegut." He sits back down in the chair. "You know as well as I do that to retract that story will raise all sorts of questions. You can't keep her hidden forever. You might as well have formally requested a new liaison because they will assign someone else to you simply because of our 'miscommunication' if that's what we choose to tell him." He shakes his head at me, a faint smile of disbelief at his lips. "You've done all of this, you've lied to The Order, you've put the entire mission in jeopardy, destroyed it actually, all because of this girl..." He sneers. "Safe House Twelve was compromised because of her."

Niklas looks right at Sarai standing behind me and without having to see her myself, I can sense the resentment boiling within her.

"So many are dead because of her," Niklas says. "Samantha. That girl back in Arizona. Reports were that she was only sixteen-years-old. Dead because of...*Sarai*." He smirks.

I see Sarai's long reddish hair whip behind her as she rushes past me. I could have reached out and stopped her, but Niklas deserves whatever retribution she can manage to dish out before he knocks her on her ass.

TWENTY-FIVE

SARAI

My face burns with contempt, tears pouring from my eyes in droves as I bolt across the short distance toward Niklas.

I don't care that he looks both surprised and faintly amused as I lunge for him, swinging my fists chaotically in front of me at his face.

In a flash, I'm on the floor on my back and Niklas is crouched on top of me, his hand pressed around my throat, rendering me unable to catch my breath. I claw at his wrist with both my hands and try to kick him but there's no way I'm moving from this spot. He glares down at me and moves his hand from my throat to my cheeks, seizing my jaw with his fingers like a vise-grip. With his other hand, he pins my wrists together, forcing them against my chest. He turns my chin to one side and then the other and I taste the chemicals leftover from his aftershave as his index finger presses against the edge of my lips.

"Get *off* me!" I growl under the weight of his hand.

"Niklas," Victor says calmly from behind. "Leave her be."

Niklas' blue eyes bore into mine and he holds me here in this position for three more excruciatingly long seconds before doing what Victor said.

I try to catch my breath when he releases me, but I think mostly I just hold it longer until he has moved away from me completely.

J.A. REDMERSKI

I raise my back from the floor, but stay sitting on it. I'm so hurt, so outraged at Niklas for the things he said, but my pride hurts worse than anything.

Because I know he's right.

I look at the floor rather than at either one of them. I don't want them to see the shame and guilt on my face although it would be evident to anyone that it's there.

"Niklas," Victor says calmly, "I am sorry to have compromised you."

I look up instantly. I feel a mood shift in the room and though I'm not exactly sure which one, I can tell by the pause in Victor's voice that it's something life-changing.

"We could devise a plan," he goes on with Niklas' undivided attention. "Let Vonnegut believe that Sarai is, in fact, dead—"

"Or we could just kill her to make it true."

I jerk my head sideways to look at Niklas, who's looking right back at me with the same condescension.

Victor shakes his head, objecting to his mordant, yet entirely serious proposal.

"We could devise a plan together," Victor continues in the same stoic tone, "or I could do it on my own and you can walk away and not be any part of it."

Niklas' eyes grow wide, his body locks up firmly. He seems at a loss for words. And so am I. I may not understand how these kinds of things work in their business, but I don't really need to know that what Victor just proposed is something very dangerous. It's suicide.

I manage to pick myself up from the floor.

"You have a choice," Victor says. "Go along with my plan to tell Vonnegut that she's dead, or tell him the truth, tell him everything that went on here to secure your place in The Order. I won't hold it against you. I'll take her away with me, set her up somewhere so that she can go on with her life. And then I'll go on with mine. It's your choice, Niklas. But I won't kill her, and if Vonnegut finds out that

184

she's alive, he will, rightfully so, question my loyalties. And you know first-hand what happens when any of our loyalties is questioned."

"Eliminated as a precaution," I say out loud, though mostly to myself, remembering what Victor said moments ago about why they ordered Niklas dead.

Niklas is in shock. He shakes his head repeatedly as if trying to shake Victor's treacherous words out of his mind.

"You of all operatives," Niklas manages to say, "...I don't understand why you're doing this, why you would throw away everything and go into hiding—" He shakes his head again, unable to finish the sentence.

"It wouldn't be the first time I risked my position and my life to follow my conscience rather than my orders."

Niklas takes in a deep breath and averts his gaze toward the ceiling. Then he looks at me and we share a moment suspended within this intricate web of lies and contempt and resentment, a moment where, despite all of that, we realize we have something in common: Victor saved us both equally, and for that we are one in the same.

Simultaneously, we look back at Victor.

Niklas finally breaks the thick silence.

"As I've always said, brother, I'll never betray you."

Victor nods and I see the relief hidden within his green-blue eyes. I wonder if he would've killed Niklas where he stands if Niklas had chosen to take the alternate route.

"I'm with you," Niklas says and glances at me once. "Whatever you want to do. But before we do anything we need to figure out who told Javier where you took her."

When Niklas' eyes fall on me again they stay there, and I suddenly feel like he's blaming me.

My eyebrows wrinkle in my forehead. I cross my arms tight over my chest. "Well, I sure as hell didn't tell him," I bark. "Don't look at me like that."

Victor walks between us and takes me by the wrist, leading me to the nearest chair where I sit willingly. My stomach swims nervously. I look up at them, my hands gripping the ends of the chair arms.

"It wasn't me!"

"I know it wasn't you," Victor says. "But I need you to think right now, Sarai. Have you at any time spoken to anyone since you left the compound? Anyone at all. Have you seen anything that maybe didn't seem right, something seemingly insignificant?"

I shake my head, my index fingers making a nervous circular motion against the cherry wood grain grooves in the design of the chair. "I-I don't know," I say breathily, desperately trying to come up with something, *anything* that he could be looking for.

But I can't.

"Victor, I-I don't think so."

He paces once and then looks over at Niklas. Then as if he was just slapped in the face by a theory, he turns his body swiftly back to me.

"Take off your clothes," Victor demands.

My heart stops.

"What?"

"Sarai, take off your clothes." He pulls me up from the chair by my hand. I try to wrench it away from him, but he applies more pressure.

"I'm not taking my clothes off!" I slap him with my free hand, right across the left side of his face.

He grabs my wrist. "I need you to trust me. I've brought you this far, now do as I say and take off your fucking clothes."

His uncharacteristic use of that vulgarity shocks me into compliance. My eyes dart back and forth between them again, my jaw tightening, my breath heavy and short expelling from my nostrils.

"Fine," I say, jerking my hand from his. "But not in front of him."

Victor takes me by the wrist and walks with me past Niklas and toward the entrance to his room.

"You have nothing I want to see," I hear Niklas say just before Victor shuts the door.

I already feel naked standing in the wide open of Victor's spacious ocean view room and I haven't even taken my clothes off yet. I want to linger as long as possible, drag it out so that maybe he'll change his mind or at least tell me what this is all about, but he wastes no more time. And he doesn't let me waste any more of it, either.

"Take them off. Now."

I start with my shirt, pulling it over my head and exposing my bare breasts. I drop the shirt on the floor beside my feet. He watches me, not with lust in his eyes, but with determination. I lean over and slip out of my pants and all that is left are my panties.

He steps right up to me.

I hesitate. The space between us is about two feet but it feels like two inches. I don't want to take off my panties, not because I'm afraid of him, but because…I'm embarrassed for him to see me that way.

When he steps up closer and doesn't demand I take the panties off, I breathe a silent sigh of relief.

"Lay down on the bed," he says and that breath is sucked right back into my lungs again before it can expel completely.

When I don't act fast enough, he wraps his hands around my upper arms and gently pushes me down against his expensive designer comforter.

I swallow a lump in my throat.

As I start to raise my arms to my breasts to cover them, I feel Victor's warm hands on me. I freeze, my eyes wide and unblinking. He raises my arms above my head and begins to feel every inch of my skin, pressing his fingers along the underside of my arms first and then down toward my ribs before making his way to my breasts.

His eyes catch mine briefly.

Maybe he wanted to ease my fear of him with that glance, but all it did was make me want him to touch me more.

J.A. REDMERSKI

The guilt of that thought sears through me. But the touch of his hands on my breasts, kneading only a small portion of them with his fingers, does something entirely different.

I picture his mouth on my nipple…

I force that ridiculous thought away and I watch him, his intent eyes and how deftly, yet at the same time, aggressively, his hands move across every inch of my body. Furtively I inhale the scent of his skin, his natural scent that somehow makes me want him to kiss me. He leans up and away from me, but he isn't done. He goes for my thighs next, starting with the left and kneading his fingers around the flesh using both hands. And then the other thigh.

When his fingers touch the sensitive skin of my inner thighs, right at my panty line, I gasp.

He stops. He looks up at me, across the naked landscape of my body. I can only wonder what he's thinking, but this time I get the feeling his gaze isn't to ease my fear of him, but instead to study my reaction to his hands being on me, so close to the most intimate part of me. I wonder why he would study my face at all, why he wouldn't take my obvious reaction and reject it by moving his hands away as I expected him to do. But instead, he leaves them there, the pad of one of his fingers I feel grazing the flesh at the bend of my leg just on the edge of my panties, conflicted about what he should do, what he might *want* to do.

He pulls away and abruptly flips me over onto my stomach.

"What are you doing exactly?" I ask, adapting to the quick change of the moment.

He pulls my panties down halfway over my butt cheeks, moves his hands here and there in the same manner and then back up to my hips.

"I'm looking for something."

"*What?*" I ask.

Then suddenly he stops, his thumb moving in a circular motion on one particular spot just above my right butt cheek, on the back

188

part of my hipbone. The same general area where I removed his bullet.

"A tracking device," he says. "You have one."

I try to twist my head around to see him better, but it hurts my neck.

The flash of a silver blade catches my eye. I panic when I glimpse the knife in his hand and start to twist my body awkwardly. But he holds me down, putting the weight of his hand on the small of my back, the hand with the knife wrestling with my left shoulder.

"What are you going to do?!" I shriek.

"I have to cut it out."

"Victor, no!"

I thrash around more violently, trying to roll over onto my back so that I can get up. Suddenly he's lying fully on top of me, and his closeness, the warmth of his breath on the side of my neck, takes my breath away. My entire frame solidifies beneath him and then begins to relax, melting into his body as his voice dances along the shell of my ear.

"I will be gentle," he whispers and my skin shivers from my ear down the full length of my spine.

He presses himself into me from behind, his hardness obvious behind the thin layer of his pants that separates us.

"I promise," he says onto my ear. "But it has to come out. Do you understand? Do you trust me?" He presses his hips toward me again and I feel me moving against him involuntarily. I shut my eyes when the tingling sensation between my legs moves through my back and into my eyelids.

"Yes," I whisper. "I trust you."

"Good," he says softly and slowly raises himself off of me.

I remain very still, thinking so much more about Victor and what he just did to me than the more imperative threat. A part of me doesn't even care about what he's going to do, that he's about to cut into me with a knife, that it's going to hurt like hell. And perhaps that's the only reason he did what he did, knowing somehow that he could control my mood, my emotions, with the hope that he might touch me more than he already has. I feel like a toy and Victor knows every button on me which to push, to touch, in order to make me do whatever he wants, feel whatever he wants me to feel. And I don't mind. I don't know how he did it, but I don't mind at all.

"Bite down on the pillow if you have to," he says.

I reach up and grab the nearest pillow, crushing it against my chest. I squeeze my eyes shut tight.

The blade goes in and I yell out in pain before burying my face within the pillow, my entire body hardening like a block of cement.

In seconds, the device is out and Victor stands at the foot of the bed looking down into the space between his bloody fingers at something as small as a grain of rice.

With his free hand, he reaches for the towel he used to dry off with after his shower, which had been lying on the floor nearby. He hands it to me. "Put pressure on it to stop the bleeding," he says and walks across the room into his bathroom.

While I press the towel on the back of my hip, I hear the water running in the sink and then the sound of him rummaging through his medicine cabinet. With one hand holding the towel in place, I get up from the bed to find my shirt, letting the towel drop only long enough to slip it on.

Victor walks out of the bathroom with an orange pill bottle clasped in his fingers and walks right past me and to the door.

TWENTY-SIX

VICTOR

"Niklas," I say coming out of the room, "does this look familiar to you?" I step right up to him and hold out the pill bottle with the tracking device inside.

He takes it into his fingers.

I hear soft footsteps behind me as Sarai emerges from my bedroom, but I keep my attention on Niklas.

He peers into the side of the bottle first but then twists the cap off and shuffles the device into the palm of his hand.

He looks up at me.

"Same type of device they use in the girls in Dubai," he says. He glances at Sarai. "You found this in her?" Then he drops it back in the bottle and tightens the lid. "I hate to ask where."

Niklas sneers and wipes his hand on his jacket.

"If it is one of theirs," I say, "this means that Javier Ruiz has a much larger operation than any of us knew. I've never known of a drug lord like Ruiz to have access to this kind of technology."

"They don't care about technology," Niklas says. "All they deal in are drugs, weapons and girls."

"Had," Sarai says and I turn around to see her. "That Javier *had* a much larger operation. He's dead, remember?"

"Yes," I say, "but that doesn't mean his operation is. It means that it'll be passed on to whoever else was in line to control it."

"Well what does that have to do with us?" Sarai asks.

I feel the urge to tell her to put on some pants while in front of Niklas, but I stop myself.

"There is no us," Niklas says.

Sarai glares at him and readjusts the bloody towel against her hip.

"Then what does it have to do with *me*?" she snaps. "Or, with either of you?"

"It has nothing to do with you," I say. "Not anymore. You were Javier's and if he had sold you or promised you to another buyer you wouldn't have been in his possession for as long as you were. He had no intention in letting anyone else have you. Now that he's dead you have nothing more to fear." I pause. "As far as what it has to do with us—." I stop right there, knowing better than to tell her any more than she already knows or I'll only put her in further danger with The Order.

And judging by the look on Niklas' face I've said too much already, in his opinion.

He slips the pill bottle into his jacket pocket.

"I'll get rid of it," he says, then without moving his head I see his eyes avert to Sarai for a split second. His hatred for her seethes beneath the calm and disciplined façade he's wearing. "So then what's our next move? Will I be covering for you with Vonnegut, or are you going rogue?"

I know what answer he wants me to give and for now, it's what I choose to do.

"Tell Vonnegut that I'm ready for my next mission," I say, making up the specifics as I go along. "And to put this house back on the market. We'll be leaving in the morning."

Sarai glances over at me with a look of confusion. Niklas nods and accepts it, because unlike her, he knows that this house has been compromised by the tracking device he's carrying in his pocket. Javier Ruiz might be dead, but the device is still in working order and someone is and has been monitoring its locations since Sarai escaped the compound. It is how Izel found us so quickly in the motel in Mexico. When I contacted Javier and gave him my location to come for the girl, Izel had arrived half an hour sooner than she should have given our distance from the compound. At the time, I assumed she had already been on the road with her men searching for us, and in fact, she had been. But I did not know until now that it was because she already knew where we were.

It was also because of the device that the two men came into the store pretending to be customers and speaking to the store owner in code. Given the fact that I killed all of the men that came with Izel the first time, I presume that Javier Ruiz wanted to play it safer by sending only two the second time. They were merely sent to gather information and to follow us until Javier devised a better plan.

When I took Sarai over the border it was more difficult to keep up with us. I imagine that he had sent more men to follow, possibly even to ambush us at some point, but that never happened and I have to believe it was due to us already being in the United States. It was even difficult for Javier to get through border patrol and he has powerful sway even with some corrupt American officials.

"I will contact you as soon as I get your new orders from Vonnegut."

Niklas steps up to me.

He strips away the unemotional liaison part of him and appears more like my brother now.

"I am sorry for what our father did," I say to him.

Niklas lowers his eyes briefly.

"I will do anything to protect you because you are my brother," he says. "Just as you did for me."

We share a quiet moment of understanding, nod and part ways.

"He hates me, as I've said before," Sarai speaks up from behind. "But he is loyal to you."

I had been staring out the large window from across the room, lost in thought listening to the waves crash against the rocks.

"Yes," I say. "He is."

She steps up to me and places her hand on my wrist.

"You couldn't have known," she says. "That it wasn't him. But that doesn't matter now. I think you cleared the air with your brother in more ways than one."

"Perhaps," I say and walk away. "But I can't concern myself with that right now." She follows me back into my room. "We should discuss you."

I enter the bathroom and she stands at the door, the towel still pressed against her hip.

"Get over here," I say.

She does without question.

I put my hands on her waist and turn her around to face the mirror. Instinctively, she props her hands on the edge of the counter, letting the bloody towel fall to the floor. Tucking my fingers behind the elastic of her panties, I slip them down over her hips, letting them rest halfway at the center of her bottom.

"Where would you like to go?" I ask as I open the closet. "I will set you up wherever you'd like, but we need to do this soon. I expect to have my new orders before the end of the day tomorrow and I won't have much time to spare between taking you where you need to go and when I must leave."

I come back over with my medical kit and set it on the counter.

Sarai doesn't answer at first, perhaps she's deciding on a place, but my gut tells me that's not the case at all.

I can see her reflection in the mirror, but she doesn't raise her head to look back at me.

"But I want to stay with you," she says cautiously. "I've already told you, I have nowhere to go, no identity—"

"And I have told *you*," I remind her, "that all of that can be remedied. You pick the place and I will take care of the rest. For now, you have the driver's license I gave you."

I clean the knife wound with peroxide and cover the area all around it with iodine. She barely winces from the stinging pain.

"I don't need your help settling me into a life I no longer want," she says.

I push the needle in and start to stitch her up. Not even this pain, although faintly obvious on her face, can deter her from the things she wants to say. I had hoped that it would, but her determination is unshakable right now.

"I used to dream about it," she says, her eyes raised to the mirror now but all she sees is the reverie. "Though I could hardly remember what Arizona even looked like, I used to picture me living in that god-awful trailer with a boyfriend and friends next door—real inspiring dream, I know," she mocks herself. "But that place, after a while, was all I could remember. I would've given anything to be able to go back there and continue with the life that was stripped from me. But after the third year or so with Javier, I stopped dreaming about it. I gave up wishing that I could find a way to escape. Slowly over time I learned to accept my life the way it was. I hated it at first of course. I hated Javier. I hated that even though he never raped me, at least not like you expect rape to happen; he knew at first I was unwilling, that I only gave in to him because I was afraid and yet he still had sex with me and I say that's rape. But I hated him and I hated that I gave myself to a man that I did not want."

I glimpse her throat move in the mirror as she swallows down the painful memory and she pauses before she goes on, trying to recollect her thoughts.

"At some point," she says, "I even stopped hating him. I-I know that sounds crazy, and-and-and I *never* loved him," she stutters over her words and I sense she's conflicted about the things she saying. "But I stopped *hating* him…"

She catches my eyes in the mirror.

"Does that make me sick? I mean…" she licks the dryness from her lips. I thread the last stitch and clean the area again with alcohol, only glancing away from her long enough to make sure of my technique. "I mean, because I stopped hating him, does that mean there's something wrong with me?"

She desperately wants me to tell her no.

I slip her panties back over her stitches and go to wash my hands.

"It means that you're human," I say.

Trying to avoid her desire to remain with me, I leave her standing in the bathroom and offer no more of my own thoughts on the matter.

But she's relentless and follows me out.

I continue about my business, intent on getting some much needed sleep. I remove my shirt and step out of my pants, flipping the light switch off as I walk past, leaving the room bathed in a dark blue hue.

"Victor," she says softly from behind. "Please take me with you. I've told you before, I can help. You can teach me, train me to be whatever you think I'd be good at."

"You don't really want that, do you?" I ask, knowing her better than she knows herself. I pull back my comforter and sheets and slip into my bed. "You just don't want me to leave you. Alone in the world. Free to be what and who you want, to make your own decisions. To have sex with men of your choosing. To have a normal life. Because it's foreign to you." I pause. "If I told you to kill someone for the sake of a job, you wouldn't be able to do it. You couldn't bring yourself to kill any human being in cold blood, knowing nothing of their crimes or their families or even why they are being killed. You could never become like me. No amount of training could make you a murderer, Sarai." I lie down fully upon my pillow, bringing the sheet up to my waist. "Now get some sleep. We'll be leaving at six a.m. and I expect you to have chosen a place you'd like to go by then."

She looks defeated. Beautiful and soft and damaged standing there before me partially clothed in the light of the moon beaming through the tall window. Beautiful, but defeated. That look in her eyes, it somehow latches onto my soul and all I want is for her to turn and walk away. Because I know that if she doesn't, if she presses me further with those soft lips and sad, vulnerable eyes that I'll succumb to the moment and either fuck her or kill her.

She turns and walks toward the door.

I stop her.

"Sarai," I say, but she doesn't turn around. "You never accepted your life with Javier, or you wouldn't…be here with me now." I had started to say: *Or you wouldn't have killed him*, but decided against that.

She says nothing and closes the door on her way out.

I lie here staring at the thick clouds covering the sky and I think about the things I told her, the *lies* I told her.

She *could* kill in cold blood. Every part of me tells me that she can and that she *would*. In a way, it pains me to believe it, to know that her innocence was taken from her so long ago and that although she still has a decent shot at living a normal life, the fact that she chooses to want *my* life, is difficult to swallow.

It's difficult mostly because I almost want to give it to her.

TWENTY-SEVEN

SARAI

I listen to the thunder and the rain for an hour, unable to fall asleep. Despite the weather it's so quiet in this house, so spacious and empty. Empty in nearly every sense of the word. I lie against the cool sheets in the spare bedroom, watching the dark clouds churn in the sky through that enormous window. I hear the waves crashing below and see the endless ocean in an eerie flash as lightning streaks across the turbulent sky.

Empty.

This house. My soul. Victor's soul. It's the only word suited for the way I feel, the way that I believe Victor feels, though him more-so than me.

How can anyone go through life so surreptitious, emotionless, so unattached to anyone or anything? When I look into his eyes I see *something* there, although dormant and completely indistinct, I know it's there. And it's powerful. I want to understand it, to feel it, to taste it on my lips.

As the thunder begins to fade as it moves off in the distance, the rain fails to a soft drizzle. I can't hear it anymore, but I can still see it streaming against the glass in poetic rivulets. The chill in the air raises goose bumps on my bare legs even underneath the covers, evoking visions of Victor lying next to me to help keep me warm.

I decide to get up.

I feel foolish and reckless for what I'm about to do, but I don't care. If he's going to get rid of me tomorrow, what does it matter how this turns out?

My bare feet move quietly across the hardwood floors and then through the center of the house. Placing my reluctant fingertips on the door lever outside Victor's room, I pause before pushing it down gently. The door clicks open and I walk inside. I see him across the large space, lying on his back, his head fallen to one side, facing me. His eyes are closed, his breathing steady. The sheet covers only his midsection and thighs, leaving the rest of his naked body exposed to the chill in the air. I recall earlier in the night when he was on top of me, pressing himself into me from behind and it makes my stomach and hips quiver.

I move closer, trying to stay as quiet as possible but at the same time wondering why be quiet at all. He's going to know I'm in here eventually, and well, that's kind of the point.

Stepping up to the side of his bed, I watch him for a moment, how his toned chest rises and falls with every quiet breath. How his lips are unopened, pressed gently against each other, signifying that whatever he's dreaming, if he's dreaming at all, it's peaceful, undisturbed by the violence that eclipses his life. Like me, the nightmares of his experiences have long since vanished, leaving only a morbid sense of normality to which nightmares no longer deem fit to visit.

I slip off my shirt and drop it on the floor.

Pressing my hands and knees against the bed, I crawl onto it, straddling his waist.

In only a second, the back of my hair is wrenched in his hand and his gun is shoved underneath my chin, forcing my neck backward so far that I fear if I move it'll snap.

I don't say a word, but I'm not afraid. I don't know for sure if he would kill me or not, but I don't fear him either way.

He winds his fingers tighter against my scalp and I feel the cool barrel of the gun trailing down the center of my neck. But more than that I feel his hardness between my legs and the knowledge of the gun being anywhere on me takes a backseat.

"If you're going to let me go," I whisper, unable to see his eyes, "then let me have this one last thing from you."

He pulls my head back even farther. The gun is pressing into my stomach now.

"I've never been with a man that I *wanted* to be with," I say. "I *want* to be with you. Just once. I want to know what it feels like to be the one in control."

He's conflicted, I feel it in the heat emitting from his skin, in his tense, uncertain movements. In one instance the gun digs deeper into my gut and I feel like my hair is about to come out within his hand. But then he relents, loosening his grip just a little, allowing my neck some reprieve. I can see his eyes now, peering up at me so deadly and yet so seductive even though I know he's not doing it on purpose.

"You can't be in here," he says, also in a whisper.

I feel his eyes on me, sweeping over my body, my bare breasts, downward to where my naked thighs are latched loosely around his hips.

"I don't care, Victor."

His gaze moves back to my face where he studies the curvature of my lips.

Then I witness something else flash over his eyes, something frightening that I've never seen before in him and I tense up within his grasp. He studies me quietly as if I'm something to be ravaged and then ultimately…killed. Despite my growing fear, I still want to be right where I am, trapped in the merciless arms of a killer.

Without releasing me he raises his back from the bed, the arm with which his hand is speared painfully within my hair is pressed against my shoulder. I sit straddled on his lap, my naked thighs touching his sides which warm my skin in the same way I pictured it. I can tell that he is completely naked underneath that thin sheet that separates us.

"If you want to kill me, then do it."

His lips move closer to mine.

"But if you do," I say breathily, "let me be with you first, please…"

My eyes close of their own accord. I wait for whatever is going to happen; death or sex I welcome both, my body stiff against his, my heart beating so fast I feel it in my head and in my fingertips. When I feel his lips brush against my own, I wilt.

But when I feel the cold metal against my temple, my eyes slowly open to look into his again.

"This can't happen, Sarai," he says.

I lower my lips to his. "Yes, it can," I whisper onto them before covering them with my own.

My thighs tighten around his waist and I feel myself pressing against his erection, tremors moving through my pelvis and down into my knees. I lift myself up and yank the sheet from between us, setting myself back down on his naked lap, instantly feeling the stark difference the sheet made. I grind myself against his cock, feeling his hardness through the fabric of my panties and it makes me tremble.

But I can tell he doesn't want this. He doesn't push me away, but he's conflicted.

"Please, let me have my way with you," I say, looking down into his beautiful eyes.

He searches my face, his fingers gently touching my cheeks, a look of uncertainty in his features as though this exchange between us is something entirely new to him. I can tell that he's probably never been with a woman he could not ravage and spoil and tame. And while I think I prefer him that way, right now in this moment I want to be the one who makes all of the decisions.

I'm unsure why, but that doesn't matter.

I feel his body relent even more.

I press the palms of my hands against his rock-hard chest and push him gently against the bed, hoping that he'll let me.

He does. He lies down, leaving his hands to rest on the tops of my thighs. We look at each other and no words are spoken. They aren't needed. Tucking my middle finger behind the elastic of my panties, I slip them off one leg at a time, and I never move my eyes from his.

Feeling him between my legs, skin on skin, alone is overwhelming. I lay forward, wanting all of him, the warmth of his chest against mine, the heat of his breath against my neck. *Everything.* I kiss him hard and deep, his tongue tangling with mine in a dance of dominance, his fingers pressing into the back of my head until he drags one hand down the length of my body and to my hip. He squeezes it, thrusting his hips toward me. He wants the control so bad, but I remind him that it's mine by pushing my hips back against him and holding them there.

When he gives back the control, I peck him lightly on the lips and then both sides of his jawline.

He watches my face, glimpsing my lips, wanting to taste them.

And then I start to cry.

I always cry when I'm angry.

I'm becoming someone else, that girl lost at fourteen-years-old, forced to live a life of bondage and pain and broken dreams. Flashes of Javier's face go through my mind erratically. I feel like I'm on a merry-go-round and it's spinning so fast, all of the faces of Javier come and go before I can reach out and grab one. I can't get my hands on just *one* so that I can beat it to death. And I just cry harder, screaming out into the night and before I realize what I'm doing, Victor has become the face of Javier that I can't otherwise catch. I swing my fists at him, beating him over and over again on the chest and on his arms and he doesn't stop me. Because I know only he can understand why I need this moment so desperately.

Yelling into the night, I let it all out. Tears barrel from my eyes.

I collapse on him and he engulfs me in his arms. I can't catch my breath as I sob into the crook of his neck.

TWENTY-EIGHT

VICTOR

Beautiful but defeated and damaged. Damaged for the rest of her life and no amount of emotional mutilation will ever fully give her back her innocence. The girl is a ticking time bomb, a danger to herself and very possibly to others. I wasn't sure before, but now I know that she is more unstable than I ever could have imagined. And because she is so skilled at hiding it, not only from me but also from herself, she is more dangerous than I am. I am discipline. Sarai is rage. I am aware of my choices at all times. Sarai's choices are more aware of her, lying in wait to decide for her based on the severity of her mood with no intention in leaving her any conscious control over it.

I know what I have to do.

I cradle the back of her head in the palm of my hand, my gun resting beside me on the bed in the other. I feel her tears soaking my shoulder, her body wracked by sobs that coalesce into my muscles. And her sweet spot still presses against my cock every time her body tenses. But I leave her there despite the moral need to pull away.

"Sarai," I whisper against the side of her head, "I am sorry."

I raise the gun slowly behind her.

She tilts her head and lies her cheek against my chest and I pause, waiting, though I don't know for what. Her sobs begin to settle, her left hand drawn up near her chin where her fingertips rest lightly against my collarbone.

"I have an aunt in France," she says softly, distantly. "My mother's older sister. I know France is a long way, but you don't have to take me there, just help me get on the plane."

I raise the gun a little higher, settling the barrel at the back of her head, but not touching it. I don't want her to be afraid before she dies and although I know she fears nothing, death is something we all fear in our final moment even if only the smallest part of us is conscious of it. I don't want her to fear it at all and she can't if she doesn't know that it's happening.

"How old were you when you became what you are?" she asks.

Caught off guard by the question and maybe more-so by the shifting of the mood, I hesitate before answering.

"I was nine."

She sniffles and wipes her eyes with the hand near her cheek.

"You were very young," she goes on. "I guess in a way like me, you never had a chance to live a life of your choosing. I guess maybe we aren't really so different from each other." She pauses. "Except I might be more like your brother than I care to admit. He's as angry as I am."

I release my finger from the trigger and slowly, so she doesn't know, move the barrel away from the back of her head.

"It must've been hard growing up with Niklas," she says.

I set the gun back on the bed next to me and before I know what I'm doing I'm cradling the back of her head in my hand again.

"Yes," I answer, "considering the unconventional circumstances."

"Instead of who's the better baseball player it was who's the better killer."

"No," I say. "Niklas never tried to be better than me, he only wanted to be my equal. We never competed with each other, but he's been competing with everyone else who has ever been close to me for as long as he's been alive."

"Close to you?" she asks.

I nod and lightly comb my fingers through her hair.

"Vonnegut, Samantha, my mother, our father," I say distantly as I picture these events, staring up at the scaling ceiling. "And now you."

I hear her sigh, but she doesn't raise her head.

"You see that you have one thing that I don't," she says carefully, though I get the feeling she's saying it more to herself. "You have someone who loves you and who is loyal to you and who will kill for you." She raises her body from mine and stands up from the bed. Then she looks down at me. "You are very fortunate to have him, Victor."

She takes her panties from the end of the bed and slips them on. Then she picks up her shirt from the floor and pulls it over her long disheveled hair and over her breasts.

"I am grateful," she says looking back, "for everything you've done for me. I guess in the end none of it will really matter, not saving my life, or sparing it. But I'll always be grateful to you."

Sarai leaves my bedroom, but in a sense she has taken me with her.

For a length of time unknown to me, I stare up at the ceiling, picturing the way she looked before she left, how she used me to take revenge on Javier. In the beginning, I know she didn't come into my room for that. She wanted to be with me. She wanted to feel something she's never felt before, but rage and vengeance were not part of her plan. Self-destruction was not part of her plan, and despite using that moment to release some of the hatred inside of her, the only thing I sense that it did was make her realize just how fucked up she truly is.

The dark, melodic sound of the piano carries softly through the house, breaking me from my trance-like daze. The piece stops three times and begins all over again as she tries to get the keys right. On the fourth try, her fingers move more confidently over the keys, fluid and careful and perfect. And before long I find myself standing beside my bed and stepping into my underwear. The piece carries on, so elegant and beautiful and heart-wrenching that it draws me from my room and I'm helpless to fight against it. I take the hallway in a quiet stride, following the sound. The music gets louder, *Moonlight Sonata* in its most sorrowful interpretation yet, filling the vast, empty space all around me.

I stand silent and still at the arched entryway leading into the piano room. And I watch her unlike I've ever watched her before. She owns me in this moment.

I close my eyes and let the music course through me; shivers sweep over my skin like faint ripples on the water's surface.

But I'm awoken from the lure all too quickly.

The music stops as Sarai becomes confused by the keys. Although disappointed that it came to an end so abruptly, I stay where I am hoping that she'll pick up where she left off and finish the piece out. Her soft form appears vulnerable, fragile in the faint moonlight enveloping her from the window, a halo-like light around her body, illuminating the ends of her hair.

Please, just play it, Sarai. Don't think about it, just play it.

She starts again from where she stopped, but after a few keys she gives up. Frustrated with herself, her upper body arches forward, her hands gently touch her forehead.

I sit down beside her on the bench.

"I'll teach you," I say, arching my fingers on the keys. "If that's what you want."

She turns her head to look at me and as she does, I know that she's wondering if I'm only referring to the music.

She nods slowly.

I start from the beginning and play the piece all the way to the point where she stopped. And then she tries again. And again, until my guidance sees her through and she's in control of the keys the way she was before, the way she brought me into this room. It haunts me, every somber second of it, so much so that my closed eyes brim with tears, but only my heart can manage to shed them.

The piece ends at the end this time and silence fills the space around the two of us.

"I don't want to sleep alone," she says gently.

And I don't force her to. Sarai falls fast asleep curled up next to me in my bed. Right where I want her.

TWENTY-NINE

SARAI

When I wake up the next morning the sun is bright through the massive window even though the curtains have been drawn. I'm alone in the bed, but I know I'm not alone in the house. It was Victor's dress shoes tapping against the floors outside the room that woke me. My heart is exhausted, but my mind and my body feel refreshed. I can't remember the last time I slept that soundly.

I don't think I ever have.

I raise my body from the mattress, untangling myself from the sheet. I can't believe I did that last night, but I did and it's over with and I can either face Victor and not be ashamed, or hide away inside this room for the rest of my life.

I choose the realistic.

As I step outside of the room, I wonder why we didn't get up before dawn to leave like he had planned.

He's sitting in the living room alone when I walk in, fully dressed in his best suit with his usual bags sitting on the floor next to his feet, minus the bag with the money. There's a newspaper in his hands and a mug of black coffee on the table next to the chair.

"Why didn't we leave earlier?" I ask walking the rest of the way into the room.

He lowers the newspaper and then decides to fold it halfway and set it on the table next to the coffee.

"I thought you could use the sleep."

My face flushes inwardly, failing at my attempt to not be ashamed of my sexual tirade, but really I doubt his answer had anything to do with that.

"Thank you," I say.

I raise my eyes to him again. "Looks like you'll have to buy me another pair of shoes," I point out, pressing my bare toes into the cool, hard floor, my hands clasped together lying on my backside.

The shoes he bought me before had been left at Samantha's when we had to get out of there in a hurry. I've not had the best of luck with shoes as of late.

"It has already been taken care of," he says crossing one leg over the other and straightening his vest.

I gaze around the room, looking for department store bags or maybe some women's clothes that had been left here for whatever reason.

A short middle-aged woman wearing a navy blue scrub uniform comes through the front door carrying a gaudy purse on one arm and several oversized store bags on the other. A set of keys jangle in her hand after she closes the door with her hip. She manages to drop the keys into her purse, twisting her wrist awkwardly to reach it.

"Oh, you must be Izabel," the woman says bright-eyed. "I'm Ophelia. It's nice to meet you." I nod and introduce myself even though she apparently already knows my name, well the name that Victor gave me, anyway.

She drops her purse in the middle of the floor and walks across the large space into the living room toward me, the store bags still dangling on her arm and by the looks of it, starting to cut off the circulation.

"You were right about the size," she says looking to Victor. She sets the bags down on the immaculate couch. "And I have a daughter your size," she says looking at me now, "so hopefully I chose wisely. Meleena was a handful growing up, that's for sure." She gestures her hands dramatically. Rings adorn her fingers. "Of course, it was my fault for raising her on Versace and Valentino but she is the most envied girl when she walks into any room, so I suppose the shit she gave me and my bank account was worth it. Here, let me see you." I try to conceal the awkward look I know I'm giving her as she pulls a cute sun dress of sorts from one bag and holds it up against me.

I decide to look across at Victor instead, hoping maybe he'll tell me exactly who this woman is and what she's doing here.

His eyes smile at me.

I do a double-take. *Did he just* smile *at me?*

"Perfect fit," Ophelia says.

But then she sets that dress aside and begins to pull other items of clothing from the same bag. The next bag is full of gift boxes where she opens each one and unwraps an outfit engulfed in extravagant tissue paper and tulle that probably cost more than it should. As she goes on and on about her spoiled, yet 'deserving' daughter she goes through each and every outfit, holding them up against me as if to imagine what I might look like in them. Or, perhaps, picturing what 'Meleena' might look like in them.

She is very odd, that one.

"Of course, after her father left us, I had to get a job," Ophelia shakes her head and looks right at me as if her having a job is the most unfortunate thing ever. "So to support Meleena and her expensive fashion sense, I went into the business. Here, try this one on. It's a pretty day so you should wear something that suits it."

"What business exactly?" I ask.

I turn around so that my back is facing them and then I slip off my shirt. I barely look at the dress Ophelia is holding out to me, more curious about her, really.

Victor sips his coffee and pretends to be reading his newspaper. Or, maybe he's not pretending. I can't tell with him half the time.

"Housekeeping," she answers.

I'm a little confused and I'm sure she can tell that.

"You can…afford to buy Versace and Valentino on a housekeeper's wage?" I ask incredulously. "No offense."

"None taken," she says, slipping the dress over my head. "But yes, I can. I only work for those who can afford to pay me. Celebrities, musicians; you know, people who have more money than they know what to do with. Wealthy people are quick to hire someone to do the pettiest of things just because they can. I profit from their foolishness." She glances back at Victor. "No offense."

"None taken," he says and takes another sip of his coffee.

"Ah, I see," I say as the cool, thin fabric rolls down over my skin. I turn around once I'm dressed.

"Yes, I'd say this one is just right," she says, propping her hands on her hips, looking me up and down. "Though you should wear a strapless bra at least."

Ophelia reaches inside another bag while glancing over at Victor. "Looks like you were right about her cup size, too," she says and I feel my face flushing again.

I guess he would have a pretty good idea of my size, considering.

"The undergarments were the only pieces I had to stop and buy on the way here. Raided the rest of it from my daughter's room. There's a purse and a few other necessities in there too." She puts the bra in my hand. "I bet there's enough money in the stuff she's never worn in her room to buy a Bentley."

I put on the strapless bra she gives me after ripping off the tag and she helps me to fasten it in the back since I seem to be having so much trouble doing it myself. Then she zips the back of the light pink floral lace dress against my back and I attempt to admire myself in it. It's very short, stopping a few inches above my knees. And it itches around the high neckline. I'm not used to wearing things like this, at least not anywhere but a few hours at a social gathering where all I had to do was stand there quietly and look pretty. With Victor, I seem to do more running for my life than standing around quietly.

Next are the shoes.

"I-I don't think anything with heels on them are a good idea," I protest kindly as she opens the first box.

There's no way I'm wearing those. Gorgeous shoes, yes, but it's not happening.

Ophelia looks to Victor again. He nods to her as if telling her that it's OK.

She closes the top on the box disappointedly and opens another one.

"Not exactly what I would've chosen to wear with this particular dress," she says, "but they match at least."

She places the cream colored thong sandals on the floor in front of me and I step into them. The bra is uncomfortable—any bra likely would be after not having worn one for so long—digging into the skin underneath my arms. I try to fight the urge to adjust it, but lose that battle after six seconds. I know I must look very unladylike right about now, pulling at the tight elastic with my arms drawn up and my face wrinkled by discomfort. When I think I've managed to fix it, I relax my arms down at my sides and stand here awkwardly.

"You look nice," Victor says from the chair, the newspaper resting on his legs.

So do you...

"Thanks," I say and look away.

I've never been so afraid to make eye contact with him before. The humiliation is stronger than I thought. The more he looks at me the more paranoid I get about what's going on inside his mind right now. I don't know what got into me last night. I went into his room with passion and lust in my eyes but at some point that I can't possibly determine, I turned into a psychotic masochist.

But he *let* me. And I'm not sure how to feel about that. I know he didn't get any pleasure out of it and I wouldn't expect him to, but the only one of us who seems to feel awkward about it is me.

Victor stands up from the chair and leaves the newspaper on the table. He reaches into his pocket and pulls out a roll of cash.

"For your daughter's clothes," he says, placing the money into Ophelia's hand. "And there's enough there to pay for your time as well."

She drops the roll into her own pocket.

"So I guess this is it then," Ophelia says. "If you ever decide to move back into this area you know how to find me. My rates will stay the same for you."

Victor nods.

"I will do that," he says.

Ophelia turns to me with a big close-lipped smile.

"You keep him in line," she says. "And just try the heels. You'd look fabulous in them."

I smile back. "I'll think about it."

She pats me on the arm as she walks past, taking up her purse from the floor on her way to the front door.

Long after Ophelia leaves, I'm still looking at the door, not with her on my mind, but I can't bring myself to look at Victor.

He walks around in front of me and fits my elbows in his hands. I stand with my arms crossed loosely over my stomach.

"Sarai," he says.

I raise my eyes to look at him and before he can say whatever it was he had planned to say, I blurt out softly, "I'm so sorry for... Victor, I'm not crazy or...well, I'm really sorry."

"Don't be," he says.

I just look at him.

"You play beautifully," he goes on. "Have you ever considered playing professionally?"

Many long seconds go by before I manage an answer.

"I did think about being up on a stage somewhere," I say and his hands fall away from my elbows. "But I really have no interest in anything like that anymore. I just like to play for myself."

To avoid eye contact again, I walk over to the couch and start arranging the clothes in a neat pile on the cushion.

With my back to him, I go on:

"I don't have any idea what I'll do when I get to my aunt's, but I'll figure something out. An education of sorts and then after that maybe I'll go into..." I can't finish because I don't know what to say. I dodge it, fidgeting the fabric anxiously in my hands now. "At least I'll look nice when I see her. Maybe she'll accept me now that I'm wearing clothes that didn't come from the half-off rack at the dollar store."

"Can you promise one thing?" Victor asks.

I turn to look at him.

"I guess I owe you that much," I say. "What?"

"Just that you'll play for me from time to time."

"What do you mean?"

He leans over beside a bookshelf and takes another suitcase into his hand. Then he walks toward me and sets it down on the couch, flipping the two latches on the sides.

When he opens it, it's empty. He points briefly at my pile of clothes.

"Our plane leaves in an hour," he says. "From here on out until I tell you otherwise, you are Izabel Seyfried and you are confident in your skin. You are strong-minded and sharp-tongued but you let me do all of the talking except when you feel the need to state your opinion on whatever matter you choose, even when it's not asked for. You fear nothing, yet you exude a sense of vulnerability that you know, privately of course, will drive a powerful man's need to know what it's like to be the one to break you. You are wealthy, though no one needs to know where your money comes from, only that you have enough of it to wipe your ass with one hundred dollar bills every time you take a shit. And the only man in any room that can tame you is me, which we will, almost certainly, have to demonstrate at least once during this mission. So keep in mind that whatever I do to you, play along accordingly. And whatever I tell you to do, do it without question because it could be the difference between life and death. Do you understand?"

I stare at him blankly.

"You're taking me with you?" There are about fifty questions swirling around inside my head, but that's the only one I could pluck from the disarray.

He steps up to me. "Yes," he answers. "I'll take you with me on one mission because I want you to see what it's like. You need to understand that the life I lead is not the life for you." He takes my hands into his and sits down with me on the couch, pushing the suitcase aside. "Hopefully, this will help you to be more accepting of a life out there instead; one with college and a job and friends and boyfriends."

He encloses his fingers around my hands more firmly and I begin to gaze beyond him, thinking about what he said, about his reasons for doing this. Momentarily, I wonder which one of us he's trying to convince.

"Sarai, listen to me carefully," he says. "If you choose to go with me you need to know that you could be killed. I will do everything in my power to keep you safe, but it's not a guarantee because no matter how much you trust me, you should never, under any circumstances trust anyone fully. In the end, you can only trust yourself. I am not your hero. I am not the other half of your soul who could never let anything bad ever happen to you. Trust your instincts first always, and me, if you choose, last."

I nod apprehensively.

"So what will it be?" he asks. "France or Los Angeles?"

I don't really have to think about it because I know what I want, but I pretend to think about it to make me appear less irrational.

"Los Angeles," I say letting out a breath.

Victor gazes into my eyes for a moment, a look of contemplation and even a bit of wavering settles on his expression.

He stands up and straightens his suit.

"Then pack your things," he says as he walks away. "We leave in ten minutes."

THIRTY

VICTOR

I had hoped she would choose France, but I knew she would choose to go with me. I could still very well take her to France and set her up with everything she needs and my conscience would be clear. But I bypassed the meaning of rational where Sarai is concerned a long time ago. She may very well die in Los Angeles, but I gave her a choice. I all but spelled out the potential consequences of her decision. I didn't exactly tell her everything, but there is a method to my madness. I can't allow her time to contemplate what she might do because in this business sometimes a life or death decision comes when you least expect it. And that is the kind of scenario she needs to experience.

Perhaps a part of me hopes she doesn't make it through the mission because then I will be free of my…shortcomings when it comes to her. But the other part of me, the part that I'm still struggling with that brought her with me as far as I have…

That's an entirely different issue.

If she lives then I'll find it necessary to confront it.

If she dies…If she dies then I will go back to my normal life and never find myself in a situation like this again.

"His name is Arthur Hamburg," I say, laying a manila envelope on Sarai's lap next to me on the private jet. "He owns Hamburg &

Sthilz, the most successful real estate agency on the west coast. But his most lucrative business is more underground."

Attracted by my silence, she looks up from the photo she removed from the envelope.

"What is his other business?" she asks, as I knew she would.

"It doesn't matter," I say. "The information that I choose to give you is all that you need."

She cocks her head to one side. "But *you* know more," she accuses.

"Yes, I do," I admit. "But as your employer, you never ask questions about the personal nature of any mark unless you're unclear as to how you're going to eliminate him. What he does for a living, who his wife is, his children, if he has any, his crimes, if he has any of those, they don't matter. The less you know about his personal life, the less of a risk there is for you to become emotionally involved. I give you a photo, tell you his frequent whereabouts and habits, designate a manner in which I prefer the hit to be carried out: messy and in public to send a message, or discreet and accidental to avoid an investigation, and then you take care of the rest."

She thinks about it a moment, the photo of Arthur Hamburg clutched in her fingertips.

"Wait," she says, "so you're saying that you don't only kill bad people. You also kill innocent people?"

A small smile, I admit unbecoming of me, lifts the edges of my mouth. "No one is innocent, Sarai," I repeat something she said to me once. "Children, yes, but everyone else, they are as innocent as you or I. Think of it this way if it makes you feel any better: to have a hit placed on you, you must've done something or be involved in something illegal or 'bad' as you call it."

"I thought you said that *I* was innocent," she reminds me. "And that's why you didn't kill me."

"You were," I say. "And I wasn't ordered to kill you by my employer. Javier's offer was considered a private hit, it didn't go through my employer first. Private hits are the ones that get innocent people killed. Wives wanting their husbands deaths to look acciden-tal so they can collect their inheritance. Scorned lovers pay private parties to kill their girlfriends out of jealousy and vengeance. I don't take jobs like those and my employer has never given me one. My Order deals only in crime, government corruption and a host of other things that make bad people bad. And sometimes we eliminate people who might be considered innocent, but who are a threat to a large number of innocent people, or an idea."

Her eyebrows crease gently as she looks to me to elaborate further.

"Would you have killed Robert Oppenheimer if you knew he was going to head the invention of the Atomic Bomb? Or, eliminate a scientist before she completes her lifelong quest to create a deadly virus in her lab that is intended only to be used against an enemy country in a time of war?"

"Yes, I guess I would," she says. "Though something like that is sort of like playing God with people's lives. You're convicting some-one of a crime before it happens."

I don't respond to that because that's exactly what it is.

"Then if they all deserve to die," she goes on, "what does it mat-ter what I know about their personal lives? What does it matter what I know about this Arthur Hamburg?" She glances at the photo.

"Because for some, the means do not justify the end."

"You mean that I might feel bad for someone because their crimes don't constitute a death sentence?"

"Exactly," I say. "And it's not for you to make that call."

"And what makes you think I'd be that soft?" she asks, her eyes full of intent and curiosity.

"I don't," I say. "Not for sure. But for someone who wasn't raised like this, who hasn't been killing people since she was thirteen-years-old, it would be a very difficult thing to get used to."

Sarai looks down at the photo one more time and then back up at me. "You've been doing it that long?" she asks sympathetically. "I can't imagine…"

"I endured several years of training as a boy before I was sent on a mission with my mentor. At that age, it's easy to be molded into whatever they want. My first kill was clean. And I slept soundly that night."

She looks away, staring off at nothing, lost in thought.

Just when I think she might start second guessing this whole mission, she surprises me.

"OK, so what am *I* supposed to do?"

I take the photo from her hands.

"This hit was designated clean," I begin. "But Arthur Hamburg is rarely alone on his estate. He throws elaborate parties three to four nights a week, only for the wealthiest of people and always by invitation only. The security at his estate is top notch. Hamburg handpicked every one of them. They are not unskilled security guards hired off the cuff. It won't be like it is in the movies where I get onto the property unseen and take out all of his men before they get a shot off. It doesn't work that way in this case."

Her face has grown weary and anxious over the course of the last few seconds.

"Then how do you get in?"

"We get in by invitation," I say. "Hamburg has a weakness, like all men, and you and I are going to use it to our advantage."

Now she looks a little nervous.

"What's his weakness?"

"Sex, of course," I say as if she should already know the answer. And I know she did.

She flinches a little underneath that soft skin.

"Is this going where I think it is?"

"Probably not," I say, "but it will still be unpleasant."

SARAI

My stomach ties up in a knot. Victor puts the photo of the old man away inside the envelope. And I can't seem to get these disgusting images out of my head of him lying naked on top of me, the creases and folds of his obvious weight problem smothering me like way too much jelly on a PB&J. I shudder. Surely Victor wouldn't expect me to sleep with this man even for the sake of a mission. I'm not a hooker in any form and I'll be damned if I become one. Not even for this. I may have slept with Javier every night for years even though I didn't want to, but that was different. That was my way of surviving. And Javier, dare I say it, was attractive despite his unforgivable faults.

That was *definitely* different...

I can't look at Victor right now, not because I'm mad at him for this even though I feel like I should be, but because...goddamn, I'm still contemplating it. There has to be something more to it, something that separates what whores do from what he expects me to do.

He won't let it go that far, I resolve to believe. Yes, that's it. It has to be.

A bit of turbulence shakes the plane and pulls me out of my thoughts. I'm gripping the armrests when I turn to see Victor again.

"So then what's the plan? It's obvious you brought me along because being the girl I fit perfectly into it."

He nods. "Yes, being a woman has its advantages in cases like these. Just remember the things I told you before: you're submissive to me but sometimes your tongue gets you into trouble. You're a wealthy, stuck up little bitch and more than anything, you fear nothing."

I laugh derisively. "Well, according to you, I've got that fear thing down pat already."

"Yes," he says retaining his serious expression, "but you might feel differently once you're there and the threat is all around you. You need to make certain that nothing will break you of the control you have over your fear. Hamburg will be turned off by you the moment he senses it. Fear to him is weakness and he likes strong, reckless young women. And even stronger men."

I feel my face distort with disgust and mild shock, but I don't ask about the obvious. I just try to let it all sink in, what exactly we're going to do and how we're going to do it. Because everything I theorized before has just been tossed out the window.

Victor did say that what I assumed would happen probably wasn't right, but I'm only slightly relieved by the truth in that. And 'slightly' will continue to be the measure because he also said it would still be unpleasant.

THIRTY-ONE

SARAI

We arrive in Los Angeles just after six in the evening. We check into the most extravagant hotel the city has to offer and Victor is in character before we even make it up to our room on the top floor overlooking the cityscape. He demands, with his chin held high and his dominant demeanor that we get the best suite and will accept nothing less. And the front desk clerk, bewitched by his dark, flickering eyes, erases a reservation a guest had booked for tonight and gives Victor the keys to the suite. He is so good at pretending to be someone else that he almost tricks me into believing he's a rich bastard who cares nothing for the people beneath him, who just so happens to be everyone. But he does it with so much grace and composure that his rich arrogant attitude doesn't induce dislike for him, but instantly demands respect.

I'm seriously beginning to doubt my ability to act compared to his. I did it for nine years with Javier. My whole life was an act and I like to think I have enough experience, but Victor intimidates me.

I straighten my back and walk alongside him in my Valentino dress and flat sandals with my head held high. I am strong, powerful, rich, and I can't be touched.

At least that's what I *hope* I'm pulling off.

"It begins tonight," Victor says setting his bags on the end of the bed and then he hangs a tall black garment bag with a zipper down the front on a hook on the wall. "If all goes as planned, it'll end tomorrow night. You'll need to wear makeup and pull up your hair. You have to look the part as well as play it. Oh, and put on the heels." Flipping the latches on his gun case he retrieves one of his handguns and starts to attach a suppressor on the end of the barrel.

"What is the plan then?" I ask, ignoring my need to complain about the shoes he wants me to wear that I hope I can even walk in.

"Tonight we go to his restaurant," he begins, still inspecting the gun. "Before we can get into the mansion, we'll need an invitation and the restaurant is where we'll get it. I'll play my part and you play along as Izabel, not as Sarai. Remember that always when in public even when you think no one is watching." He glances at me and goes back to inspecting the gun. "Hamburg is at this restaurant every Friday night like clockwork. But we'll never see him. He hides out in a private room with two other men: his assistant and his restaurant manager. But Hamburg is always observant to what goes on in the restaurant. And he's always assessing the guests. We may not see him, but it's a certainty that he will see us."

"Assessing them?"

Victor sets the gun on the bed and closes the case.

"Yes," he says. "He'll be looking for a couple. We need to make an impression."

This is worrying me more by the second.

"Well, I'm sure there will be plenty of couples in a restaurant in L.A." I meant for it to sound sarcastic, but he's not fazed by it.

"Of course there will be," he says. "But unlike everyone else in the restaurant, I know exactly what he's looking for."

He points to my bag. "Now get ready. We leave in half an hour."

I pull out the makeup kit Ophelia included with all the clothing she gave me and take it into the bathroom. I'm kind of excited to wear it. I didn't have such a luxury while with Javier except when he'd take me with him to the parties and such. And I always took my time putting it on because I wanted it to be perfect. I wanted to savor my only moment alone where I felt like an average teenage girl, standing in front of the mirror dolling myself up before another day at school. I always pretended that's what I was getting ready for and I mastered making myself believe it. That was until Izel burst into the room uninvited and dragged me out by the arm because I was taking too long.

But this time, I don't pretend I'm somewhere I'd rather be. I'm focused and determined and naturally nervous. I apply my makeup in record time and brush out my hair until it's like cool, soft silk lying against my back and then spend more time than I want trying to pull it up. After struggling for fifteen minutes, I finally manage to make it look 'rich bitch' nice, pinned to the back of my head with pretty silver hair clamps.

Victor is dressed in his usual when I emerge from the bathroom, but somehow he manages to be even sexier. I quietly gape when I see him standing there in his Armani suit, polished black shoes and tall height. I glance down at my dress and even though it had to cost a few thousand dollars, I feel like I don't compare standing next to him.

Maybe it's the sandals, maybe once I put on the heels they'll make me feel more like his equal.

"No confidence," he says and I look up. "You reek of it right now. You need to reverse that before we step out of this room." He walks up to me. He smells faintly of cologne and I inhale deeply of his scent. "You *know* you're the most beautiful and most important girl in the room," he says and for a moment I get lost in those words, not wanting to accept them as merely instruction. "You're always in competition with other women, proving to everyone around you that you can never be matched and if one ever tries, you'll snuff her out of the picture with the flick of your wrist. You don't smile, you grin or smirk. You don't say thank you, you assume you are being thanked for the opportunity to serve you. And you never raise your voice because you don't have to in order to make your point. And remember that you *always* relent to me. No matter what."

I stare blankly at him. "I'm a real piece of work," I say. "I almost feel like punching myself."

Victor grins and it sends a shiver up my back.

He holds up a finger. "One more thing," he says and reaches into his duffle bag. He pulls out a tiny ivory jewelry box and hands it to me. I open the latch and look inside. There are several stunning rings fitted in between the velvet folds on one side, two necklaces, one gold, one silver, with jeweled pendants and matching bracelets and earrings.

"Where'd you get all this?"

He hides his gun away inside his shirt, breaking apart the first three buttons to reveal a black strap down one side of his chest that I can only assume is attached to a gun holster of sorts.

"You don't want to know."

I leave it at that and slip on four rings, two on each hand, and then a matching bracelet, necklace and earring set. Then I grab my little white hand purse and Victor hooks my arm within his just before we walk out the door.

L.A. is just like it is in the movies: a vast infrastructure booming with lights and tall buildings and expensive cars and white roads lined with palm trees and multimillion dollar houses. We ride in a black convertible Mercedes-Benz Roadster, though with the top intact, through the sprawling city. It was parked at the front of the hotel waiting for us when we came outside. I guess doing what he does has its perks. It's not all about killing people for money, but having whatever he needs at his disposal that will ensure he can carry out every job he's given.

We arrive at the restaurant in the wealthiest part of town, no doubt, well after dark. A valet opens my door for me. I start to smile and tell him thank you once I get out, but I catch myself quickly and swallow my error before anyone notices. Instead, I raise my chin and don't even offer the guy a look in the eyes, much less a smile or a thank you.

Victor comes around to my side of the car and I loop my arm through his again as he walks me inside.

The restaurant is two stories with a balcony upstairs overlooking the bottom floor. The conversation all around me sounds like a constant humming, but it's not so packed that every table is full. Other than the voices, it's quiet in here with low lighting and semi-dark walls to create a tranquil atmosphere. Victor pulls me alongside him gently as we follow the waiter to a circular shaped booth with shiny black leather seats near the back. I sit down first and then Victor slides in next to me.

The waiter presents us with two leather bound menus, but before he can place mine fully on the table in front of me, I sweep my hand toward it, waving it away with a look of boredom. "I won't be eating," I say as if food might somehow ruin my path to enlightenment. "But I will be having wine."

The waiter looks at the menu in his hand and then back at me briefly, appearing confused.

Victor gives me a look which I can't quite place, but I know it's not a good one. He opens his menu and after studying it for a moment, hands it back to the waiter and says, "La Serena Brunello di Montalcino." The waiter nods, takes the menu, which is apparently the *wine menu* and I'm about to die from embarrassment, and he walks away.

"Sorry," I whisper.

Victor's eyes lock on me warningly. It takes me a second, but I understand what I'm doing wrong and wipe that embarrassed look off my face fast, straightening my back against the seat and crossing my legs beneath the table. I set my purse on the table.

This staying in character is stuff harder than I thought, but now that I've already screwed up twice within minutes, I'm more determined than ever to get it right.

In seconds, I fully become Izabel Seyfried.

I reach into my purse and pull out a compact mirror and a tube of rose colored lipstick and begin applying it at the table. I make sure to stare at myself a lot, turning my head subtly at different angles and gently pursing my lips.

"Put the lipstick away," Victor says as the rich asshole and not the man I know.

I glare softly at him and do as he says, but take my time about it.

The waiter comes back to our booth with a bottle of wine and with both hands puts it into Victor's view. Victor visually inspects it and then nods to the waiter, who then pulls the cork and places it on the table in front of Victor. He inspects that, too, and while I'm quietly wondering why so much effort is being put into this on both of their parts, I say nothing and pretend not to care. The waiter pours a small amount into Victor's glass first and then takes a step back. Victor swirls the wine around in the glass for a moment and then brings it to his nose and sniffs it before taking a sip. After Victor approves, the waiter fills my glass first and then Victor's.

I don't look the waiter in the eyes because like the valet, he's not worthy of my precious attention.

Victor declines food for the both of us and the waiter leaves our table.

"I never enjoy this city when I come here," he says, taking a sip of his wine.

I fit my fingers delicately around the swell of my glass and do the same, afterwards placing it carefully back on the table.

"Well, I personally would prefer New York, or France," I say, having no idea where I'm going with this.

"I didn't ask you what you'd prefer." He doesn't look at me.

He sets his glass down.

"Why bring me out with you then?" I ask, cocking my head. "I was only trying to engage you in conversation." I look away, crossing my arms over my chest.

Victor looks right at me. "Izabel, don't sit with your arms crossed like that. It makes you look like a stubborn child."

Slowly, my arms fall away and I fold my hands together within my lap, straightening my back.

"Come here," he says in a gentler tone.

I slide over the few inches separating us and sit right next to him.

His fingers dance along the back of my neck as he pulls my head toward him. My heart pounds erratically when he brushes his lips against the side of my face. Suddenly I feel his other hand slip in between my thighs and up my dress. My breath hitches. Do I part them? Do I freeze up and lock them in place? I know what I *want* to do, but I don't know what I *should* do and my mind is about to run away with me.

"I have a surprise for you tonight," he whispers onto my ear.

His hand moves closer to the warmth between my legs.

I gasp quietly, trying not to let him know, though I'm positive he definitely knows.

"What kind of surprise?" I ask, my head tilted back.

Just then another couple walks up to the table, a tall blond-haired woman with mile-long naked legs and an even taller man with his hand around the back of her waist.

Victor stands up to greet them. I stay right where I'm at, staying in character, yet at the same time not really having to pretend to be disappointed by their presence because I was enjoying the moment with Victor before we were interrupted; for a few minutes I had forgotten why we were even here.

"Aria," the woman introduces herself.

"A pleasure," I say with obvious distaste.

She sits down on the other side of the rounded booth. The man takes the outside seat after her, just as Victor sits.

"It has been a while, Victor," the man says with an accent that I can't place.

How do they know each other?

"Yes, it has, my friend," Victor says as he gestures for the waiter.

The waiter comes right over and takes the man's wine order.

"Izabel," Victor says, "this is my old friend Fredrik from Sweden. He'll be running my offices in Stockholm when the expansion goes into effect next month."

"Oh, I see," I say, taking another sip of my wine, sizing 'Aria' up as I look at her over the rim of my glass.

Her breasts are practically busting out of the top of her dress and I feel inadequate all of a sudden. But I don't let it show. I am the most beautiful and most important girl in the room, I remind myself. It doesn't matter in the slightest that her double-D's dwarf my C's or that she's quite beautiful and has the most magnetic blue eyes I've ever seen on a woman before.

I round my chin proudly and look away from her.

"What is my present, Victor?"

Victor's lips lengthen subtly and he places his glass back upon the table.

"Fredrik and Aria, of course," he says. "You've been so good lately and I've been neglecting you while away in Sweden that I wanted to celebrate *you* tonight."

Fredrik smiles seductively across the table at me with his lips pressed to the rim of his glass. He is gorgeous, with dark wavy hair and strong cheekbones.

"Couldn't we celebrate alone?" I ask, giving Fredrik no more of my attention. "I don't understand what you're getting at. Surely you don't mean for me to fuck them."

Victor's smile is openly sly but secretly proud by how easily I caught onto the plan.

I just hope it doesn't go farther than this table…

His hand moves away from between my legs and he places both arms on the table, bent at the elbows.

"No, of course not," he says and that surprises me. "I would never share you, you know that."

Aria smiles at me, continuously trying to make eye contact which makes me want to look at her less. Fredrik's left hand disappears underneath the table and probably between her thighs like Victor had his between mine just seconds ago.

"Victor tells us," Fredrik leans forward just a bit and lowers his voice, "that you prefer an audience. Aria and I would very much like to watch. If that is something you'd be willing to allow."

I'm not sure when the act ended for me, but right now I'm struggling to swim my way through feelings of lust and pleasure to find my way back into the real world. For a long few seconds I don't say anything at all. All I can think about is Victor having his way with me and Fredrik and Aria watching as he does it. I'm suddenly tingling between the legs. But I'm ashamed of my own thoughts and try to force them out of my mind.

"Izabel?" I hear Victor say.

I snap back into the moment, not entirely sure anymore how I'm supposed to act. Maybe Victor should've prepared me better by giving me the particulars of important details like this. I fumble over my thoughts, using my wine glass as a distraction as I finger the stem with my right hand all while still trying to exude this self-possessed personality of Izabel Seyfried that I'm not exactly feeling anymore.

"I would like that," I say. But then I glance coldly at Aria and add, "But not her. Only Fredrik."

Aria's face falls and then twists faintly into something bitter.

Victor's expression remains standard and I take that as a secret sign of his approval for my decision to exclude her.

Before I lose my confidence, I keep the dialogue flowing.

"You should've known better than to invite her, Victor."

He touches my wrist upon the table.

"Very well," he says and then looks to Fredrik. "Meet us at my hotel in two hours. Alone."

Aria goes to stand up and she angrily gestures for Fredrik to move out of her way so she can remove herself from the booth. He stands and steps over to the side, but when he reaches out to help her she pushes his hand away and snaps at him, "Get the fuck away from me," and she trots off on her six-inch heels away from the table.

It's odd how I actually feel bad about 'hurting her feelings' regardless of the nature of the situation.

Fredrik sits back down and the mood at the table changes as he and Victor start talking about this company expansion to Sweden that I have absolutely no idea about. What confuses me even more is how fluent the fictional conversation about such a fictional thing goes on between them. It seems as if they discussed this entire scenario at length and even had time to rehearse before we all came here. But I've been with Victor the entire time and he hasn't had an opportunity to go over something like this at length with anyone other than me. Fredrik seems to know more about what's going on than I do.

And quite frankly, that ticks me off a little.

"I'm ready to go," I say icily both as Izabel and Sarai.

"We'll leave when I'm ready," Victor says.

"But I want to go now," I snap. "I don't like this restaurant. It's too fucking dark. I feel like I'm in a dungeon." I take my purse from the table and go to stand up.

Victor grabs my arm and pushes me back into the seat.

"I *said* we'll leave when I'm ready. And stop talking or you can sit on your knees underneath the table between mine."

I swallow hard, a look of shock consuming my features. Seeing Fredrik in my peripheral vision, I gather my composure quickly.

I set my purse back on the table and relent to Victor fully.

And once again, I'm trying to swim my way out of my dirty thoughts.

THIRTY-TWO

SARAI

The waiter comes back over to our table to offer us more wine and to check on things. Victor indicates with a nod that we need our glasses topped off. As the waiter pours more wine into mine, I notice Victor's hand move along the edge of the table toward me and just as the waiter pulls the bottle away, my glass falls over spilling wine onto my dress. It happened so fast that if I hadn't been watching Victor I never would've known that it was him who did it and not the waiter.

I gasp and my mouth falls open. And as I go into full-on Izabel mode, the waiter scrambles to clean the wine from the table and apologizes profusely in the process.

"Un-believable," I say, standing up from the booth with my hands up and my mouth fallen open, my eyes rife with ire. "You idiot; look what you did to my *dress.*"

"I-I'm so very sorry," the waiter says.

"I want to speak with the owner," Victor demands, standing up at the booth now, too.

We have successfully caused a scene, at least.

"Yes, sir," the waiter says. "I will get my manager right away."

He starts to walk off quickly but Victor says, "No, I said the owner. Do not waste my time with anyone else."

A little bit terrified, the waiter bows and scurries off through the restaurant.

Staying in character, I ignore my need to ask about what's going on. Fredrik is still sitting with us, after all, and as far as I know…Who am I kidding? I don't know anything, really.

"Look at my dress, Victor!"

Victor picks up the cloth napkin on the table in front of him and starts wiping my dress with it.

"It's ruined," I hiss through my teeth.

"I'll buy you a new one," he says. "Or better yet, the owner of this restaurant will buy you a new one."

Fredrik sits quietly sipping his wine.

In less than two minutes, the waiter is approaching us again following behind a tall, broad-shouldered man with salt and pepper hair and a dimple in the center of his chin. The man walks with his head held high and his hands folded together down in front of him.

"I do apologize for the waiter's accident," he says. "Your wine and your meal if you have one tonight will be on the house."

"Oh, but that just won't do," Victor says stepping right up to the man. "And I am offended that you would not offer to pay for the dress along with the dining. What kind of restaurant is this? Certainly one I will never come to again. Are you the owner of this… establishment?"

The man reaches out his hand for Victor to shake it but Victor declines.

"I am Willem Stephens," he says, withdrawing his hand. "I run this particular restaurant."

"So then you're just the manager?" Victor accuses.

The waiter looks down at the floor to avoid Victor's angry gaze.

"I asked for the owner," Victor adds.

Willem Stephens nods. "Yes, Marcus here did inform me of your request, but I am afraid that is not possible this evening. Mr. Hamburg is not here."

Fredrik stands up from the table now and all of our eyes avert to him. He takes one last sip of his wine.

"I apologize," Fredrik says to Victor, "but I should go." Then he looks at me briefly. "I will meet you at your hotel in two hours."

I don't offer him any secret looks or smiles, I just nod and turn back to Victor and the issue with my dress.

Fredrik and Victor exchange quick farewells and then Fredrik leaves us at the table with the manager.

"On behalf of Mr. Hamburg," Willem Stephens says, "the dress will be paid for in full and you are welcome to enjoy a meal on the house."

Victor's hand hits the tabletop and then suddenly a bouncer in a suit is standing next to Willem Stephens as if he'd appeared out of nowhere. The skinny waiter uses this opportunity to move back several steps to put distance between him and the rest of us.

"Please, sir," Willem Stephens says, gesturing one hand toward Victor and trying to defuse the situation. "There is no need for a scene. Would you like to speak with me somewhere more privately?"

Victor steps right up to him, confidence and intolerance emanating from every pore. Likewise the bouncer steps right up to Victor. Two seconds of silent tension passes between the two, but neither of them make a move. I know Victor could easily take him and this is all part of the plan.

"I want the dress paid for *tonight*," Victor demands. "Thirty-five hundred dollars. Cash. And I'll *think* about not suing you or *Mr. Hamburg* for the dress *and* my girlfriend's emotional distress."

I find that ridiculous, but at the same time, I've heard of people suing for dumber things and getting away with it.

Willem Stephens nods. "Very well," he says. "I will go and get your funds. If you'll excuse me."

Victor's solid nod matches his and then Willem Stephens walks away, the waiter and the bouncer following close behind. Once they make their way through the quietly watching tables, Victor turns to me and gestures for me to sit down with him.

"I loved this dress," I say with gritted teeth.

With the same cloth napkin as before, Victor delicately dabs the fabric on my chest for show. "Everything will be right once we leave here," he says. Then he kisses me on the forehead. "I think you'll like Fredrik. He has control." He kisses me again a little lower between the eyes. "He'll wait until we're finished before he masturbates."

"How do you know this?"

"Because I've known him a long time," he says.

I can't believe I'm even having this conversation. Or that every bit of it is a show. I don't understand why we're even putting on a show at all with no one here to witness it. But what confounds me even more than that is how easily I've been forgetting that it's a show at all. Either I'm having way too much fun playing this dangerous game with Victor, or something is seriously wrong with me.

Victor traces my eyebrow with the pad of his thumb and I get completely lost in his eyes.

"What are you going to do to me?" I ask coyly. "You said I've been good."

He lightly kisses the eyebrow he just touched.

"Whatever I want to do with you," he says in a calm, controlling voice.

He brushes the other eyebrow with the pad of his thumb and traces it along my jawline.

I shut my eyes softly and breathe his scent in, savoring his closeness and trying to force myself not to believe the truth, that none of what he's saying to me is real.

His lips brush against mine.

"Do you have a problem with that, Izabel?"

"No," I shudder the word out, my eyes still closed.

But they pop open when Willem Stephens makes his way back to our table.

"For your troubles," he says, holding out an envelope to Victor. "There is four grand here."

Victor takes the envelope into his hand and tucks it into his suit jacket pocket hidden on the inside.

Willem Stephens then produces another, more square-shaped envelope from his own pocket and presents it to Victor next. "Mr. Hamburg would like to extend his apologies by inviting you to his mansion tomorrow evening," he says.

Victor hesitantly takes the envelope, looking at it skeptically and uninterested at first.

"It is a private affair," Willem Stephens goes on. "I can assure you that if you choose to attend, Mr. Hamburg will make it financially worth your while."

"Do I appear to need financial assistance in any way whatsoever?" Victor asks, pretending to be offended by the notion.

Willem Stephens shakes his head solidly. "Not at all, sir," he says. "But one can never have *too* much. Wouldn't you agree?"

Victor contemplates it a moment and then reaches out for my hand. I take it and we step out of the booth.

"I will consider it," Victor says and we leave the restaurant.

———

"How did you know that would work?" I ask excitedly the second we get into the Roadster and shut the doors. I can't contain it anymore. I just hope it's OK to be out of character now.

"I didn't," he says.

"But how—"

He glances over at me, one hand resting casually on the top of the steering wheel. "All of the tables in the restaurant are bugged," he says and looks back out at the road. "Hamburg sits up in that private room of his watching guests come and go, picking couples from the crowd first based on how they look. When he sees a couple that piques his interest the next phase is to listen in on their conversation."

I'm totally understanding it all now.

"But why didn't you tell me this before we went? I probably could've pulled off the acting better if I knew the guy was listening."

"Well, technically I didn't know if he was listening. And I didn't tell you some things because I wanted to see how well you could improvise under pressure and having limited information about what's going on."

"That explains your conversation with Fredrik," I say and his name on my tongue as Sarai opens up an entirely different topic. "If that's even his real name." I pause and say with warming cheeks, "He's not really going to be at our hotel is he?"

Victor's slow glance is laced with amusement.

"No, Sarai, he's not going to be at the hotel waiting for us."

Well, that's a relief. Yet the thought of Victor...

"So who was he then? Obviously he knew more about what was going on than I did."

We turn onto another brightly lit street and pass through a yellow light just before it turns red.

"Yes, his name *is* Fredrik and yes, he's really Swedish. He works for my Order, though not doing what I do. He simply aids us in times like these."

"And the woman, Aria?"

"I'm sure she was just some random woman Fredrik picked up somewhere." He flashes me a grin. "He's good at that sort of thing."

I blush and look away.

"Are you disappointed?" Victor asks.

I look back at him, flustered by his question. And that faint grin is still buried behind his eyes.

"Umm, no," I say. "Why would you ask that?"

Victor looks back out at the road.

"What, you don't find Fredrik attractive?"

I think he's toying with me.

"Well, yeah, I'd be lying to you if I said he wasn't attractive, but I'm not attracted *to* him if that's what you're thinking."

I'm attracted to you, Victor, only you...

He smiles and doesn't say anything more about it.

My face just gets hotter and hotter, and every time I see him smile or grin, because I'm completely not used to seeing that, it just makes me blush more and it feels like a hundred drunk butterflies are having an orgy in my stomach.

"So what's our next move?" I ask.

"We enjoy the downtime until tomorrow night," he says.

And that's exactly what we do.

Victor takes me out to buy a new dress with that four thousand dollars he conned from the manager. We go back to our hotel long enough to change clothes. I gape at him when I see him fully dressed. He wears a slim-fitting gray V-neck cardigan over a long-sleeved white button-up shirt. Very casual, untucked from his dark blue jeans. A pair of black leather lace-up shoes adorn his feet. I've only ever seen him wear expensive suits and dress shoes, so it's a bit of a shock to see him in anything else. Though he still manages to pull off sophistication and wealth, flawlessly.

I wear a silk sun dress and another pair of expensive flat sandals, glad to be out of those painful heels.

We do end up meeting up with Fredrik, after all, though it's entirely innocent. The three of us go out to a cocktail party on the rooftop of another luxury hotel and although I have to stay in character as Izabel Seyfried the entire time, I get the feeling that Fredrik knows I'm not really the bitch I portray myself to be. I find him refreshing and the longer Victor and I are with him throughout the night, the more I enjoy his company.

It almost feels…normal, like I've found some small way to enjoy the things around me like everybody else and to fit in with society. In the back of my mind I know that it won't last, but at least I'm experiencing it without having to constantly look over my shoulder.

We part ways with Fredrik just after midnight when Victor feels it's best we get back to our hotel and get some rest. Tomorrow night is going to be very different from this night and it should have me worried. But I'm already playing the game. I'm in too deep, too involved with my alter ego who has had more fun in one night than Sarai has had in a lifetime. I'm anxious and excited for tomorrow to get here, not afraid and having doubts like I think Victor secretly wants me to be.

No, this underground world he's opening me up to slowly isn't having the effect on me he had planned.

It's only making me want it more.

THIRTY-THREE

VICTOR

"Fredrik tells me you had a girl with you," Niklas says on the phone. "Izabel, was it?"

"Yes," I answer. "Obviously it was necessary."

He knows. I've never been so divided before. Niklas or Sarai? I feel this dire need to be selective about anything I tell him from here on out. But I can't lie to him about Izabel and Sarai being one in the same because there are too many ways for Niklas to find out the truth. He likely already has the proof he needs. If I lie to him he'll know I don't trust him with her and that could put Sarai in even more danger.

"I gave Sarai a choice of where she'd like to live and she chose California. That is the only reason I brought her along."

I hear Niklas take a concentrated breath.

"But you brought her along for a mission? Why?"

"Because for now, she is convenient," I say. "Considering the short amount of time I was given to carry this hit out, there wasn't time to fill anyone else in."

I know this is not the greatest of explanations. There are several women in Los Angeles who work for The Order like Fredrik and one of them could have easily taken Sarai's part and played it as flawlessly as Fredrik played his. But hopefully Niklas will take my word for it.

He doesn't play the field like I do. He isn't as intimate with the process of carrying out an actual hit as I am. He has killed people just as I have, but not on the same level and he doesn't have my experience.

"She will only get herself killed," Niklas says.

"Yes, you're right." I stop and contemplate my words and then decide a different approach. "It's the reason I brought her, if you want to know the truth."

I can tell right away that his concerns have changed, that I've finally offered him an explanation he can be content with accepting.

"I can't bring myself to kill her," I go on as if finally admitting this to him. "I will if I have to, but you're right, Niklas, to believe that I've been affected by her in some way. Only you noticed it before I did, or rather, you noticed it before I let myself believe it. The girl has to be removed entirely from the picture."

"I could kill her for you," Niklas says with sincerity and not out of spite or hatred for a change. He is empathizing with me and my plan is working. "Regardless of your nature, Victor, you *are* human. I understand. I can help you. Let me kill her for you."

I sigh lightly into the phone. "No. She is my problem and I will deal with it. She wants to be what we are." Niklas scoffs at hearing that. "There's no better way to make her understand that it's entirely unfeasible than to give her what she wants by throwing her into a mission head first. I'll let the mission kill her."

"And what if it doesn't?"

"Then I will do it," I say. "No matter what happens, Sarai will die in California tomorrow night."

"I am sorry, Brother," he says with real sympathy. "To have relations with women other than sex, it never works, you know this. We don't do it for a reason and this situation you've gotten yourself into with her is only proving the validity of that reason."

"I am aware, Niklas," I say and change the subject quickly. "Give me the details of the mansion."

After a brief pause and I sense his acceptance of my lies, Niklas begins, "There are ten bedrooms and a master suite which is Arthur Hamburg's room located on the fourth floor. Six bathrooms. A Jacuzzi room on the ground floor, east side. A game room with five pool tables. A theatre room is located on the back north end of the mansion. There is a hidden exit behind the projector screen that leads underneath the house and outside near the back gates. There is another hidden door on the third floor, south end near the hallway with the black marble flooring. That one we're not sure about where it leads, but the maid said that it, like the secret room in Hamburg's suite, is locked by a keypad. She doesn't have the access code. You won't have time or the opportunity to break the access code of either door so you'll have to do it the old fashioned way."

"What about cameras?" I ask.

"There is one in every room except Hamburg's suite."

"I suppose there wouldn't be," I say. "Can't imagine one like him foolish enough to record the evidence needed to put him away for life. This works in my favor."

"Yes," Niklas agrees. "Whatever you do in that room only those inside will know it."

"And the maid?"

I mentally jot down all of the information he is giving me.

"The one you should look for is a woman named Manuela. She wears a nametag like all of the staff. Meet her near the Jacuzzi room at precisely eight o'clock. But do not speak to her. She will be working near the towel shelf where the envelope has been hidden. When you make eye contact with her, simply nod once to acknowledge her and she will place a stack of three towels on top of the towels where the envelope can be found. But this cannot be carried out until eight o'clock, so if Hamburg invites the two of you to his room before that, you'll need to stall him."

"And nothing that we discussed last night has changed?" I ask.

"No. Everything is to be carried out as planned. Hamburg's gun is located in the nightstand on the side of the bed nearest the window. There is another gun in an unlocked briefcase on the floor of the closet."

I let the scene run through my mind for a moment. "This is a first for me," I say. "And I thought I have seen everything."

"I agree," Niklas says. "But it is what it is and it's no different from any other hit from our perspective."

He is right about that. Despite the unique circumstances, I have no problem carrying out this job. Sarai, on the other hand, I doubt will be able to stomach it.

"Contact me as soon as the job is complete," Niklas says. "I would like to get the information back to Vonnegut as soon as possible. Hopefully it will make up for the delays and problems you encountered and *created* on the mission with Javier and Guzmán." I hear the faint accusation in his words, but it's to be expected and I let it go.

"I will do that," I say.

Before I end the call, Niklas says, "Victor, you know it has to be done. For your sake and even for hers."

I won't kill Sarai and I'll do everything in my power to make sure that no one else in the mansion does, either, but deep down I know that what my brother said is true. I *should* kill her for my sake and hers. But I can't. And I won't.

SARAI

It's the night of the mission and my adrenaline is already pumping so hard through me that I can't sit still. After a shower I get dressed after Victor chooses which dress I should wear and once again I'm back to being bra-less.

"I feel naked," I say looking down at the thin, practically see-through silk dress.

Instinctively, I try to tug the ends of the dress down to cover more skin, disappointed that the effort doesn't magically make the fabric expand. If I were to bend over just halfway, anyone standing behind me would be able to see everything. Thankfully I'm wearing panties, at least.

Victor stands there, looking at me seemingly lost in his own mind. He appears kind of worried, sad even.

"I'm not backing out of this," I tell him, getting the feeling that's what his expression is all about. "I want to do this. Whatever happens to me, it won't be your fault."

Maybe it's a little presumptuous to think he even cares and to insinuate it out loud, but I really think he does in his own small way. And I don't care much anymore about letting him know how I feel. About everything that has happened between us. About my feelings, although I'm still not sure what they are myself. About his feelings, even though his have always been more guarded than mine.

I step up to him and curl my fingers around the lapel of his suit jacket on each side. Then I push up on my toes and kiss him softly on the lips.

"I can do this," I say. "Maybe I'm being reckless and I don't know what I'm getting myself into. No, I take that back. I *am* being reckless and I know *exactly* what I'm getting myself into. I'm crazy to go along with it, to want to be a part of it. But you know as well I do that I'm not like everybody else. And even if I had a shot at it, even if I could walk away right now and try to *be* like everyone else, I don't want to. I am afraid to die. I can't say that I'm not. And I don't want to die, but I'm prepared to."

For a moment it seems as if Victor is going to say something to me, maybe he's going to try one more time to change my mind, but instead he turns away from me and grabs his car keys from the nightstand.

"We need to go," he says and walks to the door of our hotel suite.

I feel disappointed, even a little hurt. I had wanted him to say *something* to me, anything that would verify in my mind and in my heart that he truly doesn't want me to go through with this. Maybe deep down I know that I'm going to be killed and that last desperate part of me wants to know before I die that someone cares. That *Victor* cares. Because he really is the only person in the world that I have.

THIRTY-FOUR

SARAI

On the way to the mansion, Victor reminds me one last time, "Never get out of character. No matter what happens, or how uncomfortable things might become for you. Don't break character."

"I understand," I say. "No matter what, I won't break character. I promise."

That look he just gave me, although indistinct, tells me that he has his doubts.

We arrive at Arthur Hamburg's estate at seven-thirty and are met by a tall electronic iron gate and a security guard. Victor holds our invitations out the car window to him. The guard inspects them first then walks over to a panel set in the side of a small rock security station and puts a phone to his ear. I hear him faintly through the opened window describing us and then describing the invitations. A few seconds later he hangs up and gives the invitations back to Victor.

He slips back inside his station and soon after the iron gate breaks apart allowing us access onto the enormous property. After going over the cobblestone driveway the length of at least two acres, we park our car in front of the mansion next to a plethora of equally expensive cars.

We get out and Victor loops his arm through mine and we walk toward the house. We approach the giant front double doors, passing two marble pillars on either side and then underneath a scaling balcony. We're greeted at the door by another armed security guard and this is when I notice all of the other security guards posted about the property. I remember what Victor told me about them and I start to feel a little uneasy. But after our invitations are inspected again and we walk inside, the uneasiness fades away, replaced by awe. I have been to many wealthy houses before, but this one is the most stunning by far with tall ceilings that rise four floors in the center of the mansion, opening up into a massive circular skylight. Beautiful Greek statues are displayed on the ground floor underneath it. Whenever someone walks by, the sound of their shoes tapping gently on the marble echoes as though I'm inside a museum instead of a privately owned California mansion. I hear what sounds like a small waterfall and then notice underneath a fifteen-foot archway is a beautiful white rock fountain situated in the center of that room.

Before I'm caught ogling at this place the way a girl who has never seen such wealth in her life would, I shift my expression to look mostly inattentive, narrowing my eyes gently as if a part of me is bored. And when someone does catch my eye, I pick and choose whom to nod subtly in recognition to and who to ignore. Mostly, I ignore the women, or gaze upon them briefly with disapproving eyes.

Victor walks with me through the enormous room and we are then greeted by a man, though this man is not Arthur Hamburg. He is much younger with sandy-brown hair and brown eyes.

"Welcome to the Hamburg estate," he says. He reaches out a hand and Victor shakes it. "I am Vince Shaw, Mr. Hamburg's assistant."

"I am Victor Faust and this is my lady, Izabel Seyfried."

I hold my hand out to the man, palm down and he takes it into his fingers and leans over kissing the top.

I wonder if that's really Victor's last name. He doesn't seem worried about using his real first name...unless 'Victor' isn't his real first name, either...

I can't think about that right now.

'Vince' takes a glass of champagne from a tray when a server walks up carrying it. The server presents the tray to us next.

"Please, have a glass," Vince says and Victor takes one from the tray and gives it to me before getting one for himself.

"I apologize," Vince says, "but I was curious as to where you obtained your invite."

Victor takes a sip and is slow to answer as though he's important enough to make the man wait for it.

"Izabel and I were guests at Mr. Hamburg's restaurant last evening. There was an incident."

"Oh, yes of course," Vince says with a knowing, but respectful smile. Then he turns to me. "You were compensated with interest for your dress, I presume?"

"Yes, I was," I say and take a sip. "But I must say, I think it could've been handled differently."

"Oh? In what way do you mean?"

"Well, it happened to be my favorite dress. Sentimental to me, if you must know. The waiter should've been relieved of his job."

"Ah, yes," Vince says. "Well, that certainly can be arranged. I will speak with Mr. Hamburg about it personally. That is, if you don't want to speak to him yourself about it when he meets with the two of you later."

"No," I say and bat my eyes. "I trust that you will save me from having to repeat myself."

I look at Victor who seems to be pleased with my performance.

"Of course," Vince says. "Say no more. It will be done." He smiles, revealing his straight, white teeth.

I feel terrible about being the reason that poor guy will get fired, but I make myself feel better by telling myself that he shouldn't be working for a man like Hamburg anyway. After all, if we were sent here to kill him it can only mean he's a bastard in some way, shape or form.

We mingle with Vince for a short while, but mostly I just sip on my champagne and listen to the two of them talk. Every now and then I'll bring up my hand, folding my fingernails over and into view, nonchalantly studying them out of boredom. I notice Victor glance at his watch once.

"Mr. Hamburg will be down to greet his guests in no time," Vince says. "For now, feel free to enjoy the champagne and hors d'oeuvres. Ah, there she is!" He waves a hand toward us and we turn around. "I would like for you to meet Lucinda Graham-Spencer." He smiles at Victor. "Surely you know of her?"

A stunning woman wearing a tight white dress that hugs her hourglass curves approaches with a man in a suit.

"Yes, I have heard her play," Victor says. "At a concert in London last year. She is brilliant."

"*Darrrling*, how are you?" the woman named Lucinda Graham-Spencer asks holding out her arms dramatically to Vince. Victor and I step aside and she flits between us to plant two almost-kisses on each of Vince's cheeks.

I roll my eyes. Not just in character, either.

"Lucinda," Vince says, turning to Victor, "meet Victor Faust and," he gestures to me, "Izabel Seyfried. They are guests of Mr. Hamburg."

Lucinda leans in to Victor the same way she did with Vince and they kiss each cheek. Then she turns to me. Victor's eyes narrow at me privately, but it's not enough of a hint and I sure as hell can't read his mind.

So I act as my gut tells me to.

"A pleasure to meet you," I say politely yet without letting my air of self-importance diminish. I kiss her cheeks in return, my hands fitted gently around her arms as hers are on mine.

Victor's eyes smile at me now, approving of my choice and probably relieved by it. Apparently, this woman is of a much higher stature than I could ever be, and although I have no idea what kind of musician she is or why she is so important, I know that she must be famous in her own right and I would only make myself look like an idiot if I shunned someone as respected as her. In fact, we'd probably get kicked out on our asses if I did.

Vince leaves Victor and me alone as he walks with the woman through the room to introduce her to the other guests. I listen to him, noticing that he says the same thing to everyone that he said to us and that everyone here is introduced as 'guests of Mr. Hamburg'. I start to wonder just how Victor plans to get Mr. Hamburg's sole attention with so many other people in here, couples included, to compete with.

Victor drapes his free hand around the back of my waist and we walk through the room slowly, pretending to talk about the paintings and the statues. He'll point subtly to this and that and comment on the detail or the color or the emotion it conveys. It's all pointless, uninteresting observations that really don't warrant verbal recognition in my opinion, but I play along anyway. Soon, I see that he was using that time to get across the room without looking lost or as though we needed the company of someone else to make us feel more welcome.

"I need to find the facilities," Victor says, placing his glass of champagne down on a table at the hallway entrance. "Will you be all right on your own?"

"Of course," I say with an air of annoyance. "I'm perfectly capable of standing by myself."

He kisses my lips and then walks down the hallway. I watch until he turns the corner at the end. I know he's not looking for the 'facilities' and I start to get nervous when he's gone for more than a few minutes and I'm still standing here alone. I hope I don't look in need of social rescue.

I get it anyway.

"I'm Muriel Costas," a woman says stepping up to me with another woman and one younger man. "I've never seen you here before."

"Izabel Seyfried," I say and sip my champagne very slowly, letting her know it has more of my attention than she does. "And I suppose you wouldn't since I've never been here before."

She smirks, bringing her own glass to her rose-colored lips. She has long jet-black hair cascading over both shoulders that ends just below her plump breasts, her cleavage is pushed into view by the tight gray dress she wears. The woman standing beside her glances at her once, probably wondering if she's going to let me get away with the attitude I gave her. I smirk back at her and turn my attention to the young man who can't be much older than me.

I offer him a faint, seductive smile just to spite Muriel and he catches it. But then his gaze strays submissively when she looks over.

"Where does it come from?" she asks me.

"Where does *what* come from?"

She and the other woman glance at each other with soft grins, obviously sharing an opinion of me.

"Your money," Muriel says as if I should know the lingo.

She sips her champagne.

"You are wealthy, though no one needs to know where your money comes from."

My whole face darkens with a confident grin. "Only someone who feels threatened ever asks that kind of question," I say and glance at the other two briefly to quietly flaunt my win of the control. It's apparent to me they are Muriel Costas' lost dogs and depending on whose hand offers the better scraps, they're not immune to influence.

Victor re-emerges from the hallway.

Muriel's face lights up when she sees him. She introduces herself immediately, offering him her hand for a customary kiss which I know has nothing to do with custom and everything to do with challenge. Victor accommodates the gesture and gazes into her dark eyes as he comes out of his half bow, which he holds a little longer than I like. But Muriel is pleased and she makes it a point to look me straight in the eyes to let me know just how much.

They introduce themselves and start the pointless mingling conversation all over again. But instead of showing an ounce of jealousy, because I know nothing would satisfy Muriel more, I walk away from the four of them with my chin raised in an important manner and find my own small group of men to mingle with. I'm not sure if this is an act that Victor approves of, but I don't look back at them once to find out. If I do that, it would pass me off as jealous as much as blatantly displaying it would. And Izabel Seyfried doesn't *get* jealous easy. She gets even.

I don't offer my hand to these three men, just my charming, confident conversation that I would never offer a woman. I least expected for this to happen, but it's in this moment when I take things entirely upon myself that I see not only am I more into this role than I thought I could be, but I'm beginning to give Izabel Seyfried her own traits. Traits that Victor never technically told me to give her. I choose—because it feels right—to make her despise women a little too much and love men a little too intensely.

After all, if I'm going to play the role of someone else I might as well fill in all of the missing pieces of her personality and make her entirely realistic.

During my conversation with these men whose names I've already forgotten, Victor joins us. I feel his hand around my upper arm, squeezing it harshly.

"You know I don't like it when you walk away from me," he says.

The men say nothing, but listen to us intently as if intrigued by Victor's display of dominance over me.

I smile slyly. "I know you don't like it," I say, "but it was getting… stuffy over there with your great-grandmother."

Muriel's eyes lock on mine on hearing and I smirk at her faintly in return. She and her sidekicks walk in the opposite direction toward another small group of people.

Victor wrenches my arm, causing the champagne in my class to slosh around.

The spiteful smile disappears from my face in an instant.

He leans toward my ear and says in a low voice, "I can't bear the thought of doing it, Izabel, but if I have to, I *will* let you go." His breath dances along the side of my neck, raising chill bumps to the skin.

"I won't do it again," I say breathily, turning my neck at an angle so that my mouth reaches his.

I close my eyes to kiss him and feel his lips near mine so close that I can almost taste them, but then he pulls away. The men standing next to us are gawking in their own private way when my eyes open again.

Arthur Hamburg emerges from the fountain room with four men in suits and all attention turns to him.

THIRTY-FIVE

SARAI

The man looks even older than he does in his photo. And heavier. I estimate he must be in his late sixties, average height but not quite six-feet tall and no less than three hundred pounds, most of it in his stomach and cheeks. As he stands there at the head of the room with his henchmen at his sides, I don't see a simple overweight man of mature age, I see an evil man who is going to die tonight. It's all I can think about: he's going to die. And I'm going to be there to witness it. Suddenly my insides lock up, my chest constricting, my stomach a hard knot, and I feel like I can't breathe. I suck in air through my parted lips and let it out very slowly through my nostrils. Calm Sarai. Just remain calm.

I didn't think it would affect me this way, knowing a man's fate, practically controlling whether he lives or dies simply by having the knowledge that he doesn't have. But despite the anxiety I feel as the reality of the situation catches up to me, I don't regret coming here. I may not know what Arthur Hamburg has done to deserve death, but I trust in Victor's words and I know that he is far from innocent or we wouldn't be here.

Arthur Hamburg addresses his guests, thanking us all for coming tonight and he carries on and on about superfluous things to which everyone nods and agrees and smiles and offers their own input. And he makes jokes to which he laughs at before anyone else, but they always laugh, too, because it would be rude not to, of course. Even I find myself chuckling lightly at a joke that everyone else seems to find funny and that I really don't.

Victor moves me around to stand in front of him, pressing the back of my body against the front of his. His mouth explores my bare shoulders, his hands rest on my hips. But the affection is brief, just for show, and his attention is back on Arthur Hamburg, who I notice in that short timeframe singles us out with his gaze fixed on us from across the room. I can see the deliberation in his eyes, the sudden shift in his demeanor. After a few more announcements, he wraps up the small talk and leaves everyone to mingle and enjoy themselves the way they had been doing before he came into the room.

Next thing I know, he's walking straight toward us.

VICTOR

Arthur Hamburg shakes my hand as I introduce myself and Izabel.

"My assistant tells me that you encountered a problem in my restaurant last night."

He knows very well that it was the two of us. He watched us from that private room of his, listened to our interactions at the table through the tiny microphone situated inside the table centerpiece.

"Yes," I say with a nod. "Forgive me for saying it, but I believe a change in the way your management hires your staff is in order."

Hamburg smiles to cover up what he's really doing: studying me and Sarai, getting a feel for us more than he already had at the restaurant, imagining us with him in his room. He couldn't care less about the incident at the restaurant or being sued. That has nothing to do with why he invited us here.

"Are you from L.A.?" he asks.

"No," I say, pulling Sarai closer to me with one arm around the back of her hip, my hand resting near her pelvic bone. Hamburg's eyes stray to see it there. "Stockholm."

He looks intrigued.

"You don't sound foreign," he says.

I respond by saying in Swedish, "I am fluent in seven languages." And then I repeat it in English, so that he understands.

He nods with an impressed smile. Then he looks to Sarai.

"And what about you?"

"She is from New York," I answer for her.

Sarai keeps quiet this time.

Hamburg turns to me again and asks, "Is she your…" he searches his mind for the safest way to ask the question.

"My property?" I say for him, letting him know that it's perfectly acceptable to talk about otherwise taboo things. "Yes, she is. And for the most part, she enjoys it."

He raises a bushy graying brow. "For the most part?" he asks inquisitively. "What does the rest of her think?"

He glances at Sarai, a faint grin at the edges of his aged lips.

"The rest of me has a mind of my own," Sarai says as Izabel.

I sigh and shake my head, brushing my fingers along her hipbone. "Yes, that she does, I admit," I say. "I prefer a woman who puts up a fight."

"So you've already been down the other road, I take it?" Hamburg asks and I know he's referring to full submission, owning a woman who will do anything and everything she's told without cracking the slightest expression of discomfort or refusal.

"Once," I answer. "I am content with Izabel, regardless of her mouth sometimes."

Hamburg watches her more closely now, as well as me. He likes both women *and* men, after all. And he also likes women who put up a fight, like Izabel. The only difference is that the ones he's enjoyed were forced here against their will.

Suddenly Hamburg raises his chin proudly and says, "I would very much like to speak to you privately. In my suite. If you're interested in lucrative offers. You *are* interested in lucrative offers, aren't you?" He smiles and wets his lips briefly with his tongue.

I think on it a moment, playing with his head, letting him know just by the look in my eyes that I'm interested but I'm not desperate.

"I am willing to hear the offer, at least," I say.

His eyes light up. He turns to the man in the suit beside him, whispers something in his ear and turns back to us as the man takes the glass elevator up to the top floor.

"Walk with me," Hamburg says and the two of us follow him toward the elevator.

Hamburg tells us about the construction of his mansion while we wait for the glass elevator to make its way back down empty. And he rambles on about how much money he has put into it as if to covertly explain to me that he can spare whatever my price. I can sense Sarai getting more nervous as we rise toward the top floor. At one point, she clutches my hand and I glance down to see her delicate fingers tangled in mine. I squeeze her hand gently, letting her know that I'm here and that I'm going to do everything in my power to keep her safe. I glance over to see her eyes and right now all I see is Sarai looking back at me, the brave but anxious and complicated girl that I've grown very protective of.

We walk down one massive hallway where out ahead is the entrance to his room, intricate and overdone like the rest of the house. Two men in suits stand guard outside of it. Each of them, like the ones downstairs, carry guns hidden beneath their clothes. But I don't. Not this time. Because I know Sarai and I will be checked before we're let inside and to find one on either of us, two wealthy but otherwise simplistic individuals that have no reason to be carrying firearms, would change Hamburg's initial assumptions about us. He might feel threatened and change his mind about letting us inside.

We stop at the entrance and I raise my arms out at my sides to let one guard pat me down.

Sarai does the same, but isn't so quiet this time.

"Is this really necessary?" she hisses while the other guard pats her down.

"Sorry, my dear," Hamburg says as he pushes open his suite doors, "but yes. Can't be too careful."

When the guards find nothing, they step aside and just before Hamburg closes the three of us off inside his room he says to the guards, "You may go. I'll need a bit of privacy for the next hour or so."

The two guards nod their acknowledgment and leave their post outside his room.

THIRTY-SIX

SARAI

The second the large double doors lock behind us, I feel my heart sink into the pit of my stomach. But I shake it off and do my best to retain my Izabel Seyfried façade.

As I'm letting my gaze sweep the vast room I'm surprised at how fast Arthur Hamburg gets right to the point.

"I will tell you what I'd like and give you the opportunity to name your price." He gestures for Victor to sit down in the nearby leather chair.

Victor sits and I find myself being left to stand here alone.

The masks have come off now that the two of them are alone together in the privacy of this room. Arthur Hamburg is no longer the disgustingly charming man he pretended to be out there in front of everyone. No, he's the evil, sick bastard that Victor was sent here to kill. He's no longer looking upon me as a guest of his mansion who deserves a glass of champagne and respect; I'm merely a pawn in his sexual game who isn't worthy of his eyes or his conversation anymore. Only Victor is worthy of such luxuries. Victor is the one he wants. I see that now. But there's so much more to it than I know. And it takes no time at all for the rest of it to unfold.

"What is it that you want?" Victor asks calmly, cunningly.

He rests his back against the chair and props his left ankle on the top of his right knee.

Arthur Hamburg takes the matching chair across from Victor, a devilish smile slides across his harsh features.

"I like to watch," he says. "But none of that missionary position bullshit." He pauses and adds, "You fuck the girl, every now and then do what I ask you to do to her and then afterwards, if you're up to it—and for extra money—I'll get on my knees in front of you."

He grins and for the first time since I walked in here, his eyes skirt me.

While I'm secretly having an anxiety attack, Victor ponders it for a moment, making it seem as though he's taking the offer into consideration.

Victor glances at me.

"No way," I say right on cue. "He's disgusting, Victor. I don't agree to this."

Victor stands up and casually takes me by the elbow.

"You'll do what I tell you to do," he says.

I shake my head back and forth, looking between them, trying not to break character, but finding it more and more difficult to achieve.

I can do this, I tell myself as the loud pounding of my heart rises over my voice in my head. *Victor won't hurt me. In any way. I have to believe that.*

Why doesn't he just kill the pig now? I don't understand...

With my elbow still clenched in his hand, Victor turns to Arthur Hamburg and says, "Fifteen thousand," and Hamburg's face lights up. "And it'll be another fifteen if I let you go down on me."

I feel my eyes widening in my skull.

"It's a deal."

"No," I say and try to wrench my arm free, but then Victor narrows his eyes at me and I give in.

"Bend over the table," Victor says.

What?

He looks at the heavy square marble table, moving nothing but his eyes.

"Now, Izabel," he demands.

Oh my God...

Hesitantly I step over to the table and lay my stomach and chest across it from the waist up. Already I feel the air in the room brushing against the fabric of my panties. I swallow hard.

Victor comes up behind me and raises my short dress the rest of the way over my butt, resting it on my lower back. One of his hands squeezes my cheeks.

"Make her cry," Arthur Hamburg says from the chair behind me. "I have things you can use if you'd like."

"I can make her cry without them," Victor says, pulling my panties down and letting them fall around my ankles. I gasp uncomfortably as I'm exposed. "But I might use them still. It's been a while since I really hurt her."

Arthur Hamburg makes a strange noise I've never heard before. "Oh yes, I'd very much like to see that." He smacks his hands together and adds with creepy delight, "How small is she? I have a rubber bat."

I freeze against the table, his comment sucking the breath right out of my lungs.

Are you fucking kidding me?

I'm ready to kill him now. He could be my first kill. I'm ready to do it!

My hands begin to shake underneath my chest.

Stay in character, Sarai...no matter what.

Then suddenly as if we're no longer in the room with this sick fucking bastard, I feel Victor's fingers slide into me and I'm instantly wet. I gasp sharply, the warm breath emanating from my lips coats the marble table inches from my face with moisture. I watch it appear and disappear with every rapid breath I take.

"Spread your legs," Victor instructs.

At first I don't, but when he wedges both hands between my thighs and forces them apart, exposing me fully, I don't fight him, I just grapple the edge of the table with my fingertips and straighten my back.

My mind struggles with the wrong in this. I know it's wrong and disgusting because that man is sitting there watching this happen. But the other part of me, the part that is starting to block Arthur Hamburg's presence from my mind entirely, *wants* Victor to have his way with me. I try to shut my eyes and picture only Victor in the room and it works a minute or two until I hear Arthur Hamburg's voice again.

"Yes, she's very pink. Very small," he says and I grit my teeth.

Victor begins to stall.

"You know," he says, "maybe you could show me what you have. I'll fuck for a little bit first, open her up some, and then—"

"Say no more," Arthur Hamburg says with a sadistic smile in his voice.

I hear him get up from the chair and then his dress shoes tap against the floor as he walks by. I see his pants have already been unbuttoned, his shirt untucked sloppily about his grotesque stomach. He's already been touching himself. As he approaches what looks like a large closet, he stops about midway and turns back to Victor. He seems to be contemplating intensely until he says, "Would it be OK if I allowed my wife to watch with me?"

After a momentary pause, Victor answers, "An extra person wasn't part of the deal." He mulls it over. "But I suppose that would be all right. Is she downstairs?"

"Oh good," Arthur Hamburg says, rubbing his fat hands together. He continues onward toward the closet, opening both enormous doors to reveal a walk-in bigger than an average bedroom. "No, I keep her in here."

Huh? You keep *her in there?*

Sensing that this has gotten more than just Victor's attention, I look up just as he walks past me. Having no idea what he's doing, I'm not sure if I should stay like I am, or do what I'd rather do and stand up to let my dress drop back over my ass. I wait it out a few more minutes.

"Don't be too shocked when you see her," Arthur Hamburg says. It looks like he's punching in a series of numbers on a silver keypad in the wall on the inside of the closet. "In a way, my Mary is just like your Izabel."

"Is that so?" Victor says stepping into the closet with him.

Another massive door breaks apart from the wall inside the closet to reveal another room.

"Yes," Arthur Hamburg goes on. "Though she's much more submissive than yours."

Then I hear a loud *thump* and a *bang* as the two of them disappear somewhere inside the hidden room. I scramble to pull my panties up and run across the space to see what's going on, nearly tripping on my way there because of the heels.

"Victor!"

"Get in here, Izabel, now!" I hear him shout and though he called me Izabel, I know by the urgent tone in his voice that he's speaking to me as Sarai.

Once I make my way past the tall shelves inside the closet and burst through into the hidden room, I'm shocked and confused by what I see, unable to form thoughts much less words. Victor has Arthur Hamburg pressed face first against the wall with a tie wrapped tightly around his thick neck. His face bulges over the restricting fabric, his skin turning dark red and purple. A woman lies on a cot next to the wall wearing a long, see-through white cotton gown that has been soiled by urine and blood.

"In the closet," Victor says, pressing his body against the struggling man, "there's a briefcase on the floor with a gun inside. Get it."

I nod rapidly and run back into the closet behind me to search for the briefcase, finding it in seconds. I take the gun out and rush back inside the room.

He frees one hand and I give it to him.

Victor shoves the gun against Arthur Hamburg's temple and releases his body. He gasps for air, making desperate choking sounds as he tries to regain control of his breathing. Then Victor pats him down, checking for weapons. When he's satisfied there are none, Victor reaches into his pants pocket and pulls out a pair of rubber gloves and tosses them to me, indicating for me to put them on.

I do so quickly.

"Now here are how things are going to happen," Victor says to Arthur Hamburg. "Unfortunately, you get to live. If it were my choice, I'd of killed you last night at the restaurant, or any other Friday night before that. But you get to live."

What. Is. Going. On? I can't wrap my mind around this unexpected turn of events.

"If you didn't come here to kill me," Arthur Hamburg says, his voice shaking with fear but laced with amusement, "then what the fuck are you here for? Money? I've got plenty of money. I'll give you anything you want."

Victor shoves Arthur Hamburg onto the floor and keeps the gun trained on him. Sweat is pouring from the man's face and neck, soaking his white dress shirt. Then Victor reaches inside his hidden suit jacket pocket and hands me a small yellow envelope.

"Open it," he instructs.

As I'm doing that, Victor turns back to him.

"The death will be ruled as a suicide," Victor says and I'm growing even more confused. "She left a note signed by her hand. All you have to do is wait one hour after we leave to call it in."

"What the fuck are you talking about?" Arthur Hamburg snaps, despite a gun being pointed at him.

I can't decide who to look at more, the sick man on the floor or the poor woman lying on the cot.

Suddenly she looks up at me with sad, weak, tormented eyes and a chill runs through my body.

"Victor we have to help her." I start to move toward her.

"No," Victor says. "Leave her be."

"But—"

"Remove the contents of the envelope," he interrupts.

I take out a folded piece of paper first, trying to grasp the feel of it through the tight rubber gloves sealed to my hands.

"Read it," he says.

Carefully, I unfold it and look down into the pretty handwriting in a blue ink flourish. And as I begin to read the letter aloud, I start to feel queasy and my heart hurts.

My Dearest Husband,

I can't do this with you anymore. I've shamed my family, our children, we've shamed ourselves, Arthur. I don't love you anymore. I don't love myself. I don't love anyone because I can't. I haven't been able to feel a valid emotion in twelve years of the thirty I've been married to you for. I can't live like this anymore. So many times I wanted to seek help, maybe get on medication. I don't know, but after so long, after years of wanting to get help I started not to care.

I am so sorry that you had to see me this way. I'm so sorry that I couldn't come to you for help. But I didn't *want* help. I just wanted it to end.

And that's what I'm doing.

I'm ending it.

Goodbye, Arthur.

Sincerely,
Mary

The man can't take his eyes off his wife. His flabby chin vibrates as he tries to hold in his tears. But I still don't feel a shred of remorse for him. Not only because I'm still struggling to figure out why this has happened, but because I know he's a sick man and doesn't deserve remorse.

"Why are you here?" he asks, his husky voice shuddering.

Victor looks to me. "Give me the SD card," he says.

I pull the tiny square card from the corner of the bottom of the envelope and place it into Victor's free hand. He holds it up to Arthur Hamburg wedged between his thumb and index finger.

"All of the information on this card has already been transferred to my employer. The names on your extensive client list, the locations of your underground operations, the video evidence that your dear wife recorded that you knew nothing about. It's all here." He throws the SD card onto Arthur Hamburg's chest. "If anyone comes looking for me or Izabel for the death of your wife and it's not ruled a suicide, all of that information will be released to the FBI. We are to walk out of here unharmed and as welcomed as we were when we walked through your front doors. Is that understood?"

I'm shaking I'm so confused and nervous and unsure. Unsure of everything.

Arthur Hamburg nods, sweat still dripping from his chin and eyebrows.

The woman reaches out her hand, but then it drops back to her side. Two syringes lay empty near her legs. She's heavily drugged. My eyes sweep the rest of her, seeing that the bends of her arms and around her ankles are painted by needle marks.

I can't help it anymore, I rush over to her fully intent in helping her up. But Victor reaches out and grabs me by the arm, stopping me. He looks fiercely into my eyes, the gun still pointing at Arthur Hamburg.

"She is the target," he says to me, pulling me closer to him. "Go into the room to the nightstand on the side of the bed where the window is. There is another gun in the drawer. Bring it to me."

I want to say no, that I won't do it, but the stand I take only goes as far as my mind. I do it because a part of me still trusts Victor as much as the rest of me wants to stop this before it goes too far.

"OK," I say and run back into the main room. I find the gun right where Victor said it would be and I pick it up nervously by the handle and carry it so carefully back into the hidden room it's as if I'm terrified it's going to explode in my hand. Maybe it's because I know what he's about to do with it. It feels heavier, deadlier, more ominous than any gun I've ever held. Even the one I used to shoot Javier with didn't feel like this.

I feel my heart beating in the bottoms of my feet.

"Now trade with me," Victor says.

He's wearing a pair of black gloves now.

I step up to him, wobbling on my shaking legs, and hand him the gun. I take the other one and make sure to keep it pointed at Arthur Hamburg. I can barely hold it straight. I feel like I did when I hid in Victor's car, the gun so heavy in my hands that I just wanted to drop it and be free of it.

Victor looks at me, his green-blue eyes intense and faintly empathetic.

"Do you trust me?"

I nod slowly. "Y-yes. I trust you."

"Plug your ears," he instructs and I don't hesitate.

Without another word he walks over to the wife and leans forward, lifting her from the cot into a slouched sitting position. Her body is so weak and disconnected that she can just barely stay upright on her own. Her eyes open and close seemingly from exhaustion or the drugs as Victor puts the gun into her hand, folding her fingers around the handle and her index finger on the trigger. I feel like I'm going to be sick, but the adrenaline won't let me.

Victor positions his body in front of her and shoves the gun underneath her chin and pulls the trigger with her finger. I hear the shot reverberate through the thick-walled room, but my eyes close before I see the blood.

Arthur Hamburg cries out his wife's name and then slumps over onto the floor, his oversized body trembling with emotion.

Victor stands behind me in a way that makes me think he's trying to shield my eyes from the gruesome sight of the wife. It's a quiet gesture that I find unexpected and sheltering.

"You have one hour," Victor says. "You might want to get your story in order."

"Fuck you! Fuck you!" Arthur Hamburg shouts, spit spewing from his mouth. He points at us coldly, barely raising his face from the floor an inch. "Fuck you!"

"It never would've happened," Victor adds.

Then he wraps one arm around my shoulder and walks me out of the hidden room, still shielding me from the sight as best he can. I want to break away from him long enough to run back over and kick the disgusting bastard in the stomach with my heels, but I can't knowing the woman is lying dead just feet away from him. It's not the bloody sight of her that makes looking at her so chilling—I have seen too much death to be affected in that way—but it's the terrible feeling of her being innocent and in need of help that makes it unbearable.

What has Victor *done*?

THIRTY-SEVEN

VICTOR

I stop Sarai at the doors to the suite and turn her around to face me, my hands on her arms. I shake her. "Listen to me," I say and she raises her eyes. "You're still in character when we walk out of here. Act as you did before any of this happened. Do you understand?" I shake her again.

She nods erratically and then takes a deep breath, swallowing the lump in her throat.

We step out into the hall and I turn the lock on the inside of the suite door before closing it. How safely we get out of this mansion and off this property all now lies in the hands of Hamburg. If he decides he wants us dead more than he wants to stay out of prison and lose his entire fortune, then the next five minutes are going to be complicated. I have one weapon, the gun from the briefcase in the closet. Nine bullets are in the chamber. I'm not entirely confident that I can take out the guards who will be shooting at us, with only nine bullets. If I were alone and didn't have Sarai to protect, I could pull it off.

"Head up," I whisper harshly to Sarai.

She raises her chin and I slip my hand around her waist as we walk casually toward the glass elevator. The two guards who had been positioned outside Hamburg's room are nowhere to be seen, but there is one at the end of the hall. Like the others, he's wearing an earpiece. We walk by him casually and Sarai works her charm, smiling a venomous little smile at him. Beguiled by her, he grins like an idiot until the elevator drops us below his floor.

"Ah, there you are," Vince Shaw, Hamburg's assistant says as we exit the elevator on the ground floor. "Are the two of you leaving already? You should stay a while longer. Lucinda is going to play for us tonight." He stands with his hands folded neatly in front of him.

I smile and shake my head. "I would love to, but I have an early flight to catch."

"But I want to stay," Sarai says as Izabel and with a little whine in her voice.

"Not this time," I say. "You know I always miss an early flight when I don't get at least six hours of sleep the night before."

"Please, Victor?" She lies her head on my arm.

I ignore her artificial efforts altogether and reach out to shake Vince's hand.

"It was a pleasure to meet you," I say.

"You as well. Perhaps you can enjoy the party longer next time."

"Perhaps."

I pull Sarai along next to me as we head toward the exit. Just before we make it to the tall double doors, I hear Hamburg's voice carry through the mansion from the balcony of the fourth floor and we stop cold in our tracks.

"Victor Faust," he calls out over the crowd.

I feel Sarai's heart beating in her hand as she grasps mine.

I step away from the door and back into the light so that I can see him fully. He has cleaned up nicely in such a short time, his dress shirt tucked back inside his slacks, his gray hair that had been drenched by sweat, slicked back over his head likely by his fingers rather than a comb.

The moment of silence, although only a few seconds at best, is tense. I think Sarai has stopped breathing.

Hamburg smiles down at us, his hands resting over the balcony railing.

"I look forward to seeing you again," he says.

I nod. "Until then," I say.

The doorman swings one side of the door open for us as we exit the mansion. Neither of us feel safe until we drive the length of the two acre driveway and are allowed past the front gate without being stopped or shot at.

I drive around the city for thirty minutes before going back to the hotel to make certain we're not being followed. Sarai is silent the entire time, staring out the windshield. She doesn't have the look of someone who is traumatized. She's doubting me. She's regretting her decision to have taken part in what happened.

"Sarai—"

"What *was* that?" she shouts, her head snapping around to look at me. "Why was that woman the hit? She was harmless, Victor. She needed our help! She was innocent! It couldn't be more obvious!"

"Are you sure about that?" I ask, retaining my calm demeanor.

Sarai starts to yell at me more, but she stops and drops her chin.

"Maybe not," she says, second guessing herself now. "But he kept her in that room. She was drugged. Helpless. A prisoner. I don't understand." She looks out the windshield again.

"It appeared that way, yes," I say. "But Mary Hamburg was just as deserving as Arthur."

"Then who ordered the hit?" she asks, her gaze fixated on me. "Why kill her and not him?"

"Mary Hamburg ordered the hit on herself," I say and Sarai's eyes cloud over with disbelief. "The two of them have been involved in numerous cases of rape and murder, accidental deaths caused by erotic asphyxiation, but murder nonetheless, all covered up by their big bank accounts. They've been involved in this lifestyle for most of their marriage. A year ago, Mary Hamburg—according to her—decided she didn't want to be a part of that life anymore. Her demons caught up to her. When she tried to talk to Arthur about them getting out of it, seeking help and straightening out their lives, he turned on her. Long story short, he got her addicted to heroin and kept her locked inside that room so she couldn't destroy everything they had. But he loved her. In his own demented way, he loved her. That was apparent to me by his reaction to her death."

Sarai shakes her head slowly, trying to take in the truth.

"How do you know all of this?"

"I read the file," I say. "I usually don't, but in this case I thought it was necessary."

"Because I was with you," she says and I nod. "You knew I'd have questions."

"Yes."

She looks away.

"How could he keep her out of the public view for so long? Somebody would've had to know something. Their kids. The letter said they had kids."

"Yes, they did," I say. "Two children who both live in Europe somewhere and wanted nothing to do with either of them. And Hamburg didn't keep Mary out of the public eye entirely. He claimed she was on her deathbed. Terminal cancer. Every now and then, when a public appearance was necessary to keep any suspicion away, he would dress her up, drug her up and wheel her out to sit beside him in a wheelchair for no more than a few minutes. It was enough of an appearance for people to see that Mary Hamburg did indeed look to be dying of cancer because of her weight and the effects the heroin had on her. No one asked questions."

I bypass the valet and pull into the parking deck of our hotel and I turn off the engine.

We sit in silence for a moment, shrouded by the dim blue-gray lighting embedded in the concrete beams above us.

"But how did she order the hit on herself?" She runs her hands through the top of her hair. "I just don't—"

"There were few people allowed inside the room where she was hidden. Maids only. Illegal immigrants. Fearful for being sent back to their country, and likely for their lives, Arthur Hamburg knew they wouldn't speak. At least, that's what he thought because it was one of the maids who helped Mary Hamburg set up the hit."

"She should've just killed herself," Sarai says. "If it was me, I wouldn't go through all the trouble."

"You would if you couldn't bring yourself to take your own life. There are many people like that out there, Sarai. Ready to die, but afraid to do it themselves."

She doesn't respond.

"Do you think they'll come after us?" she asks.

I open my door and get out and then move around to her side, opening hers. "Right now, no. He would've done it before we left if that was the case." I reach out my hand to her. She places her fingers into mine and I help her out of the car.

After shutting the door I add, "Hamburg has far too much to lose. But that's not to say he won't devise some kind of plan to take revenge on me in some way that he believes he can't be linked to it."

"Or me," she says and looks at me hopelessly. "He could take revenge on me."

I hit the alarm on the key ring twice and the car beeps, echoing loudly through the parking garage.

This time I don't respond.

I walk with her to the elevator and up to our room on the top floor. I don't think much at all about Arthur and Mary Hamburg or what went down tonight. Mostly I think about Sarai and what she went through with me. She didn't die, but I feel like another part of her did. And it's one hundred percent my fault. I knew I shouldn't have taken her there. I am fully aware of my own actions and how inexcusable they are. I came to terms with it the moment Sarai didn't back out of the last chance I gave her. It should've been me, right then, who put a stop to her having anything more to do with it.

I chose a different path.

And I don't regret it.

There are a few more things that Sarai and I need to talk about and I fully expect the way I touched her in Hamburg's suite to be among the first. I prepare myself for it, but when we walk into the room and she kicks off her heels, she stuns me when she says, "I want to kill him." She sits down on the end of the bed and turns her head to look up at me, resolve at home in her eyes. "That man needs to die, Victor. He needs to pay for what he's done. He needs to pay with his life. Just like she did."

There is my proof. Sarai has the blood of a killer; there's no mistaking it anymore. I know I didn't make her that way. Life did that, not me. But I know I'm the one who ultimately pulled the shroud from her eyes to make her see it.

"It's only a matter of time before a hit is ordered on him too," I say.

I take off my jacket and tie, draping them over the back of a chair.

"We should've done it when we had the chance," she says.

Breaking apart the buttons of my dress shirt, I glance over at her sitting there, staring off at the wall, and I wonder in what way she's imagining she's killing Hamburg. It's bloody. It's vengeful. I'm sure of it.

I lay my shirt over the chair with my jacket and walk toward her, stepping out of my shoes on the way.

"If we did it tonight," I say, sitting down on the end of the bed beside her, "we wouldn't have made it out of there alive. It wasn't part of the mission. Every mission must be planned precisely. Stray from any part of it and you triple your chances of exposing yourself or getting yourself killed."

We sit in stillness, both looking out ahead, both married to our thoughts. I wonder if hers are about me. I can't help but for mine to be about her.

THIRTY-EIGHT

SARAI

I never want Victor to leave me. I couldn't bear the thought of it before, but now…now things are so much different. Our souls have become intimate, whether he wants admit it to himself or not. We are one in the same and I don't want to imagine being on my own without him. Ever.

"Sarai, I'm sorry for what I did."

I look over. I know what he means, but I'm not sure yet what to say in return.

"I hope you believe me when I say I got nothing out of it. It was merely for show. I hope you understand that."

I do believe him. I know I couldn't look a normal person in the eye and tell them what happened without them thinking I've lost my mind, or that I've succumbed to Stockholm syndrome. But Victor could've had his way with me many times over. He could've raped me. He could've given in to me the few times I've shown an attraction to him. But he never did and he always pushed me away. Up until a few nights ago when I slipped into his bed. He didn't push me away then, but I know deep down that he was more attuned to the rage I was feeling in that moment than even I was.

Without looking at him, I ask in a quiet voice, "If he hadn't put in the access code to the room sooner…would you have fucked me?"

I notice him glance over but I don't meet his eyes.

"No," he answers in a quiet voice to match mine. He sighs. "Sarai, I couldn't force him to open the room. He might've punched in a panic code and alerted the guards in the house, or—"

I look at him finally, locking my eyes with his. "But would you have *wanted* to?"

He becomes quiet. I watch the struggle shift in his face.

"Not there," he says. "Not like that."

I lift my dress over my head and drop it on the floor.

"Will you now?" I ask.

He doesn't answer, but I've learned by now that the only way to get what I want from him is not to relent.

I get up from the bed and move to stand in between his legs. His hands move up my thighs slowly and he tucks his fingers behind the elastic of my panties. His lips touch my belly, the tip of his tongue grazing the skin between my ribs so softly it raises chills all over my body. I run my fingers through his hair as he slides my panties over my hips and down my legs.

Then I straddle his lap.

I kiss him softly and whisper once more, "*Will you*, Victor Faust? If that *is* your name." I nudge the side of his face with my chin.

"Only under one condition," he whispers hotly onto my mouth.

"What condition?"

He kisses my lips slowly.

"That I'm the one in control this time."

I part my mouth near his, teasing him with a kiss that I want him to take from me, my fingertips gently enclosed around his jaw. He gazes into my eyes for a moment, reading my thoughts. And then his arms wrap possessively around my body, crushing me against him. His kiss is ravenous, his strong fingers digging into the skin of my back and I can feel the hardness of his cock so distinctly through the fabric of his pants that it makes me tremble. My lips part and my whole body shudders just feeling him there, wanting him inside of me more than I think I've ever wanted anything in my life.

He spears one hand within the back of my hair, forcing my head back and exposing my neck to him. He kisses my throat upward in a perfectly straight line until he finds my mouth again and takes my bottom lip into his teeth.

I feel two of his fingers slip into me below.

I gasp, my head still forced backward in his grasp, and I thrust my hips gently against his fingers.

"I want you inside of me," I say breathily.

I can't fucking take it anymore.

With my lips on his, our warm tongues tangled, I fumble the button on his pants and then slide the zipper down.

He flips me over onto the bed, crawling on top of me and never breaks the kiss while stripping off his pants with one hand. And when I feel the warmth of his naked body, I wrap my legs around him, crushing him with my thighs, pushing myself toward him so I can feel the swell of his cock against my wetness. His mouth searches my neck and my chest until his teeth find my nipples and he bites them just hard enough to make me whimper.

"This goes against everything that I am, Sarai," he says and then kisses me.

"No, it doesn't," I whisper and kiss him back. "It's you becoming more of who you really are."

And then he slides his cock inside of me slowly. I can barely keep my eyes open anymore. My legs tremble and my body shudders with tiny tremors that explode and infiltrate my insides. I gasp and shove my hips forward to force him deeper.

I never imagined that sex could feel like this, that the way my body is reacting to him could *ever* feel like *this*.

He raises his body from mine, still on his knees between my legs and he grabs my thighs tight in his hands, pulling me toward him. He fucks me slowly at first, so slowly that it drives me mad. With each thrust he pushes deeper until my thighs are trembling and I can't hold them steady around his body anymore. The back of my head arches against the pillow and I moan and gasp and dig my fingers into the flesh of his hips. He starts to fuck me harder and I grip the pillow above my head before pressing my hands against the headboard, forcing myself against him, feeling his cock swell inside of me.

He collapses over me again and I feel the wetness of his mouth on my breast. My throat. My lips. His chest heaves with rapid breath and I can feel his heart beating against mine. He begins to pace himself and while he fucks me slowly, his kiss deep and hot and hungry, he reaches one hand down between my legs and moves his fingers in a steady, persistent motion on my clit. I wind my fingers in his hair, gripping it so tight, moaning into his mouth, tasting his tongue.

So attuned to each other, we almost come together. He pulls out to finish, but doesn't stop moving his fingers until my shuddering body finally eases and my trembling legs dissolve into mush on both sides of him.

He rests his sweating head across my breasts and I brush my fingers through his hair. We stay like this for the much of the night, in stillness and in thought.

And all I can think about is how I never want to leave this room with him.

———

I lay tangled in the sheets with Victor. The curtains on the window are fully opened and I gaze across the room at the bluish-black sky faintly illuminated by the city lights beneath it. Victor fell asleep sometime after he made love to me. Made love? I'm not sure I understand the true meaning of that phrase. I don't think that this thing between us is love, or even lust. It's something else, something powerful and unmistakable that neither of us have been able to ignore. But it doesn't have a face. Or a name. Maybe he didn't make love to me, but he didn't fuck me either.

It was definitely something else.

I hear his heart beating calmly against my cheek. I feel his breath emit lightly against the top of my hair. His body is so warm, almost hot, as I lie wrapped within his arms. His natural scent, it's faint but comforting and draws me closer to him like a bee to nectar.

"Where do I go from here?" I whisper my private thoughts aloud and then bury myself further beside him when I don't have an answer.

"We'll figure it out," Victor says and his arm gently squeezes around me.

I had no idea he was awake. I raise my head from his chest and lay down against his arm so that I can see his face.

"You're not going to leave?"

It's a long-shot, but I'm hopeful.

A second of quiet passes between us and his bare chest rises and falls with a deep and steady breath.

"Sarai, you know that I can't take you with me," he says and my heart sinks. "It's just not realistic. My life is in The Order. It always has been. It wouldn't be like waking up one day and deciding I hate my job and want to find something better. If I were to leave my Order—because that is precisely what I would have to do—the next hit that would be arranged would be on me. And on you."

I want to cry, but I don't.

I lay my head back on his chest, too disheartened to look at him anymore. I stare out across the spacious room, my fingers arched on his upper chest muscle.

"I think the only thing I can do is to let you live your life—"

"But—"

He squeezes me again.

"Let you live your life," he goes on, "but I'll visit you from time to time. Make sure you're doing OK, that you're safe and you have everything you need."

I'm not satisfied with that, but I know too that it's all I'm going to get out of him. And it's better than nothing. He's right and I can't deny it. I want to be with him always, in whatever way he'll allow himself to have me, but I can't expect him to risk either of our lives to make that happen.

I have to let him go…

"That is if you *want* me to visit," he says.

I detect a shift in the moment to something more lighthearted. It strikes me as odd coming from him. I raise up from his arm and prop my upper body on the weight of one arm, looking down at him.

He's smiling. Not just his eyes, but his lips, too. He's so beautiful to me. So dangerously beautiful.

I go with the moment and shove my free hand playfully against his side, laughing lightly under my breath.

"Of course I want you to," I say.

Then he takes my wrist and carefully pulls me down on his chest. He runs his fingertips down one side of my face and then the other, all the while peering into my eyes, though beyond them. I wonder what he's looking for in their depths. Whatever it is, I hope he never finds it so that we can stay like this forever.

He places his hands on the sides of my face and draws my lips to his.

"What have you done to me?" he says.

"I was going to ask you the same question."

I nibble his bottom lip. He presses his cock against me gently.

"It seems we've created a bit of a problem," he says and pushes against me a little harder.

I do the same. I gasp lightly, my skin breaking out in shivers and heat.

He kisses me, but then pulls his mouth away an inch from mine, teasing me. I lean over farther, pressing my breasts against his chest, wanting the taste of his mouth but he only gives me a little. He thrusts his hips again, holding his cock against me, his firm hands gripping my ass. He's so fucking hard. I want it. My mouth parts halfway and my breath shudders through my lips.

"Do you want me to fuck you?" he whispers. "Is that what you want?"

I gasp at his words on my ear. I can't answer. I can't think straight.

"Do you, Sarai?" he adds, the heat of his breath dancing on my parted lips.

I force my hips against him, trying to position myself on his cock in a way that I can push it inside of me without either of our hands having to do it.

"Yes…" I gasp. "Fuck me like you would've fucked Izabel."

"Are you sure?"

"Yes…"

I can't breathe.

"Say it again…Izabel."

My eyes open heavily as I look down at him. I pant lightly through my lips. He touches them with his.

Before I can respond, he lifts up from the bed into a sitting position, keeping me on his lap. The tip of his tongue moves along my collarbone. My breasts are crushed in his hands.

"Say it, Izabel," he demands and flicks his tongue against one nipple. "Tell me you want me to fuck you."

"I want you to fuck me."

He twists the back of my hair in his hand and stands up from the bed with my legs straddled around his sculpted hips.

He carries me to the table by the window and forces me on top of it on my belly. My arms come out ahead of me knocking his cell phone and his gun onto the floor, my hands gripping onto the rounded edge of the table. His fingers dig into my hips as he jerks my body backward toward him. He squeezes my ass. Hard. I inhale sharply when I feel his hands between my legs, spreading me apart for him. The heat of his hard body encompasses me when he leans over across my back, dragging the tip of his tongue across the back of my neck. I feel his cock right there waiting for me and I try to force myself backward against him, but his hand braces the back of my neck, forcing my cheek against the tabletop.

"Please, Victor," I say breathily, every part of me opening up to him.

I gasp and moan loudly when he shoves his cock inside of me, my teeth clamping down on his index finger as his hand presses gently against the side of my face.

No, I never imagined that sex could be like this...

THIRTY-NINE

SARAI

We oversleep the next morning and are awoken by the housekeeper knocking on the door outside the room. I guess he wasn't just putting on a show at the Hamburg mansion when he said he always misses an early flight if he doesn't get enough sleep the night before. Or, maybe it was just my fault. I guess I have thrown him completely out of his normal routines.

Victor gets out of the bed and I can't help but admire his naked form before he gets dressed quickly. He opens the door to tell the housekeeper that we'll be leaving late and not to come back for at least an hour. I don't want to go anywhere. After last night, I just want—

"You get ready to go," he says walking back into the room with me. "I'm going to take you to stay with a lady I know in San Diego. You'll be safe there until I can get the rest sorted out, get you set up in a place of your own. But right now, I have to make a call to Niklas to let him know about last night. And I'm fairly certain I'll be making a trip to Germany soon to meet with my employer."

I just want to talk about last night, or do last night over again right now.

"That doesn't sound good," I say as I get out of the bed. I got a bad feeling when he said the part about meeting his employer.

He steps into his shoes and drops his duffle bags on the foot of the bed.

"No, it's usually not," he says, rummaging through the bag. "These last two missions have created a lot of questions about me and my ability to carry them out as ordered. I'll have to report to him face to face to give him a more thorough explanation of what went on and why things happened the way they did."

"What are you going to tell him about me? Do you think he'll know I'm still alive?"

He finds a small handful of bullets and starts loading his 9MM.

"I'll figure that out on the way."

That too, gives me a bad feeling.

"OK, so who's this lady in San Diego?" I look at him now with a wary eye. "She's not someone you—"

"No," he says, hiding the gun in the back of his pants. "She has nothing to do with my Order and doesn't know anything about what I do. She's just a friend. Met her and her husband on a mission five years ago. It's a long story, but no, it's nothing like that."

"What about her husband?"

He looks up at me once.

"He's not there anymore," he says.

"Why not? Did he die? Are they elderly?"

I can't help but ask all these questions; I want to know as much as I can about the place he's going to take me.

Victor pauses and then says, "Yes, he's dead. He was my target."

"Oh…"

I don't feel so confident anymore about going there.

"You'll be fine," Victor says, noticing the worry on my face. "She doesn't know that it was me."

He walks over to me, placing his hands on my shoulders. "I'm going to go downstairs to the front desk and get the room squared away and call Niklas." He leans in and kisses my forehead. "Take your time. I'll be back in a few and then we'll leave."

I nod, looking into his eyes. "OK."

Victor leaves the room and I grab a more casual dress this time and a clean pair of panties and head for the shower.

VICTOR

Niklas is angry with me. I can hear it in his voice though he's trying hard not to be too obvious, which in itself is out of character for him.

"You said you'd contact me as soon as the mission was over," Niklas says into the phone. "If it was carried out last night as planned then why are you only now calling me half a day later?"

I let out my breath through my nose.

"Take it for what it is, Niklas," I say, growing as irritated with him as he has been with me. "You've got to stop concerning yourself so much with me."

"I am your liaison," he snaps.

"Yes, but the part of you that has become so painfully assiduous about how I choose to do things, is my brother. Perhaps you should reacquaint yourself with your liaison half, that way we can both go back to a simpler, strictly professional relationship."

"I see," he says. "You don't need a brother anymore now that you have that girl. Obviously she's still alive."

I should've seen that coming but I didn't.

"You have not been replaced, least of all by a woman," I say.

Maybe Sarai hasn't replaced my brother, but she's become something so much more to me and I can't explain it. Not to myself and definitely not to Niklas.

"I have new orders," Niklas announces, leaving the bitter topic alone. "They are last minute, but I think it's best to get them over with before you head to Germany to meet with Vonnegut. Don't give him any more reason to doubt your abilities."

"Is it a mission?"

"It will be one," he says. "The client is there in Los Angeles and would like to meet with you personally."

"That is not standard," I say. "First Javier Ruiz, now this one wants to meet face to face?"

I prefer to go only through Vonnegut and never meet a client in person, but unfortunately sometimes bigger risks must be taken.

"She's a very meticulous woman," Niklas says.

"What are the orders?"

"Meet with her outside at 639 South Spring Street. She will be wearing a white blouse with a silver butterfly broach on the left breast. She'll be there at one-thirty."

"That's in less than an hour," I say, glancing at the clock high on the wall in the lobby.

I lower my voice to a whisper when a hotel guest walks by.

"You have plenty of time to get there from the hotel," he says. "And please…contact me this time the moment the meeting is over."

I sigh quietly. "I will," I say and hang up the phone.

After paying for another full day for use of the room since it appears we'll be here for longer than another hour, I take the elevator back up to let Sarai know of our minor change of plans. Afterwards I head out, leaving her in the room so that I can meet with the client privately. I drive toward the location, arriving with several minutes to spare and park in a side lot just feet from where I am to meet her.

I stay inside the car and wait.

And all I can really think about is Sarai.

SARAI

I've never been to San Diego before. Technically, this is my first time in California. I wonder what this lady will be like, what she knows, how she and Victor are friends. I have a lot of questions, as usual, that I won't let Victor get away without answering while on the way there.

I swipe my hand over the mirror in the bathroom, clearing a path through the humidity fogging up the glass. And I smile in at my reflection. For the first time since I met Victor, I'm starting to feel content, relieved by the outlook of my future. Because before, all I could see of it was blackness, a void that had no beginning or end, everything hanging there in uncertainty. But now I have something to look forward to. I have a purpose. And I'm not going to waste a second of it.

I squeeze the water from my hair with a towel and then pin it up sloppily at the back of my head. After drying off and getting dressed, I head into the main room and start to turn the television on when there is a knock at the room door. I glance at the clock beside the bed.

It hasn't been an hour already.

Setting the remote control back on the bed, I walk toward the door to answer it, but just as I set my hand on the lever, the voice on the other side freezes me in place.

"It's Niklas. Victor sent me to get you."

My fingers fall away from the lever very slowly. I take one step away from the door.

He knocks lightly again.

"Are you in there? Sarai? Come on and let me in. I know you despise me, and quite honestly I'd rather be having a beer in a quaint little bar somewhere, but Victor needed my help."

He's lying. Victor would've told me if he had sent Niklas here. He would've told me before he left, or he would've called.

I glance at the phone by the bed. Maybe he did call while I was in the shower.

I take another step away from the door, my instincts pulling me backward like a dozen reaching hands. There's one more series of knocks and then it's silent. I stand in the center of the room, perfectly still, perfectly quiet. The only sound I hear is a faint, buzzing coming from a light bulb. Moving quickly across the room I press my face near the door and try to peer out through the peephole. What I can see of the hallway is empty. He's gone. But then if he's really gone, why am I still so afraid that he's right outside the door somewhere, waiting for me to stick my head out and look? I press my eye at an angle against the peephole, trying to get a better visual to the left and the right. Then I hear voices and see a shadow moving along the wall. My heartbeat speeds up and I hold my breath until two men walk past. I let the breath out long and heavily.

But the relief is short-lived when I see Niklas again.

I jump back and away from the door fast and rush over to Victor's duffle bag, rummaging through it to find Arthur Hamburg's gun. Victor left it for me. Just in case. But I get the feeling he left it in case of Arthur Hamburg. Not his brother.

There's nowhere to hide in this place. Absolutely nowhere that Niklas couldn't easily find me in under a minute.

I inhale a quick, sharp breath when I hear the tiny clicking sound of a card key being slid through the door and unlocking it. He must've taken the housekeeper's master key. In half a second, and too late for me to realize and remedy my mistake, I see the chain on the door is still unlocked. I make a run for it, knowing in my heart that I won't make it to the door in time to slide the chain lock in place before Niklas is inside the room. And just as the door opens, I'm falling against the wall behind it, gripping the gun in both hands up against my chest, my heart pumping blood so fast through my veins that my eyes twitch near the corners and I feel my jugular throbbing.

The door shuts and locks automatically and Niklas and I stand face to face, each with a gun pointed at the other.

"Ah, there you are," he says with that glaring look in his eyes that shows just how much he hates me.

I keep my finger pressed against the trigger and although I'm shaking, I manage to hold the gun steady and pointed right at his head.

"I *will* kill you," I warn.

"Yes, I know," he says, exuding more confidence than me by far. "You were the one who shot Javier Ruiz, after all." He sighs dramatically and shakes his head. "Sarai, I want you to know that I don't get off on this, on killing innocent women. I never wanted to kill you or hurt you for that matter, but what you've done to my brother...well, I can't have that."

Keeping the gun trained on him and my finger firmly on the trigger, I start to back away from the door. He moves with my movements.

"Why do you care what Victor does with his personal life?"

He cocks his head to one side. "Victor doesn't *have* a personal life. None of us can have that. It's like oil and water. Surely you know that by now."

"He's taking me somewhere today," I say quickly, losing any confidence I had, which wasn't much to begin with. "He's getting rid of me. He already told me that I can't stay with him. Why can't you just leave it at that? He's doing what you want."

"It's not what I want, Sarai." We've managed to steer far away from the door and are in the center of the room now. "I'm only trying to protect him. He's my *fucking brother!*" His sudden anger makes me tremble. I notice his trigger finger twitch.

"Niklas, please just let me go. You're right and I know it. I've known it for a while, that I'm only making things harder for Victor."

"You're going to get him *killed!*" he cries out, pushing the words through his teeth and the barrel of his gun toward me. "Even if he leaves you alone today, even if he never sees you again—*fuck*, even if he *kills* you—what has already happened is enough for The Order to kill *him!* Don't you see?" His face is red hot with anger, his expression distorted by pain. "They will kill him! If he goes to Germany he's dead, Sarai. Did he tell you that? I bet he didn't tell you that."

I don't want to believe it. I shake my head and almost lose focus, gripping my gun tighter.

"You don't know that," I say, but deep down I believe him. "If that's true then why would he even go?"

A sneer crinkles the edge of Niklas' mouth. His teeth grind together behind his closed lips.

"Because Victor is stubborn," he says. "And a little too trusting when it comes to Vonnegut. Victor has always been his Number One, he's always been the best. He's better at what he does than all of the ones under Vonnegut who came before him and he's *still* the best. But being the best doesn't make him immune to the Code. He has fucked up far too much since he's been involved with you that there will be no exoneration."

"Then let me talk to him—"

"You've done *enough!*" he roars.

FORTY

VICTOR

The client is late. Five minutes late, but even one minute by someone who Niklas described as 'meticulous' doesn't sit well with me. Two more minutes and I'm leaving.

I watch people walk by on the street and I study them from the clothes they wear to the way they hold their heads when they talk to those walking alongside them. Are they really just tourists and residents? Or, are they decoys? Spies? I can never be too careful. This could be a setup, like any mission, but ones like this that put a knot of uncertainty in the pit of my stomach—

Wait…

I recall my phone conversation with Niklas earlier:

"Meet with her outside at 639 South Spring Street. She will be wearing a white blouse with a silver butterfly broach on the left breast. She'll be there at one-thirty."

"That's in less than an hour," I say.

"You have plenty of time to get there from the hotel."

I had plenty of time to get here from the hotel…

I grip the steering wheel with both hands, my mind running a hundred miles per second. How would Niklas have known that?

He had no idea where in Los Angeles Sarai and I were staying. He couldn't have known that I could make it to that address from where I was in that amount of time.

Unless he knew exactly where we were all along.

SARAI

"Niklas…if you kill me, you'll make an enemy of your brother." My throat is dry like sandpaper, my lungs heavy. "If everything you're saying is true, if Victor's fate is already sealed then what would killing me accomplish?" I raise my voice out of desperation and fear. "It won't solve *anything*!"

He doesn't want to kill me. I don't know whether it's because of what I said, about making Victor his enemy, or if he's just conflicted, but whatever it is it's the only thing keeping me alive right now.

"Look what you've *done!*" He shoves the gun in the air toward me, his hand gripping the handle so tight his knuckles are white.

He moves forward. I move backward.

"Niklas…*please*," I beg him. I don't want to shoot him. I know he's more likely to kill me, but I don't want to shoot him.

Anger flickers through his eyes in an instant and he rounds his chin defiantly, his jaw clenching, his eyes narrow and his nostrils flaring.

Yes, he *does* want to kill me after all.

The door swings open and I hear a shot just as Niklas turns his head to see Victor storming through the room. And then another suppressed shot zips through the room, but Niklas, already running toward Victor too, manages to keep from getting hit and I hear the bullet move through the air just feet from me and embed inside the wall.

My gun falls from my hand and I fall to my knees. It takes a few seconds for me to realize that I've been hit, and once I do, I feel the burning hot pain in my stomach. Warm blood soaks the fabric of my dress. I lay on my side, both hands pressed firmly over the wound.

The table out ahead of me wobbles on its wooden base as Victor and Niklas crash against it. My little jewelry box falls from it and hits the floor, breaking apart the latch and scattering the jewelry about. Victor, on top of Niklas, rains his fists down on him, blow after blow until the table can no longer hold their weight and tumbles over onto its side, sending them both crashing onto the floor with it. The tall lamp that stood over the back of the chair hits the table, the cord ripped from the wall and the light bulb shattering into pieces.

Niklas is on top of Victor now, hitting him repeatedly in the face, but Victor reaches up and grabs Niklas' throat and lifts him off of him, slamming his back hard against the floor. Victor stands up and kicks Niklas in the face before forcing his way through the room to get his gun.

In seconds, he's standing over his brother's surrendering body with the barrel pointed at his face.

"Victor, don't kill him!" I manage to shout through the pain.

He blinks back into focus having been momentarily lost in a blind rage, and he glances at me.

"Please, don't kill him," I repeat in a soft, desperate voice.

"He tried to kill *you*," he says, looking at me with a confused expression as though he can't believe what I'm saying. "He *shot* you."

I press my right hand harder over the wound, blood moves in between all of my fingers. I'm starting to feel faint.

"Victor, he's your brother. He's only here because he was trying to protect you."

He looks back and forth between me and Niklas, both of us lying bloody and helpless on the floor on opposite sides of the room. His face is consumed by conflict and pain and things that I can't possibly understand because I've never had a brother or sister, I don't know what it feels like to be loved in that way. Maybe Victor never knew either, until now.

I try to lift my head but I'm so weak that my cheek stays pressed against the scruffy carpet.

"Niklas is all that you have, the *only* family you have left," I say. "I would do anything to have someone who cares for me as much as he cares for you. *Anything.*"

The room gets very quiet. I can see Victor's eyes, clouding over with…I'm not sure. Is he even really looking at me at all? I feel like I can hear Niklas speaking but it sounds muffled and distant in my ears. I see the ceiling now. Just the ceiling. Thousands of minuscule holes open up to me from within the material and I feel like I can see every single one of them as they push down on me from high above. That warmth. What is that warmth I feel all around me like a blanket?

"Sarai?" I hear a voice say, but whose voice it is I can't tell.

All I see is blackness. I try to lift my eyelids, but they're too heavy.

I hear the voice again and a shot of pain radiates through my body when I feel like I'm being lifted into the air. I try to cry out, but I don't think anyone can actually hear my voice.

I try to cry out…

FORTY-ONE

SARAI

I feel like I've been dreaming for days. The same constant series of images and voices all around me always sound calming yet persistent. The images, they're what tells me that it's not real because everyone I see are already dead. Javier. Izel. Lydia. Samantha. My mother. They walk by me in a sort of quiet, contemplative state as if I'm not even here. I can almost touch my mother's hair when she passes.

I must be dreaming.

But the dreams are slowly fading and the strange, unfamiliar voices I hear are becoming more distinct. I feel like I'm trapped inside my own mind and it has forgotten that it controls my body. Because I can't move anything. Not my eyes or my lips or my hands. I can't even tell if I'm breathing on my own. But mostly what I think about are the voices, how clearer they're becoming. I find myself concentrating as hard as I can so that I can focus on their words, but I never get further than the sound.

At least not until I hear Victor's voice in the distance.

"I won't be here long today," I hear him say to someone.

I try to wake up, but I think the effort has the opposite effect because in an instant I'm consumed by blackness and all of the voices disappear.

More time passes. More dreams. More voices.

And then just like that as if a switched had been flipped in my brain, my eyelids break apart and I see that I'm lying in a hospital bed.

Victor is sitting next to me in a chair.

"You're awake," he says and smiles down at me.

"How long have I *not* been?" I'm still trying to put my mind back together.

"Three days," he says. "But you're going to be fine. They kept you sedated most of the time you've been here."

I try to raise my back from the pillow, but the pain in my stomach is too much. I wince and my hands come up to put pressure on the area, but Victor takes my hands and guides me back down. "You can't be moving around yet," he says and stands up. He takes the extra pillow from a nearby chair and positions it underneath the back of my head. Then he pushes a button on the side of the bed to raise it to allow me to sit upright. An IV snakes along the top of my hand, plastered to my skin with white tape. It itches like mad.

"The bullet missed every organ," Victor says as he sits back down in the chair. "You were lucky."

Niklas' face flashes in my mind.

"Or your brother is just a bad shot."

I look down at my arms resting on the bed at my sides. I want to know what happened to Niklas and I feel like I should hope that he's dead, but I can't.

"Is he—?"

"No," Victor says. "Half of me wanted to kill him, but the other half couldn't do it. I just wonder which half would've won if you hadn't been alive in that moment."

I reach across the bed a few inches with my hand in search of his. He interlocks his fingers with mine.

"I'm glad you didn't," I say, pushing a faint smile through to the surface of my face. "I couldn't live with myself if I had been the reason you killed your brother. I-I never should've come between you. I didn't know what I was doing, Victor. I am so sorry."

He squeezes my hand.

"You did something that no one else could," he says and I eagerly wait for him to tell me what that could possibly be. "You made me remember that I *have* a brother, Sarai. He and I have practically sat side by side at a table as strangers for the past twenty-four years. And I see now that despite his faults, he has never once betrayed me."

He pauses and his gaze veers off.

Then he looks back at me.

"In a sense he did betray me when he went there to kill you," he goes on. "He betrayed me when he misled me so that he could get to you. Yes, that is a betrayal. But it's a very different kind of betrayal."

"I know," I say. "Look at me." He does. "You did the right thing. Regardless of what he did to me, you did the right thing and I don't ever want you think I'll feel differently."

He doesn't speak, but I know that look on his face, it's the conflict that's always there. I wonder if he'll ever be rid of it.

Then he says, "But you did something else that no one else ever could." His features soften and my heart is slowly melting. "You made me feel real emotions. You unlocked me."

I reach out and touch his lips with my fingers, my hand cradling his chin.

The subject changes all too fast.

"Niklas will never hurt you again," he says. "He gave me his word. And besides, he knows that if he ever tries that I won't hesitate to kill him the next time."

Then suddenly he adds, "You're just as important to me as he is."

I'm quietly stunned.

Victor stands up and walks to the window, crossing his arms looking out at the brightly lit day. I can see that there are so many things he wants to say, so many loose ends he wants to tie up with me. But things have changed since Niklas shot me. I can feel it. And I won't fight him anymore because I know that it has to be the way it is, that it has to end the way it's going to end.

"I don't expect to ever see you again, Victor, and I understand." I swallow hard. I don't want to say these words. "It's better this way, I know."

"Yes, unfortunately it is," he says distantly with his back to me. "I can't keep you safe with the life that I live. I wanted to, but in the end, I couldn't. I knew better, but I…"

I wait quietly.

"…but I was wrong," he says, though I feel like he wanted to say something else. "I'm sorry, but there's no other way."

My heart is *breaking*…

"Promise me one thing," I say and he turns only his head to look at me. "Don't go to Germany. Don't go to that man, your employer or whatever the hell he is. Niklas told me about what will happen if you go there. *Please* don't go there."

I hear him sigh softly and he looks back out the window.

"I can't promise that," he says and my heart crumbles. "But I can promise that I won't just stand there and let someone kill me."

That doesn't make me feel any better, but I know it's all he'll give me.

He leaves the window and produces a package from a briefcase lying on the nearby table. He walks back over beside me and places it in my hand. It's an elongated black box stuffed inside a tattered paper package that had been covered in tape at some time. I pull the box from the package and open the lid. A single stack of cash is inside along with an envelope that has been folded over length-wise to fit and a few other random pieces of paper.

"What's all this?"

"Your real birth certificate, social security card, shot records, which you are behind on a few that you should get taken care of soon." He points to the folded envelope as I'm opening it to see the contents.

I look at my birth certificate first. Sarai Naomi Cohen. Born July 18, 1990. Tucson, Arizona. I say my full name over in my head three times just so that it might feel real to me, real like it used to feel.

It doesn't.

"How'd you get this?" I look up at Victor.

"I have my ways," he says with a smile behind his eyes. "I also set you up a bank account. The details are on the rest of the documents in the box."

"Thank you, Victor," I say, setting my birth certificate down on my lap. "For everything."

I mean what I'm saying to him. I would've been dead many times over if it weren't for him. But saying these things to him, these good-byes, are shredding every last bit of what's left of my heart.

"When are you leaving?" I ask.

I don't really want to know the answer.

I put the documents back into the envelope and close them away inside the box.

"In a few minutes," he says and I choke back my tears. I want to be strong for him because I know this is hard for him too. "But there's one more thing before I go."

He goes to the door and opens it. In walks Mrs. Gregory, more a mother to me than my own mother ever was. I'm so shocked that the only part of my body that moves are the tears streaming down my face. My hand comes up over my mouth. I look back and forth between them. They're both smiling, Victor less so, but smiling nonetheless.

Mrs. Gregory, looking so much older than I remember her, walks toward my bedside with open arms and she envelops me in a hug. She smells of Sand & Sable perfume. She always wore it.

"Oh, Sarai, I have missed you so much." She squeezes me gently, knowing just how to without hurting me. Her voice is heavy with emotion, but she's vibrant with joy.

"I missed you too," I say, squeezing her back. "I never thought I'd see you again."

She pulls away and sits beside me on the bed, running her long, aged fingers through my hair.

But then my smile fades and my heart finally dies completely when I look back at where Victor stood to see that he's gone. For a long moment the things that Mrs. Gregory is saying to me sound muffled, forced somewhere far off in the back of my mind. I want to leap out of the confines of this bed and run after him. I swallow hard, pushing my scarred emotions down into the very depths of me and pull myself together as much as I can for Mrs. Gregory's sake.

I turn back to her and enjoy our reunion.

FORTY-TWO

SARAI

That was six months ago.

Today life is very different. The bank account Victor set up for me had two million dollars in it. When I got on the plane with Mrs. Gregory four days after Victor left, only then did I find the strength to look at the other documents he left inside the box. One was my bank account information and on the back, scrawled in Victor's handwriting:

Your profit for executing the job.
Sincerely,
Victor

He gave me his portion of the money Guzmán paid to have Javier killed. I guess it's only fair since I'm technically the one who killed him.

But life is definitely different. I'm living back in Arizona with Mrs. Gregory. Over in Lake Havasu City. And I have enough money that I don't have to work, but to keep my mind busy and try to conform to this life of normalcy I work nights at a convenience store. Mrs. Gregory doesn't like it. It scares her. She says it's dangerous working in places like that which are open at all hours of the night.

She happened to be right.

I was robbed my second week there, but as the guy stood on the other side of the counter pointing that gun at me, all I could do was watch his eyes. When he glanced down at the money I put into his view, I smacked the gun aside, managed to grapple it from his hand and then I hit him in the face with it. It was stupid, really. But it was instinct. I'm not much intimidated by low-life meth-heads that rob young women in convenience stores.

That's child's play.

But I'm definitely not some kind of reformed badass created by my extraordinary experiences, either. Just ask the spider that crawled on me the other night while I was reading a book in bed. Mrs. Gregory about had a heart attack I screamed so loud.

I went to school to obtain my GED and passed the test two months ago. It wasn't very hard for me, although I struggled with the math. Now I'm enrolled in community college taking Computer Science, though I don't know why. I really have no interest in it out in the 'real world', but…well, normalcy. That's my excuse for everything these days, for hanging out with my new friends, to pretending to be interested in their life goals. It makes me feel like an awful person that I have to pretend these things at all, but I can't force myself to like something just because I should.

But not everything is so unbearable. I love Mrs. Gregory and I spend most of my time with her. She has arthritis so bad that her fingers are gnarled and she can't play the piano much anymore, but she still teaches me and I still play, sometimes for hours until my fingers are cramped and my back is stiff. I finally mastered *Moonlight Sonata*. And each time I play it I think of Victor and the night he sat with me at the piano.

Mrs. Gregory's health is getting worse. I take care of her, but I know she won't be around forever and that one day I'm going to be alone again. I like to think that maybe Victor is still out there watching over me and sometimes I trick my mind into believing that he is. But the reality is that I don't even know if he's still alive. I try not to think about that, but it ends up being all that I *ever* think about except when I'm lost in the piano.

I miss him. I miss him so much. Some people believe that when two people separate that over time they heal. They start to find interest in other people. They go on with their lives. But that hasn't been the case with me at all. I feel a deeper void now than the one I felt when I lived at the compound. This is more painful, more unbearable. I miss everything about Victor. And I'd be a liar if I said I didn't think about him sexually on a daily basis. Because I do. I think I'm addicted to him.

It has been so hard for me to adjust to just about everything, but in the grand scheme of things, six months isn't a very long time. Not compared to the nine years I was at the compound. So I'm hopeful that by the time another six months rolls around, I'll be better. I'll be 'normal'. My friends, although I can't tell them about my life—and I think that's why I've had such a difficult time getting close to them— are really great. Dahlia is a year older than me. Average beauty. Average intelligence. Average car. Average job. We are alike in the ways of average, but we couldn't be more different when it comes to everything else. Dahlia doesn't jump at any sound that remotely resembles a gunshot. I do. Dahlia doesn't look over her shoulder everywhere she goes. I do. Dahlia wants to get married and have a family. I don't. Dahlia has never killed anyone. I would do it again.

But I'm grateful no matter how often I dream of being somewhere else. Of being *someone* else. I'm grateful because I got away. I'm grateful because I'm home. Though 'grateful' is very different from 'satisfied' and despite finally having a normal life that a lot of people would love to have, I'm as far away from being satisfied as I can be.

Victor Faust did much more than help me escape a life of abuse and servitude. He changed me. He changed the landscape of my dreams, the dreams I had every day about living ordinarily and free and on my own. He changed the colors on the palette from primary to rainbow—as dark as the colors of that rainbow may be—and not a day goes by that I don't think about him or about the life I could've had with him. Although dangerous and ultimately short, it's what I want. Because it would've been a life that better suited me and, well, it would've been a life with Victor.

I'm just not ready to let him go…

"There you are," Mrs. Gregory says from the doorway of my room. "Are you going to come and eat?"

I blink back into reality.

"Oh yeah, I'll be there in a second. I need to wash my hands real quick."

"All right," she says; her smile bright.

I truly am the daughter she never had. And, I guess it's safe to say that she's the mother I never had.

Mrs. Gregory, or Dina, always cooks chili dogs on Friday nights. We sit together at the kitchen table watching the HD television mounted on the wall in the kitchen. The news is on. It's always on around this time.

"So have you and Dahlia decided on a place to vacation this summer yet?"

I wash my food down with a swig of soda. I start to answer when something on the news catches my eye. A reporter is standing outside a very familiar mansion talking to a very familiar man.

Absently, I set my fork down on my plate.

"I sure wish I could tag along with you two," Dina goes on. "But I'm too old for that stuff anymore."

I'm too engrossed in the television to give her my attention:

"Yes ma'am," Arthur Hamburg says into the microphone. "Every year I do my best to contribute. This summer I'm planning an event to raise one million for my new charity, The Prevention Project, in honor of my wife."

The reporter nods and looks faintly remorseful, repositioning the microphone in front of him.

"And is that drug or suicide prevention?"

"Drug prevention," Arthur Hamburg says. "In my heart my Mary didn't commit suicide. The drug addiction is what killed her. I want to do my part in helping others who are addicted to drugs and also to help prevent drug abuse before it starts. It is such a terrible disease in this country."

So is lying and sexual violence and murder, you bastard.

"Yes, it is, Mr. Hamburg," the reporter says. "And speaking of disease, I understand that you've also been giving money to cancer research because of—"

"I have," Arthur Hamburg cuts her off. "I still feel awful about lying to everyone about my wife's disease and I doubt I'll ever feel as though I've apologized enough for it. But as I've said before, I was only protecting her. People can accept cancer, but they're not so accepting of drug use and I did what I had to do to protect my wife. But yes, I feel it's only right that I also give to cancer research."

You are such a piece of shit.

I grit my teeth.

"Sarai?" Dina says from the other side of the table. "Did you decide on Florida or New York?"

The rest of Arthur Hamburg's words fade into the back of my mind. I think about Dina's question for a long time, staring right through her.

I look at her finally and pick up my fork and answer, "No, actually I think we'll be taking a trip to Los Angeles this summer." I cut a piece of hot dog from the bun on my plate and scoop it up with some chili and take a bite.

"Los Angeles?" Dina says inquisitively and then taking a bite of her own. "Going to do the Hollywood thing, huh?"

"Yeah," I say distantly. "It's going to be great."

I have unfinished business there.

I smile to myself thinking about it and cover it up with another drink of soda.

Look for the continuation of Victor and Sarai's story in
book #2 in the series, *In the Company of Killers...*

REVIVING IZABEL

OTHER BOOKS BY J.A. REDMERSKI

Speculative Fiction/Contemporary Fantasy
DIRTY EDEN

Crime & Suspense
KILLING SARAI (#1 - *In the Company of Killers*)
REVIVING IZABEL (#2 - *In the Company of Killers*)
THE SWAN & THE JACKAL (#3 - *In the Company of Killers*)
SEEDS OF INIQUITY (#4 - *In the Company of Killers*)
THE BLACK WOLF (#5 - *In the Company of Killers*)
More to come...

New Adult Contemporary Romance
THE EDGE OF NEVER (#1 - *The Edge Duology*)
THE EDGE OF ALWAYS (#2 - *The Edge Duology*)
SONG OF THE FIREFLIES
THE MOMENT OF LETTING GO

Young Adult Paranormal Romance
THE MAYFAIR MOON (#1 - *The Darkwoods Trilogy*)
KINDRED (#2 - *The Darkwoods Trilogy*)
THE BALLAD OF ARAMEI (#3 - *The Darkwoods Trilogy*)

ABOUT THE AUTHOR

J.A. (Jessica Ann) Redmerski is a *New York Times, USA Today* and *Wall Street Journal* bestselling author, and award winner. She is a lover of film, television, and books that push boundaries, and is a huge fan of AMC's *The Walking Dead*.

To learn more about Jessica, visit her here:
www.jessicaredmerski.com
www.inthecompanyofkillers.com
www.facebook.com/J.A.Redmerski
www.pinterest.com/jredmerski
Twitter - @JRedmerski

CPSIA information can be obtained at www.ICGtesting.com
Printed in the USA
LVOW07s1358270716

497997LV00008B/266/P

9 781490 436524